PROBLEMS IN

...othy found a stranded crab pot on ...e beach below Talland church, then his ...ister said it had been baited with part of a ...an's leg muscle.

Bun and Phipps agreed, so it seemed ...atural to search for the rest of the body, ...ithout bothering the County Constabulary.

Convinced they are looking for a one-...gged ex-soldier tramp, the Hydes enquire ...the Cornish Times, Liskeard police and ...ally the man's only surviving sister.

She panics and this starts a full scale ...arch by the newly formed County CID.

Timothy scatters bloodstains in a ...ghbour's car boot - then tells the police; ...acon bones, believed to be human ribs, are ...ound in another man's garden; and a ...dent's demonstration skeleton appears in ...omebody's coal shed . . . to be further ...rculated during the hours of darkness.

...n between times: smugglers smuggle and ...o undergraduates circulate poison pen ...tters . . . for the fun of the thing.

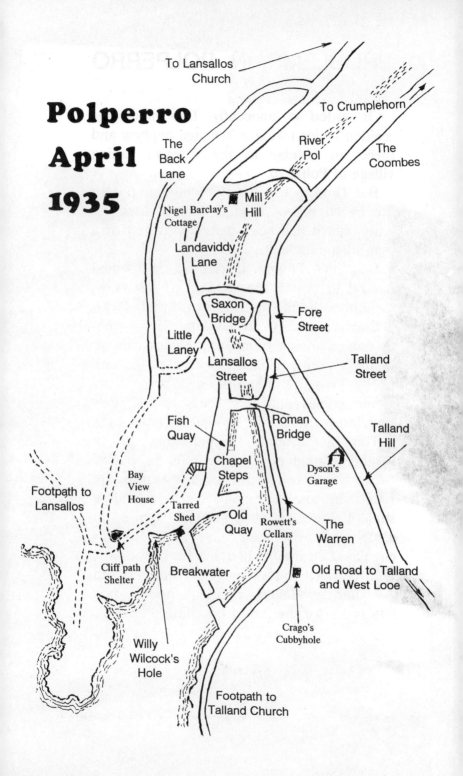

PROBLEMS

IN

POLPERRO

HARRIET HICKS

TREVIADES   **TP**   CORNWALL
PRESS   TR11 5RG

First published in Great Britain 1999
by
Treviades Press, Falmouth, Cornwall,
TR11 5RG

A CIP catalogue record of this book is available
from the British Library.

ISBN 0-9534323-1-9

Printed and bound by T.J.INTERNATIONAL LTD
Padstow, Cornwall, PL28 8RW.

Typesetting and design by Treviades Press.

Chapter One

The afternoon express - Waterloo to Plymouth - slowly ground to a halt on arrival at the Southern Railway's Queen Street station, in the middle of Exeter. Doors flew open and passengers hurriedly left the train, shouting for porters or waving to friends, as they struggled through dozens of waiting people - bound further west - who surged forward to occupy any vacant seats.

Miss Philippa Hyde, whose christened name had been abbreviated to 'Phipps' by her older sister almost forty-three years before, scanned carriage windows from a vantage point on the platform scales, her head anxiously swivelling from one side to the other like a spectator at a tennis tournament.

Bun - originally named Anthea Eulalia - stood nearby.

She was also scrutinising the train, but doing so with a solemn expression and economy of movement.

Glancing down at her sister, Phipps smiled momentarily as she thought how much that matronly figure, with its above average height and magisterial head motion, proclaimed a previous occupation. Bun only needed a whistle, slung from her neck on a piece of grubby string, to personify the school mistress watching her children at play during morning milk break.

Phipps shook her head and resumed her frantic search.

She was on the lookout for a nephew and niece.

Debbie and Timothy should have joined the express at Salisbury, for two weeks holiday in the Cornish fishing village of Polperro . . . consigned to the care of their two maiden aunts by Theo Hyde, when he found himself unable to leave his Lewes solicitor's practice - back in Sussex - due to pressure of work.

"I can't see them at the back of the train," Phipps babbled wildly, "and the guard's out on the platform with a green flag in his hand! What shall we do?"

"Keep calm, pick up your case and follow me. They're right up front . . . near the engine," her older sister responded.

Phipps jumped down onto the platform, picked up her overnight case and scurried after Bun, thanking her lucky stars that they had sent most of their luggage on in advance. Getting a porter in this mad scramble would have been hopeless.

As she followed her taller sister's broad back, Phipps regarded the crowds of people with amazement. Where had they come from? Where were they going . . . in such numbers? Then she gave a grimace of resignation. Inevitable really, wasn't it? The Thursday before Good Friday. Everybody wanted to make the most of the coming Easter Bank Holiday weekend.

Phipps caught up with her sister just as she reached an open carriage door where Timothy stood waiting.

Tall for his seventeen years - with dark wavy hair like his father - the youth seized his aunt's case and carried it through to where he had been sitting. Bun followed. Debbie gave her a kiss in passing, then reached down to help Phipps.

"Hello Auntie Phil. You're looking terribly hot and bothered. Come along to our compartment and sit down. We've got it all to ourselves now that those other dreadful people have gone."

Phipps smiled up at the girl. Fifteen - nearly sixteen - and beginning to speak with that same censorial tone of voice as her mother was wont to use. Oh well . . . perhaps she'll grow out of it when she gets away to college.

"Been having a difficult journey?" Phipps asked, handing her small case up and following after it.

Debbie reminded her aunt that reaching Salisbury from Lewes, by train, involved a very long and tedious drag through boring old Brighton, ponderous Portsmouth and soporific Southampton; with no chance of getting anything to eat or drink en route.

"Then this family of sixteen-stone gluttonous Gorgons pushed into our compartment, just before the express left Salisbury."

"You make them sound like something straight out of Greek mythology," Phipps laughed. "Did they have wings, enormous teeth and writhing snakes in place of hair?"

Debbie replied that she hadn't really noticed. Their travelling companions had got out a very large Melton Mowbray pie as soon as the train left the station, divided it up and eaten every last crumb without offering the young Hydes as much as a sniff.

"And you know what it's like, when you're starving hungry."

"Seeing food makes it worse?"

"Sheer agony!" Debbie moaned. "I only had eyes for that pie."

"Then we shall have to take you both along to the restaurant car for an early tea," Phipps replied, entering their compartment.

Before she had time to take her coat off, Phipps heard the sound of carriage doors being slammed shut, followed by warning shouts, then a guard's whistle. There was an answering 'toot' from the engine, carriage brake-rods creaked and their train lurched forward, soon disappearing into the blackness of St David's Tunnel, as it descended to the Great Western Railway station.

There was a brief halt, to pick up more passengers, before the express headed out into open countryside for the long haul around Dartmoor and down the Tamar Valley towards Plymouth.

Immediately after a steward passed along the corridor, calling out that afternoon tea was now being served, the Hydes went in search of the restaurant car.

Bun and Phipps exchanged family news with Debbie and her brother over plates full of toasted tea-cakes. Phipps cautioned her neice about such liberal use of strawberry jam. Bun reminded the girl about the dangers of 'puppy fat'.

"I'm too active," she replied with a cheery shake of the head. "I can eat as much as I like. Never put on weight. I expect I take after Auntie Phil: little and good."

Her brother punctuated this part of their conversation with a single derisive snort.

Asked if they had been to Polperro before, Debbie said no; but she was looking forward to lots of fresh crab sandwiches when they got there, since it was a well-known fishing port.

Timothy immediately gave voice to the old nautical myth that all the tastiest crabs fed on the bodies of drowned sailormen. This was how they got that distinctive flavour. Debbie grimaced with disgust while deftly kicking her brother's ankle beneath the table. Bun sententiously observed that young ladies did not kick their older brothers.

"Ah! But I'm still a growing girl, Auntie," she laughed. "Fully entitled to kick, bite, scratch and gouge right up to my eighteenth birthday . . . always providing I keep it in the family," she concluded, landing another stinger on the the injured ankle to drive her point home.

Phipps smiled to herself as Bun stood up - every inch the class mistress she had been for many years in Miss Crawford's Brighton prep school before taking early retirement - and suggested they return to the relative privacy of their own compartment before they were all turned off the train for disorderly conduct.

Timothy said he wasn't at all sure he could still walk.

Bun, starting to move away, replied that was all right. He could remain where he was . . . and settle their bill when the waiter became available.

To Phipps' amusement, this effected an instant cure.

Making her way down the corridor, behind Debbie, she recalled the consternation over breakfast on the morning their eldest brother's letter arrived, proposing that Bun and herself should drop everything and take a fortnight's holiday in Polperro.

He had arranged to rent an old smuggler's cottage for the children's Easter holidays, but pressure of work was now making it impossible for him to leave Lewes. Bun and Phipps could take up the booking - all expenses paid - if they would keep an eye on Debbie and Timothy.

"Here we are, just finished settling into a perfectly delightful riverside cottage on the Exe," Bun had complained, "and looking forward to enjoying the coming spring weather, when we are asked to turn our backs on Tozers Quay, say goodbye to Topsham and head for the wilds of Cornwall. Frankly: I don't see why Theo's wife can't take her own children on holiday."

Phipps had smiled grimly, pointing out that Dear Rosamund was so house-proud she would fret herself to a shadow whilst away from home, worrying over the mess she might find upon her return.

"Yes. Theo says as much in here," Bun replied, waving the letter. ". . . 'sees it as her wifely duty to remain in Lewes, looking after husband and home'."

"With emphasis on the latter," Phipps snapped.

However, the two middle-aged, unmarried sisters had finally accepted their brother's invitation, mainly to avoid disappointment for their nephew and niece if the holiday had otherwise been cancelled. And now Phipps was beginning to enjoy herself. She had not travelled down this line before and was fascinated by the changing scenery.

Once beyond those innumerable cuttings which had obscured most of the countryside, between Sampford Courtenay station and Okehampton, Phipps had caught brief glimpses of Dartmoor's wild hillside turf with small groups of sheep or ponies grazing . . . when they weren't sheltering beneath stunted, wind-arched hawthorns.

And now the train was south of Tavistock, high above a wooded valley, following its serpentine contours along towards Bere Alston. According to a map, on the wall of their compartment, one should soon be able to see the River Tamar.

"I think I'll stand in the corridor for a little while," Phipps called to her sister, who had returned to their compartment. "We should be running beside a river for the next couple of miles, before the track turns inland - through St Budeaux - heading up to North Road station."

Timothy joined his younger aunt in the corridor soon after they had passed through Bere Alston without stopping.

"The next station is Bere Ferrers!"

"You sound very excited at that prospect?"

"Scene of a terrible accident . . . back in The War."

Phipps pointed out that when her nephew reached her age he would be less likely to glorify those four years. Timothy chose to ignore this rebuke, hurrying on to recount how soldiers from a stationary troop train had been crossing the other railway line in the dark, when an express had roared through the station without stopping . . . leaving a trail of dead and dying men behind.

"Entire place littered with legless bodies! Shouldn't much care to be around after sunset on anniversary night. Might bump into a ghost looking for his head!"

Phipps, disregarding the improbability of a legless body running about to look for something without the use of its eyes, was instantly reminded of a young Canadian infantry lieutenant, whom she had met whilst helping at a Brighton convalescence centre. He had been one of the survivors of that dreadful night, and eventually returned home with an artificial leg.

She shook her head at the tragic waste. Young men, who had left their own country to fight in Flanders, losing limbs or lives within a few hours of reaching Plymouth Sound.

Phipps decided on a change of subject matter, telling Timothy they would probably see some battleships in Devonport Dockyard, just before their train pulled away from the river towards North Road station.

"Not terribly interested . . . since I failed my interview for Dartmouth," her nephew drawled indifferently, before leaning closer to add in confidential tones, "Frankly, I don't think the old admirals are frightfully keen to have solicitors' sons in their wardrooms. Probably regard us as being about the same level as grocers' boys."

"Oh I shouldn't think so, dear. After all: grocers are said to be in trade . . . whereas soliciting is a respectable profession."

Timothy mumbled something about 'not when practised by ladies in Piccadilly', which was almost lost on his aunt as their train rattled over an iron girder bridge spanning the River Tavy.

Before Phipps could ask for clarification, her nephew declaimed airily that he had to see a man about a dog before they drew into Plymouth, and swayed off to find himself a vacant toilet.

"Men!" She tut-tutted under her breath. "Always have to draw attention to themselves when needing to spend a penny. A lady would simply excuse herself in a low voice and fade away. Let's hope he remembers to lift the seat before commencing his performance."

Then Phipps was struck by a sudden thought . . . the Cornish train might be made up with non-corridor coaches. She quickly followed her nephew's example.

A needless precaution, she discovered when they changed at Plymouth North Road, because the Hydes found themselves joining another express for the final leg of their main line journey. However, on alighting at Liskeard, they were directed right out of the station.

To their bewilderment, they were told to cross a road.

Debbie asked what was happening.

Her brother said they would have to walk the last ten miles.

Bun declared most firmly: "Not in these shoes!"

Phipps asked who would carry their cases.

But to everyone's relief, they found themselves - together with a handful of other travellers - almost immediately entering another, much smaller and entirely separate station, built at a right angle to the main line platforms.

A tiny engine - blowing off steam as if in a hurry to be on its way - stood waiting, coupled to a single coach. Fortunately for passenger comfort, there were less than a dozen other people travelling down to Looe, so there was plenty of room for all; including a couple of farmers' wives who were each carrying home a week's supply of groceries in large, square-shaped wicker market baskets.

Once settled in their seats, Debbie drew her aunts' attention to an old countryman who held a small sack across his knees.

There was stealthy movement inside.

Then snuffling noises.

And finally an ear-piercing scream!

"My God! He's got a baby in that bag!" the girl shrieked.

"That ain't no babby, m'dear," one of the farm women called across the carriage with a laugh. "Ole Jack's bringing 'ome the bacon. That's right, id'n it Mister Jago?"

"'Ess. Picked up a lil' ole weaner, over to Liskeard Market."

At this point, the hidden animal redoubled both its screams and struggles . . . eventually forcing its snout out into the open.

"My Gor Missus Richards! You didn't orter said 'bacon'. Proper upset 'im, you 'ave. I reckon 'ee's goin' ter git away!"

"Well shut that door, somebody!" Mrs Richards shouted.

A gentleman in plus-fours hastened to oblige . . . then climbed up to stand on his seat.

Bun observed this seemed a most sensible precaution and followed suit . . . to be joined by her sister and their niece. Other female passengers did likewise . . . while calling to each other that they didn't know what all the fuss was about.

"'Tis only a lil' ole pig. Let un out for a run, Jack!"

"It would appear," Bun began, "that he has no option."

The three Hydes watched transfixed, as the tiny animal wriggled through its owner's frantically clutching arms, fell to the carriage floor, struggled to its feet and made off at a run.

Mr Jago said, "Aw dang the silly beggar!"

Mrs Richards shouted, "Mind yer feets, up front there!"

Her friend said, "An' you mind me baskit. I got eggs on top!"

Outside, on the platform, men called out and whistles blew.

There was a brief reply from the engine, and they were off.

Timothy shouted, "Yoiks, tally-ho!" and dived after the pig.

Unfortunately, two men at the front end of the coach tried to grapple the runaway creature . . . which instantly took fright, turned and headed back the way it had come.

Human head met snuffling snout.

Piggy screamed and collapsed in a dazed heap.

Timothy said something which was quite unprintable at the time of the incident - Easter 1935 - and his Aunt Anthea Eulalia exclaimed, "I didn't hear that." Which, in her sister's view, indicated Bun had heard it only too clearly.

Another male passenger, sitting nearby, wrenched off his unbuttoned hacking jacket, threw it over the pig and held on until Mr Jago was able to struggle it back into the sack.

"We do see life," Bun commented as she stepped down.

"Can't beat these branchline trains, for rural fun and frolic," the gentleman in plus-fours called over upon resuming his seat.

"It was a couple of nanny goats, last time I travelled this route! And you know what they're like: poor bowel control. We had their droppings rolling round all over the carriage . . . much the same as little brown marbles to look at, but make a bit of a mess when trodden on with a pair of size ten veldschoen. I tell you: anything can happen on the Looe line. . . and generally does!"

This seemed to be borne out within minutes of their train's departure from Liskeard station. Having negotiated a steeply curved track which wound down round the hillside to a valley floor, it stopped at a tiny halt.

Nobody made any attempt to leave, though Phipps could hear a man's voice calling, "Coombe! Coombe! Anyone for Coombe?"

More shouting was followed by a shrill blast from a porter's whistle, answered by a 'toot' from the engine.

Then their train set off in the opposite direction!

"We're going back to Liskeard!" Debbie exclaimed.

"Probably left the guard behind," Timothy suggested.

The gentleman in plus-fours explained that this train always ran backwards, coming downhill, then changed to normal running for the remainder of its journey towards Looe.

As Timothy was quick to point out, shortly afterwards, 'normal running' did not appear much better than a horse's brisk trotting pace. Then they found the brakes going on again and the train stopped at another tiny station. This happened all the way down the line; Coombe being followed by St Keyne, Causeland, and Sandplace.

"A bit like the polka," Debbie observed as their track crossed the head of a tidal creek to follow a riverside embankment, giving everyone wide views of low tide mudbanks, "One-two-three: hop! But instead of hopping, we stop."

"One must live in hopes that our old carriage doesn't hop off the rails," Timothy drawled. "Shouldn't fancy landing upside down in that mud. Looks pretty 'niffy'. Probably full of dead fish heads and general offal . . . thrown over the side by people cleaning their catches at the town quays, in Looe."

Phipps, recalling her brother Theo's letter, reminded her nephew that they were going to stay in a smuggler's cottage, and wondered if people still did that sort of thing in the 1930s.

Timothy replied he should certainly hope so.

"I've mentioned this Cornish trip to close friends, been given a few tips on what to look out for, and told to bring back a couple of cutlasses or flint-lock pistols."

"You'll be lucky," his sister mocked.

Timothy put on his sneering expression, betting her that it was only a matter of perseverance. However, if he could not find evidence of a genuine home-grown mystery . . . then, by gosh, he'd jolly well create one of his own making.

He informed his aunts that he would be commencing with a thorough examination of their holiday cottage.

Bun asked what he had in mind.

"Tapping all walls and floors with a small hammer, listening for hollow echoes. There may be a secret passage, or priest's hole, or something."

"So that's why I saw you sneaking a hammer from the garden tool shed, when we were packing!" Debbie exclaimed.

"Well of course. Got it in my suitcase. I came prepared."

Phipps, recalling what had happened to Bun and herself, back home at Tozers Quay earlier that same year - when they had discovered a woman's body concealed in a hidden wall cavity at their cottage - suggested Timothy should confine himself to poking about the local caves and beaches.

"Yes! Quite agree, old girl," Bun said in a tone of voice which brooked no argument. "If you find any unpleasant relics from a bygone age, in a public place, you can always walk away and disclaim all knowledge or responsibility. Just remember, young man: cutlasses were used for fighting . . . "

"Chopping off heads . . . and all that sort of thing," Debbie interrupted, her face tightly set in a serious expression.

"Oh that's OK. My friends and I have already considered skeletons. A few bleached bones would be perfectly acceptable."

"You wouldn't be allowed to keep them," Debbie warned. "Have you forgotten about those bits and pieces, found near the cross-roads, at Haywards Heath?"

"When was this?" Phipps asked.

"Some time last year, Auntie. Boy scouts - out camping - dug them up when they were excavating a pit to bury their rubbish."

"Probably an eighteenth century highwayman," Timothy said.

"Hung in chains!" his sister continued. "Well anyway: the police took them into protective custody."

"The bones or the boy scouts, dear?"

"The bones, of course," Timothy answered. "But that was only because their stupid scoutmaster reported the find." The boy shook his head despairingly. "That's the trouble with the scout movement: over emphasis upon honesty and personal integrity. Rather cramps individual enterprise. Well I've got more sense. If I found a skeleton I should simply bring it back to the holiday cottage bit by bit - safely wrapped up in a bathing towel - and lock it away in my large suitcase, underneath any dirty clothes. Shouldn't say a word about it."

Bun turned to her sister, observing drily: in that case they must hope the smugglers of a previous century had cleared up all their dead bodies, after any fracas with the local Excise men.

By this time, the train had arrived at East Looe railway station. The Hydes gathered up their cases - called for a porter with no result - then made their way towards the exit.

Bun asked the elderly ticket collector about transport to Polperro. She was pointed in the direction of a small motor bus, which was rapidly filling with a variety of country folk. All appeared to be heavily laden with bulky items of hand luggage.

When she noticed that Mr Jago - complete with pig - was to be one of them, the elder Miss Hyde drew a firm line with her feet, by leading the way straight across the forecourt to commandeer the one and only taxicab.

"What's wrong with the bus, Missus?" the driver asked.

"It appears to be full . . . and I'm a MISS , not a MISSUS!"

"Oh arr. Missed the bus in more ways than one, by the sound of things! Aw well, come-us on. Git yer gear aboard . . . MAID. I don't want to be out 'arf the night . . . "

Phipps almost laughed aloud on hearing her forty-five year old, staid and matronly sister - with hair as straight as a pound of candles - being addressed in this manner.

Everyone heaved their cases into the decrepit old vehicle, then followed up themselves. Timothy whispered that they should keep their feet off the floor . . . in case it disintegrated and they had to run most of the way to Polperro, like actors in early American comedy films.

To his further amusement, the engine refused to start when their driver pulled knobs on the dash-board, which meant the old man had to crank up by hand.

Once moving - when engine noise ensured he wouldn't be able to hear what was being said amongst his now-hilarious passengers - Phipps asked her sister if they were all like this, down in Cornwall.

"Are you referring to the car . . . or driver, old girl?"

"That man! The way he spoke to you!"

Her sister nodded thoughtfully. "Let's just say the indigenous population enjoy a well-deserved reputation for exhibiting a rather determined independence of spirit . . . whilst still nominally declaring allegiance to the House of Windsor."

"And in times of crisis they tend to gather together, in public places, to shout 'UP TRELAWNY'," Debbie added.

"How very odd," said Phipps.

"Sounds downright rude, to me," observed her sister.

Timothy, ever practical, asked, "Why?"

"Because he was one of their home-grown bishops."

"Oh yes," Bun mused aloud. "Wasn't he one of those seven who fell out with James II, over the Declaration of Indulgence, back in sixteen-something-or-other?"

"That's right. A proper old barney. Really fraught. The King put them all on trial. Half the male population of Cornwall downed tools, right-shouldered pitchforks, then marched on London singing 'And shall Trelawny die?

'Here's twenty thousand Cornishmen
'will know the reason why!'"

"Well you're wrong there, Debbie. Our school Glee Club used to sing that ballad. Their choirmaster said it was written nearly two hundred years later, by some bloke called Hawker."

"Born in Plymouth, went up to Oxford - where he won the Newdigate Prize for poetry - and later became vicar of Morwenstow, on the north Cornish coast," Bun told them.

Phipps watched her sister's face darken, before she added, "He ended up a traitor to the cause . . . went over to the Church of Rome twelve hours before going aloft to meet his maker."

The phrase: 'better late than never' crossed Phipps' mind, but she forbore from verbal utterance. Bun could be very stuffy about papists and popery.

Instead, she gazed out of the car's window noting they had finally reached the crest of a very long, steeply winding hill. Their road had been hemmed in by dense woods on the right and a steep cliff to her left, but now they were travelling through pleasant farming country. Low, well-trimmed hedges bordered modest-sized fields of grass or young corn, with small groups of stone-built barns and cottages dotted about the landscape.

Bed and breakfast signs hung swaying beside the road, while hedgerow notice boards pointed the way to Private Camp Sites. Phipps thought their route must have described a wide circle for much of the next two miles, before the contours dipped away and she heard their old car grinding down another steep hillside.

Shortly after turning a corner, she saw the village of Polperro ahead - cottages crowding the valley floor - and a quaint old whitewashed public house on her left.

Phipps caught the name 'Crumplehorn Inn' as they rumbled past, constantly descending towards the sea. A parade of small shops and cafes was followed by another licensed premises: the 'Mermaid Hotel'. Then their car turned right, soon after passing the 'Ship Inn', to cross a tiny river. Another sharp left turn brought them into a narrow street of shops and cottages which soon ended at the beginning of Fish Quay.

"Right! This is as far as I goes. Git yer bags out . . . or you'll make me late for me tea," the driver said, turning round in his seat after parking at the head of a boat slipway.

"But where's our cottage?" Bun demanded.

"You wants The Warren! That's what you telt me, earlier on."

"And this is it?"

Their driver shook his head, explaining the obvious: that this was the Fish Quay. They would have to walk the rest of the way.

"You goes across that lil' ole' 'umpity-back bridge, to yer left, then turns right at the top of that there 'nip'. But you doan't need me to tell 'ee where to go. The boy'll take 'ee."

"But why can't you drive right up to the door?"

"Because that there road's too narrer . . . an' there ain't much room for turning when you gits where youm goin'."

The driver lowered his window and called over a couple of ragged urchins. Phipps thought them no more than eight years old. They had been waiting beside a plank and orange box mounted on four old pram wheels.

"These people wants one of they 'oliday cottages . . . out along The Warren. You want-ter earn yerselves a couple o' bob?"

Phipps, thinking she might as well accept the situation and set a good example, opened her door and got out. She approached the local porters to make a closer inspection.

Number One boy was wearing down at heel boots tied with broken laces, brown socks riddled by large moth holes, dirty grey flannel shorts - with a badly frayed hole in the seat - an oversize blue guernsey and what appeared to be a man's cloth cap jammed down on top of his ears.

Number Two boy - although dressed similarly - was not a boy at all . . . but a little girl. This tiny creature scuttled across to the open door, grabbed the first case she could reach and carried it away to the box on wheels, her pinched little face set in a grim expression of desperate determination.

Phipps felt so upset by the sight of such obvious poverty that she resolved to give the poor little waifs three shillings and sixpence. After all . . . Theo was paying their expenses, and he had plenty of money.

Her three companions quickly followed her out of the car. Bun paid their driver, while the two children loaded all luggage onto the cart. The four Hydes faced the harbour, took deep breaths, breathed out and said 'Ugh! Fish!' in unison. Then they walked slowly after the children - as Phipps saw it - like four mourners at a very peculiar funeral.

Chapter Two

The two children, acting as guides in addition to general carriers, pointed out The House On Props as the Hydes re-crossed the river by the 'umpity-back bridge.

Timothy irreverently murmured something to the effect that it was only a spare room perched on a few mouldy old tree trunks.

Phipps hurriedly said, "Oh isn't that marvelous!" in a loud voice, so the children wouldn't feel hurt by her nephew's insensitive remarks.

Then, shortly after they found themselves walking along the narrow street known as The Warren, Number One boy pointed to the steps and walls of a cottage which had been decorated by hundreds of seashells being set into the plaster saying, "And that's the Shell House, all done by Mr Sam Puckey!"

Timothy drawled, "Well, who would have ever guessed?"

His sister stuffed her hand in her mouth to control giggling.

And Phipps called, "Yes. Very nice, dear," to their guide.

When they could see over a low wall, the little boy - who was a boy - pointed once again, explaining that the low-roofed buildings beneath them were fish cellars, where the men pressed pilchards into wooden barrels for sale to the Italians.

Debbie whispered, "Why don't the Eyeties catch their own fish?"

"Because they're too busy making wine . . . when they aren't making love," her brother replied.

Bun told her nephew to shut up or walk ten paces to the rear.

Shortly after this, the children stopped at a gap in the wall on their right. Phipps saw steps leading to a slipway, with more fish cellars either side. On her left, she found tall, three-story cottages lining a curve in the road.

Number One boy pointed with obvious pride and said to Bun, "There y'are, Missus: CRAGO'S CUBBYHOLE! Shall us go neckst-door an' git yer key?"

Bun nodded her head in silent acquiescence.

The boy touched his raggity cap and scuttled away.

Phipps thought the property disappointing. Its original stonework had recently been covered with new plaster, thereby destroying all character, and she felt the name too 'contrived'. However . . . time would tell, on that point, in due course.

Once the key had been produced and the Hydes obtained entry, Phipps discovered the interior had been modernised every bit as severely as the front facade. She found bedrooms on two floors, with kitchen, small sitting-room and toilet facilities at ground level.

A whispered remark, overheard when Timothy was speaking to his sister, summed it up perfectly: 'Cleaner than a cat's arse'.

Bun - busy allotting bedrooms - after she had secured the best first floor back for her own use in hopes of avoiding early morning harbour noises, observed that all this up-dating had put their nephew's nose right out of joint.

"He certainly won't find any hidden passages down below," Phipps said. "I noticed all the ground floors are new concrete when I turned back a corner of their dreadful linoleum."

"Good job! Now he can take his toffee hammer off to the Great Outdoors when he feels the need to dig up bits of Polperro's more lurid past. Are you quite sure about having that front bedroom? Fishing harbours work according to the tides. You could find yourself being woken at four in the morning!"

Phipps replied disturbance would be compensated by the view.

Once Timothy had collected the advance luggage from next door, he began complaining of hunger pains.

Bun pointed out the larder was bare . . . except for two loaves, a jug of fresh milk, tea and sugar. He had better get along to the shops, before they closed for the night, and buy something.

"Such as . . . ?"

"I'll write out a list," Phipps told her sister.

"Right. In the meantime Debbie: put the kettle on! I'm parched."

The ladies were just finishing second cups of tea when Timothy returned, laden with fresh lettuce, new potatoes, ham, cheese, a bag of mixed biscuits, a fruit pie from the village baker, together with a rich fruit cake, and half a pound of cream.

Grabbing a handful of biscuits, and accepting a cup of stewed tea, he said that they must go to Talland Bay tomorrow.

"A hotbed of smuggling! And a vicar - back in the seventeen hundreds - who was a regular old ghost-buster!"

"How do we reach it," Debbie asked. "Boat or bus?"

"Neither. Shanks's pony. It's only just round the next corner. Less than a couple of miles by public footpath. I thought we might take a picnic lunch."

Bun, turning to address her sister, said it sounded a bit of a dogs' walk. "There and back again."

Phipps asked Timothy if it involved crossing muddy fields. On being assured their path followed the cliffs, she said it might be a good idea. "We'd get lovely views out to sea."

"Hmmm. I suppose so and, if there's been a vicar, one presumes we should find a church to look around," Bun said.

"Oh, there is! Centuries old! Positively ancient and steeped in history," their nephew declared enthusiastically. "And you don't have to return by the same path, if that's the only thing bothering you, because I'm told there's another way back into Polperro. Up the mysterious Bridals Lane . . . where the constant passage of smugglers' carts has carved wheel-ruts in the very rock, itself!"

"And what about ghosts?" Debbie asked.

"They only come out at night . . . but I doubt there's any left."

"You mean your old vicar scared them all away?"

"Something like that, Debs. Legend has it that the Reverend Doidge used to chase them downhill and out to sea by running behind - dressed in a black coat and white periwig - while lashing the air with a huge whip."

Bun observed drily that she had always been given to understand Men of God recited prayers, when exorcising evil spirits. Use of a whip was a new one on her.

Timothy was quick to provide reassurance, by mentioning the case of the spectral coach and four. "Old Doidge has gone down in history as the man who banished it from local turnpikes. A first class example of the power of prayer."

"And where did one meet this apparition, dear?" Phipps asked.

"It used to belt around a nearby village called Lanreath, about four miles up the road from us, drawn by four headless horses at full gallop . . . and driven by The Man In Black!"

"Hmmm. Makes a change from the usual coach stories Phippsie."

"Yes dear. I've always thought it was the driver who went about headless when the clock struck midnight."

Bun agreed, but reminded her sister they were now in the Duchy of Cornwall, suggesting this story might be yet another example of how the natives did things differently.

Debbie, pointing out that her brother had never crossed the River Tamar before today, demanded to know how he had suddenly acquired so much local knowledge within an hour of arrival.

"Met an old seaman . . . just down the road . . . sitting on his front steps near Mr Puckey's Shell House . . . and we got talking. Told me he's known locally as Chuggy Williams."

"Because he talks a load of hot air?"

"No! Because he used to drive the council's steam-roller!"

Bun nodded wisely, observing the sobriquet appeared to fit the known facts . . . as was often the case with village characters.

Timothy grabbed up another generous handful of biscuits.

Debbie told him to stop, or there wouldn't be any left.

Phipps supposed they had better get a proper meal together.

Bun, rising to her feet, said her sister supposed correctly.

It was dark by the time the Hydes had eaten, washed up the dishes, unpacked suitcases and hung up their clothing, so no one wanted to go out on that first evening. A few games of gin rummy were soon followed - by common consent - with biscuits, milky drinks, and then bed.

Phipps was the first to wake up next morning. She shrugged herself into a warm dressing-gown, shuffled her feet into her slippers, then crossed the bedroom floor to pull back curtains and look out upon the harbour.

The sun was already shining out of an almost cloudless sky, giving the promise of a pleasantly warm day for their first picnic. She dropped her gaze. High tide, though just beginning to ebb. Water beneath the Fish Quay was glass calm, reflecting the shapes of boats and dinghies riding to their moorings.

Whitewashed walls of fishermen's cottages, both beside and above the quay, gleamed brightly and Phipps thought even their roofs looked attractive in this early morning light, with that growth of yellow lichens adding a touch of colour to the normally drab grey slates.

Behind the village, she noted a green, scrub-covered hill rising steeply to above the three hundred foot contour line, before gently curving downwards to either side.

Could be oppressive on a dull day, she thought, but not with the morning sunshine streaming across its gorse and bracken.

Black-backed gulls called to each other from rooftop vantage points, ready to dive into the harbour the moment anyone threw fish offal out from quay or boat, whilst a raft of terns floated quietly to and fro in the centre of the inner harbour.

Movement caught her eye as Phipps turned slightly to push up the window sash. She narrowed her gaze, looking towards a small blue motorboat. The 'Three Sisters' was tied up alongside a short length of quay which jutted out at right angles to the opposite shoreline. An old man, dressed in the regulation guernsey and stained grey flannel trousers of a local fisherman, was bending over his starting handle, about to crank the engine.

Proof of his success came when Phipps heard a noise like a Monday morning mangle shatter the formerly peaceful scene, followed by a series of more staccato coughing sounds as cooling water was blown out of the exhaust pipe in the stern . . . to the disgust of the terns who moved further up the harbour, in the direction of the slipway and 'umpity-back bridge.

A woman, wearing a wrap-around pinafore, came out of a front door from one of the small cottages standing on this quay. She carried an enamel washing-up bowl, full of dirty grey water, which she threw into the harbour.

The terns immediately flew out to sea, screeching a vociferous protest as they went.

"'An'some weather, you," the woman called out.

"'Ess, proper job!" came the fisherman's shouted reply.

The woman threw back her work-rounded shoulders to take a deep breath of the fresh morning air, then returned to her cottage and banged the door shut.

The man in the 'Three Sisters' climbed arthritically onto the quay, lifted the loops of his mooring lines from square, creosoted posts, then dropped back aboard. Phipps watched him coil down the ropes, before pulling an engine lever. His boat moved astern to manoeuvre briefly off the end of the quay before chugging out of sight, to her left, headed for the open sea.

With the departure of the 'Three Sisters', she felt as if the spell was broken. It was like watching the end of an American travel film, she thought, where the commentator speaks those immortal words: 'And so they sail away into the western sunset.'

With reluctance, Phipps turned back into the room, brushed and combed her hair, then crept silently downstairs to make a pot of tea. Timothy joined her, shortly afterwards, asking hopefully what they were all having for breakfast.

"Dry bread, dear."

Timothy looked appalled and asked, "Why?"

"Because you forgot to buy any butter, yesterday . . ."

" . . . or eggs, or bacon, or tomatoes. Don't worry, Auntie Phil, I'll slip round to the shops as soon as I've had my mug of tea."

Debbie was next to arrive for tea and biscuits, saying she had slept like a log . . . until woken by some butter-fingered old fishwife dropping a metal dustbin lid in her back yard.

Bun came into the kitchen five minutes later. To her sister's surprise, she was already washed and dressed, declaring their noisy neighbour richly deserved a hundred lines stating: 'I must not drop my dustbin lid before ten o'clock in the morning'.

When she heard Timothy telling Phipps that he was ready to do the shopping, Bun said she would come too because they needed picnic food, in addition to breakfast necessities.

From then onwards, Phipps was amazed how the time flew by. She washed, dressed, and made their beds, returning to find her sister was back and breakfast nearly ready to serve. All hands helped wash up afterwards, and make sandwiches, then the four Hydes set out for Talland Bay.

They turned left, from Crago's Cubbyhole, to walk along The Warren, passing a further scattering of attractive cottages. Then, at the foot of a hill, found the street narrowed to become a footpath at the top. This followed the cliffs past a minature lighthouse, indicating the harbour entrance, then several small vegetable gardens carved out of steeply sloping marginal land.

The granite cross of a War Memorial marked the headland, from where the cliffs curved back to their left. After pausing to admire the view across Talland Bay towards the next headland, with St George's Island beyond, the family set off again.

Phipps was soon able to make out a tiny beach ahead . . . with the parish church tucked into folds of a nearby hill. To everyone's relief, they saw a small cricket pavilion style wooden hut - constructed of creosoted weatherboarding - built on a patch of neatly mown grass at the back of the cove.

"Cream teas . . . ," yipped Debbie, reading aloud.

" . . . and Walls Ice Cream!" her brother joined in.

"With coffee for two . . . ?" Bun enquired of her sister.

"And chocolate biscuits, dear?"

"Of course . . . Brother Theo's paying!" Bun replied.

Accepting their aunts' dictum that eleven o'clock in the morning was not the right time for eating cream teas, nephew and niece settled for sixpenny choc ices instead. Then they left Bun and Phipps sitting at a veranda table to linger over coffee, and walked off to examine flotsam cast up by the receding tide.

Phipps idly watched boy and girl conferring over a stranded crab pot. Suddenly, Debbie jumped backwards, arms waving, and very obviously engaged in spirited argument.

Chapter Three

They had wandered over to the wickerwork crab pot because Timothy said he might be able to salvage a useful length of rope, always handy for cliff climbing . . . or tying driftwood together to make a raft.

Debbie, looking forward to her picnic lunch of crab and lettuce sandwiches, had peered into the stranded pot, hoping to find a fresh crab and been disappointed. She saw the bait remained untouched, and still securely fastened into place.

She thought it looked oddly familiar, picked up a stick and used it to push a frond of bladder-wrack clear, thereby obtaining a better view. She cocked her head on one side, then reached out a hand and tilted the crab pot so that sunlight shone directly onto the bait. She peered closer and prodded it with her stick, shuddered, let the pot fall and called to her brother.

"Hi . . . Tims! Come and look at this, a minute!"

He had begun unravelling rope, intending to coil it up and carry back to their holiday cottage. So he was reluctant to stop and waste time. Debbie clutched his arm, shaking impatiently, telling him he could muck about with his old rope afterwards.

Timothy, failing to shrug off his sister's hands, heaved a theatrical sigh of exasperation and let her draw him across to the stranded crab pot.

"Take a look inside. Tell me what you see."

Timothy stared blankly, as instructed, then straightened up.

"Bit of dead fish, species unknown . . . but obviously unfit for human consumption or it would have been sold in the market. Remember when we were down in Sidmouth last year: the locals always used the poorer stuff for bait . . . either in their pots, or stuck on hooks for the 'long lines'."

Debbie pointed out that this flesh was pinky-red with an almost white skin - though she could see a lot of reddish-brown blotches - and there were no scales . . . only hairs.

"So it's a bit of butcher's offal. Maybe a bit of belly pork."

"What about those blotches? Pigs are white!"

"Not all of 'em. What about The Black Boar, outside Lewes?"

Debbie replied public house signs didn't count because everyone knew a lot of their illustrations were based on mythical creatures.

"If you want my opinion . . . I'd say that's a half a pound of human flesh. Cut from the bone!"

"Come off it Debs. You've been reading my Sherlock Holmes books again. Tell me: do you suppose it was cut from that part nearest the heart . . . as per 'The Merchant of Venice'?"

His sister replied no, it was more probably a thick slice from the back of a leg.

"Right or left?"

"Oh stop playing the fool!"

"Of course . . . it could have come from an arm. Plenty of juicy muscle on the top parts."

"No. You get hair growing on the lower section, but not much above the elbow."

"Any further observations?"

Debbie pointed out that she hadn't had a close look, but if she was right - and the slice of bait had come from a man's calf - he would have been about forty years old.

"And a manual worker or athlete, Tims."

Her brother said she was making it up as she went along. He didn't believe a single word. To prove his point, he took out a penknife to cut the fishing twine securing bait to basketwork, at the bottom of their crab pot.

This was shaken until the bait dropped through to fall on the beach. Timothy turned it over thoughtfully with the toe of his shoe, said "Hmmm" a couple of times, then looked up towards the top of the tideline.

Debbie followed his gaze to see that her aunts were now wandering about, apparently picking up sea shells for souvenirs. Her brother suggested Debbie should try out her theories on them.

"After all: they must know something about human flesh. I mean to say: they did part-time nursing - back in The War - with the Red Cross, or V.A.Ds. They ought to be able to recognise a bit of leg when they see it."

"It may upset them. Bring back old memories of shattered bodies and lost loves. Remember: they both lost their sweethearts in Flanders. Mummy told me. All very sad."

Timothy, turning aside to unravel more of the lines attached to their crab pot, told his sister to get Aunt Anthea to have a look first.

"But don't go rattling on about half pounds of human flesh. That's what the lawyers call a 'leading question'. Just ask if she's got any idea what sort of fish has been cut up for bait, in this pot. They're bound to know a fair bit about fish - living in Brighton for so many years - and now settling in that waterside cottage near Exeter."

Debbie waved and shouted for her aunts to come and look at what she'd found.

Bun and Phipps straightened their backs, the older sister asking why her niece couldn't bring whatever it was up to them.

Phipps smiled as Debbie hopped from one foot to another a couple of times - for all the world as if she was desperate to spend a penny - while replying that IT was not something which she cared to handle.

"Oh children!" Bun muttered softly to her sister.

"You mustn't call them that, dear. Debbie would be most upset. She's nearly sixteen . . . "

" . . . and never misses an opportunity of reminding us, but don't worry Phippsie. I remember what you were like, at that age. Don't think it would bother that boy, though. Master Timothy is too confident for his own good."

"Oxford should help to put him in his proper place, dear."

"If he manages to scrape past the examiners." Bun shook her head. "And I wouldn't care to wager money on his chances of success . . . having already failed Dartmouth."

Phipps suggested this was more probably due to prejudice on the part of the interviewing officers, rather than deficiency of character being displayed by the candidate.

Bun replied with "Humph", placed her shells carefully beside their picnic bags and walked down the beach towards Debbie.

Shown the crab pot bait, now well-covered with sand, Bun retraced her steps to the high tide mark. She picked up a tattered corner of some child's shrimping net and returned. Rolling Debbie's specimen into the net, she took it across to a nearby rock pool and washed it clean before carrying out a closer examination.

There was an almost instant reaction.

"Good God!"

Bun stood up.

"Phipps! Come here!"

Taken completely by surprise, at receiving such a peremptory command, Phipps hurried to join her sister, wondering what on earth could be wrong.

She was shown the specimen of crab pot bait.

"What d'you make of this, old girl?"

One glance was quite enough!

Phipps turned her head away saying that - when she had been helping out at the local officers convalescence centre, during The War - she had specialised in beverages, books and bed-pans.

"I left wound dressing to hardier souls, dear."

"Bit of leg, though?" her sister pressed. "Filleted, of course."

Timothy pricked up his ears on hearing this and re-joined the group, casually mentioning to his aunts that Debbie had been playing at detectives.

"Thinks she's Sherlock Holmes. Been trying to tell me the age of the chap who grew that grisly exhibit."

Phipps listened with growing amazement as her sister replied anyone with reasonable intelligence could see this flesh came from the leg of a full-grown man . . . and he would have been between twenty and forty-five years of age.

"Tell me more," Timothy encouraged, somewhat mockingly to Phipps way of thinking.

Bun gave her nephew a superior look.

"If you're really interested: I should say he had spent a lot of time on his feet . . . postman, milkman, ploughman. Something like that."

"Or a counter-jumper perhaps?" the boy suggested.

"No! Shop assistants stand in one place, often leaning against a shelf or cupboard when there are no customers present. This is part of a well-developed muscle. I think its owner must have walked a lot . . . or perhaps he was a keen cyclist."

Phipps watched breathlessly as her sister bent down to make a closer inspection, then stood up once again nodding her head as if confirming a previously held belief.

"Ginger hair. But that goes without saying, doesn't it?"

Chapter Four

Phipps thought Timothy appeared momentarily disconcerted at this authoritative display on the part of her sister. But their cheeky young nephew rallied splendidly within seconds by innocently enquiring whether Bun's ginger gentleman had parted his hair on the left, right, or centre.

"I pause to remind our nephew of something to be found in chapter seven of Galatians . . . 'for whatsoever a man soweth, that shall he also reap'," Bun intoned grimly.

Reluctant to be put down so abruptly, Timothy asked mildly if anyone could supply a paraphrase.

Debbie was quick to oblige, snapping, "In your case: 'He who asks a silly question will surely receive a silly answer'!"

Phipps moved smoothly into the silence which followed, by saying she understood the preference for manual workers, because muscular development followed such occupations, but wondered about her sister's choice of ginger hair.

"Ah! Puzzled because time and tide have bleached out all the colour from what we have on our specimen?"

"Yes dear. Are there any other bits of this poor creature lying about, further up the beach?"

"Not that I know of, Phippsie. I was going by those blotches on the skin. People with that amount of pigmentation are invariably red-heads."

"And how can you be so precise about this man's age?"

"Because a male below the age of twenty would probably not be so hirsute . . . and those in their late forties would have started to lose it. Happens when coarse material constantly rubs the leg while walking. The calves go 'bald'."

"But why does it have to come from a man, at all?" Timothy asked. "Could just as easily be a bit of woman's leg."

Bun said she entirely disagreed, for no woman would let hair on her legs grow to that length in 1935.

"Skirts are too short," Debbie butted in.

"Something we didn't have to bother about in dear old Teddy's reign," Phipps added, speaking as much to her sister as the others.

"So we ought to be keeping our eyes peeled for signs of a ginger-haired gentleman . . . walking with a pronounced limp?" Debbie asked with a laugh.

" . . . or a local undertaker who goes crabbing on his day off?"

"Don't be so beastly, Timothy!" his sister shouted in disgust. Turning towards Phipps she entreated, "Make him stop, Auntie Phil. He's only saying that to put me off crab sandwiches for life!"

But Timothy was unrepentant, addressing his older aunt upon the question of where they could obtain some formalin, to preserve their evidence. To Phipps' relief, her sister began scraping a shallow depression in the sand, saying they would be better off burying their specimen where it lay.

"There's nothing more to be learnt from this lump of flesh. And if we take it back to the cottage we'll attract every blowfly in Polperro. Next thing you know: the place will be crawling with maggots. Not going to have that!"

"But it's a mystery! Perhaps there's been a murder! We ought to investigate," Timothy pleaded.

Phipps was in silent agreement with her nephew but found no need to give vocal support because her sister was obviously of the same opinion.

"Well of course we'll look into things," Bun said, covering the dead flesh with beach sand. "I suggest you hide this crab pot, together with its marker float and two green canvas flags, under a convenient bush. Then I think we should split up to carry out a thorough search around the nearby shoreline as soon as we've had our lunch."

"What are we looking for?" Debbie asked when they had finished this alfresco meal on grass at the top of the beach.

"Dead bodies!" Her brother answered with what Phipps considered to be an unnecessary display of relish.

Debbie told her brother there was no need to drool so, when mentioning dead bodies. Phipps pointed out their bit of leg muscle might have been cut from the body of some unfortunate walker who had strayed from the path and fallen to his death.

Bun said it was far more likely the body was elsewhere, though they might find another pot with similar bait.

"Such as a human head . . . with blankly staring eye sockets!"

Debbie pointedly ignored her brother's remark, asking Phipps if they could team up together . . . and go off in the opposite direction. This divided the Hydes into three groups. Phipps and her niece elected to examine nooks and crannies amongst low tide rocks, beneath the cliff path leading back to Polperro.

Timothy set out to follow weed-covered rocks on the other side of the cove, eventually rejoining a cliff path beneath Talland Church; while Bun walked along this same narrow track towards Looe, for something over a half a mile . . . peering down at intervals to see if there was any suspicious object lodged in a rock fissure or gully below.

All returned to their picnic baskets empty handed.

By common consent they moved across to the beach cafe for an early afternoon tea, before returning to Polperro.

Timothy wanted to conceal himself amongst cliff top undergrowth, in case the owner came round to collect his crab pot. He could stop all night . . . providing his sister would bring out sandwiches and a flask of hot coffee.

Debbie reminded her brother that their evening meal would include roast chicken, with apple pie and lashings of real Cornish cream to follow. She was not going to miss the chance of a second helping through having to walk all the way back to Talland with his supper.

Phipps was amused at how quickly cheese sandwiches lost their appeal.

Timothy very generously offered to shelve his idea - of standing a night-watch - so that his little sister could enjoy her dinner undisturbed. "She must have regular meals," he explained. "Still growing! Needs lots of nourishing food."

But he fooled no one. Bun and Phipps exchanged secret smiles while his sister called him a smooth-tongued twister.

However, by the time they got back to Crago's Cubbyhole, Timothy had another line of enquiry to pursue. He suggested Debbie should accompany him for a look around the quays, in hopes of finding more crab pots bearing the same double green flag markers.

Bun warned nephew and niece against boarding any suspect boats. "And when one of you is looking over a pile of fishing gear . . . make sure the other is gazing about in the opposite direction, as if admiring the view. That way: you'll soon see if anyone is watching."

Once they were alone in the kitchen, Phipps asked her older sister if she expected the youngsters to find anything.

Bun replied that she very much doubted it, thrusting her hand into the fowl's carcase, to withdraw it moments later triumphantly clutching a handful of giblets. Phipps studiously refrained from watching this performance, bending her head low over the sink as she peeled potatoes.

"Silly, isn't it dear?" she murmured after a while. "We warn Debbie and Timothy not to get into any mischief on the fishing boats, yet encourage their endeavours on the grounds that it will give them an interest." She shook her head. "I wonder how long they will keep up this search for the body of a ginger-haired gentleman?"

Bun replied it would probably depend upon whether they turned up any further clues to help sustain curiosity. "Move over, a minute, old girl," she demanded, then held the fowl's carcase under a tap to fill it with water. Once clean, Bun returned it to the kitchen table and began forcing handfuls of bread stuffing into the gaping hole which had once held the bird's rectum.

Phipps began cutting up a locally grown broccoli - and diligently searching for baby slugs - while carefully avoiding her sister's activities. Bun, still mauling the limp carcase, observed that they were both working quite hard, considering the fact that this was supposed to be as much a holiday for them as for Theo's two children.

"But they'll have to fend for themselves tomorrow."

"Why? Are you going on strike dear?" Phipps asked.

"No. But you and I are both invited to dine at the Pickfords."

"Who . . . ?"

"Colonel Pickford - Royal Horse Artillery - but he was only a captain when we knew him. Early in 1918: one of our convalescent patients at Brighton."

"Oh yes . . . but how did you know he was living down here?"

"I didn't, old girl. Came as a complete surprise. Walking out of the greengrocer's, when a hand grasped my shoulder, while a horsy voice shouted 'Nurse Hyde' in my ear."

"This morning?"

"While you were washing and dressing."

Phipps said she would have thought her sister could have mentioned the meeting before this. Bun asked why? Did she need a fortnight's notice before accepting a dinner invitation?

"Of course not!" Phipps replied crossly.

"Anyway: I've told you as soon as I could. Useless trying to have a sensible conversation - or make arrangements - with Master Timothy larking about all the time."

Phipps nodded her head, observing that this was the first moment they had spent together, since joining their charges on the train, at Exeter, during the previous afternoon. "We must try and introduce ginger-haired men into after-dinner conversation, at the Pickfords. May hear that some local character is missing."

"Without mentioning the fact that we appear to have found a small portion of their body in an old crab pot," Bun cautioned.

"Actually dear: I shouldn't think our victim was resident in the district. Why . . . even the pot could belong to a fisherman from Looe or Fowey."

Bun supposed the ginger-haired man might even have been French, because Brittany crabbers often crossed The Channel.

"But don't mention that to Tim. It might put him off. Frankly: I regard the contents of our crab pot as a bit of a God-send."

"Encourage the pair of them to use up their boundless energy on a wild-goose chase?"

"Less wearisome for us, old girl." Bun straightened up and stretched. "Personally: I'm all in favour of finding a sheltered corner on one of the quays. Want to set myself up with another cardigan before winter. Knitting in the spring sunshine will suit me very well."

Phipps watched as her sister put the bird in the oven, washed her hands and began making pastry for their apple pie. She said she was going to look around the shops for a book on smuggling.

"This is just the place, dear. I believe Polperro was quite famous for smuggling in previous centuries. I shall be able to read all about it then - by looking over the top of my book - I'll be able to see the very cottages where it all happened."

Bun stopped to peel and slice apples, saying that - if Timothy failed to find any further clues - she would jolly well make some up herself. They were in a fishing port, weren't they? Then a dish of good red herrings would not be at all out of place.

"Anything to keep them occupied . . . and out of our hair!" Bun looked across at her sister. "Finished the vegetables, have you? I should think you ought to go down for the cream. Better make haste or the dairy'll be shut."

Phipps hurried upstairs to get her coat and hat, because ladies of her generation obeyed an older sister's command as readily as they once obeyed Mother.

On her way back from the dairy, Phipps left Talland Street at The House on Props, walking down to the 'umpity-back bridge on her right. Looking up at a wall-plate, she found this part was known as Roman Bridge and shook her head in amazement.

Surely the Roman legions never marched through Polperro, let alone stop long enough to build a bridge? Looking down the harbour, she saw the tide was coming in once again, slowly driving a small flock of feeding terns towards where she was standing. Gulls wheeled and dived overhead, every so often settling on a telegraph pole or nearby roof to scream at each other, shoulders hunched, heads thrust forward and down, as if the effort was choking them to death.

Phipps smiled and shifted her gaze to the Fish Quay.

To her delight, she saw Debbie walk into view, soon followed by her brother. They waved to their aunt and hurried along to join her. Predictably, Timothy's first words were, "How's the chicken getting on? I'm so hungry I could eat a horse . . . shoes an' all."

Debbie said they had found some more of those green twin-flag crab pot markers.

Phipps told them to wait until they were inside the cottage before chattering about that, in case somebody was listening.

They found Bun had finished making the apple pie but not yet cleaned up. Timothy perched himself on a clean corner of the kitchen table, picking up a length of discarded apple peel. He put it into his mouth and began chewing idly.

Pressed to tell them all about his discovery, Timothy replied that there wasn't much in it. He and Debs had walked down The Warren and crossed Roman Bridge to stroll through Fish Quay as far as Old Quay.

"That's the short one - opposite us - jutting out from the harbour side," Debbie interrupted. "The one with those cottages built along the back."

Her brother went on to say they had continued up a slipway to the new quay, or breakwater, without seeing much in the way of pots lying about.

"We were just about to give up and come home when I saw some fishing stuff piled against an old tarred shed," Debbie said.

"Built on a flat rock which has been made level with a bit of concrete," Timothy added, "beyond those three waterside cottages which face this way."

"And there they were!" Debbie rushed on when her brother paused to draw breath. "Half a dozen pots; all with two green canvas flags on their marker sticks."

Timothy explained this shed appeared to have been built as a lean-to, directly against the face of a cliff - more easily seen from their bedroom windows - with a cave beneath.

"Local folk call it 'Willy Wilcock's Hole'," Debbie told them.

"Which makes our next move all too simple for words," her brother continued.

Phipps looked towards her sister.

Bun said she hoped Master Timothy was not thinking of making what the Americans called a Citizen's Arrest.

Phipps cautioned: "For 'Vengeance is mine; I will repay, saith the Lord' . . . Romans 12:19 if you're interested."

Her nephew replied, "Not in the least, dear Auntie Phil. Only thinking of keeping observation from the comfort of a front bedroom window . . . with your birdwatching binoculars, if I may? Surely our next step must be: identify the owner of those crab pots?"

At this point Debbie broke in to suggest that, whilst she did not want to be thought a spoil-sport, they really ought to tell the police of their discoveries.

Her aunts thought not . . . firmly and in unison.

Bun told nephew and niece they should keep well back and on no account be seen to become involved. "Village folk tend to inter-marry. Harm one and a dozen take up his cause, regardless of whether he's right or wrong."

Phipps nodded, tight-lipped. "We shall be in the wrong for interfering, dear."

"Cross one . . . cross 'em all!" Bun added.

Phipps reminded Timothy they had only just started their holiday. "We don't want to make life unpleasant for ourselves, at this stage. Different if we were going home again, tomorrow."

"Gosh, yes!" Debbie exclaimed. "We could write an anonymous letter to the Chief Constable . . . and post it at Liskeard station when we're changing to the Paddington express."

Her brother took up this point immediately, saying he would write a letter after dinner. Then he could slip out to post it last thing at night. Nobody would see him and be able to make any connection, when the police arrived in force, on the following morning.

Phipps wondered what startling information could be conveyed, considering the inescapable fact that they had not - as yet - found the body from which their bit of leg muscle had been originally carved. They didn't even have the bait, which would no doubt have been eaten by prowling crabs as soon as the tide came in, that same evening. "The bobbies will think it's a hoax."

"All the more reason to keep an eye on that gear, opposite. D'y'know: I wouldn't mind betting our body's inside that shed."

Phipps, anticipating his next suggestion, murmured, "Oh dear."

Debbie, obviously thinking along the same lines, told her brother he needn't expect her to go sneaking a look in that dirty old shed as soon as the clock struck midnight.

Bun, made of sterner stuff, asked if she might have her nephew's complete and undivided attention for a few brief moments. Timothy turned towards her.

"I shall send a telegram to your father, first thing tomorrow morning, if you as much as open our front door between the hours of ten p.m. and eight a.m."

"Congratulating him upon having such an intelligent, adventurous and resourceful opportunist for a son?"

"No! Advising him to order you home immediately, before you get yourself knocked on the head, then cut up for next week's crab pot bait by some equally enterprising Cornish fisherman!"

Timothy accepted this formidable threat with good grace, assuring his aunts that he was - as everybody knew - one of those chaps who went early to bed and slept late on the following morning whenever possible.

"As Ecclesiastes put it: 'The sleep of a labouring man is sweet, whether he eat little or much' . . . but if it's all the same to you: I'd like large helpings, when you get the dinner on the groaning board. Don't want to keep waking up in the wee small hours, suffering from night starvation."

Phipps asked how her nephew had come by this biblical quotation, to be told it was a favourite of his English master, when enjoining pupils to work harder.

Bun, more concerned with Timothy's fear of night starvation, instructed that he should place his faith in a mug of Horlicks. Portions would be small tonight, because there had to be enough chicken left over for two salads tomorrow. "Your Aunt Phil and I shall be dining with a friend: Colonel Pickford. Met up with him this morning. One of our patients, back in The War. Asked after you, Phippsie! Wanted to know if the little lady who helped save his life was with me. First time I've known the fetching and carrying of bedpans to be described in such terms."

"Somebody had to do it, dear. But Pickford could hobble to the toilets . . . so I expect he was remembering all the cups of tea I used to bring him when Matron wasn't looking."

Encouraged by Debbie, Bun and Phipps reminisced about their time as auxiliary nurses while the dinner finished cooking.

Timothy went upstairs to keep watch over those crab pots, outside the tarred shed, above Willy Wilcock's Hole.

Chapter Five

Polperro rests at the base of a letter 'Y', two inland valleys converging at Crumplehorn, where a stream known as The Pol cuts down through the narrow floor of a third valley, eventually flowing into the harbour beneath Roman Bridge - shortly after passing The House on Props.

The Hydes' holiday cottage stood beside a tarmac road - no wider than a cart track - which followed the northern side of the harbour. There was no road beyond Fish Quay on the opposite side of this water, all cottages further seaward being reached by steep steps and narrow footpaths. These led to a rocky promontory beyond the breakwaters, where a stone-built net store faced the harbour entrance.

The tarred shed above Willy Wilcock's Hole was situated about midway between this isolated building and the breakwater.

Timothy Hyde carried a Lloyd Loom chair over to his chosen bedroom window and settled down to observe the opposite shore.

He raised the binoculars to his eyes . . . and let out a howl of dismay. Crab pots, coils of tarred rope, together with those double green flagged marker floats, had all disappeared.

Petulantly tossing his aunt's binoculars onto the nearby bed, he hurled himself downstairs in a fury of personal afront and resentment to inform the rest of the party.

Making it clear that he felt himself to be the most hard done-by person in the county, Timothy grumbled that one couldn't turn one's back on anything for five measly minutes without somebody else interfering. Now he'd lost his most significant clues and would have to start all over again!

"Good job Debs was with me, when I found those other pots, or you wouldn't have believed a word I said."

Bun calmly told her nephew to stop clucking about the kitchen, as mad as a wet hen, because she was just about to serve up. "Clear off to the dining-room, if you wish to throw a fit."

"All very well for you . . . "

"And it will be even worse for you, young man, if I spill hot fat or boiling cabbage water over your precious person. Come on! Hurry up and get yourself out of my kitchen . . . and take Debbie away too."

Timothy slunk out, making the very predictable assertion that it would be quite impossible for a chap to eat a single mouthful after suffering the shock of such sudden disappointment.

But Phipps smiled knowingly, at the end of their meal, after watching her nephew clear his plate minutes before anyone else.

When the final spoonfuls of pie and cream had been consumed, dishes cleared to the kitchen and coffee placed on the table, Bun raised the subject of the missing fishing gear.

"You didn't see any signs of a boat putting out into the bay, did you Timothy? Or perhaps a lorry or van moving about on Fish Quay?"

"No. Hardly any men hanging around, either. All home for tea, trotters in the trough, I suppose."

"What about those two old gaffers who tottered down Chapel Steps . . . heading for the Three Pilchards?" Debbie reminded her brother.

"They couldn't have moved those crab pots. Hardly able to put one foot in front of another. Shouldn't be at all surprised to hear they've been cut up for bait before long."

"There was that young couple on the breakwater seat, Tims," Debbie pressed him.

"Would that be the same pair we passed on our way to Talland - just before we reached the War Memorial?" Bun asked.

"Yes. Sick-making, wasn't it?" Debbie said scornfully. "Billing and cooing all over the place like a pair of collared doves."

"Perhaps . . . but they're staying in the village. About three or four doors along from the post office," Bun told her niece.

Phipps said it should be obvious that this must be Timothy's starting point when making further enquiries.

"I suppose I have to creep up on them when they're kissing, then ask my questions the minute they come up for air? Could be embarrassing!"

"Oh get along with you," Phipps exclaimed, "and take Debbie too. Anything's worth a try."

Bun suggested they also walked along to the tarred shed.

"Take a closer look at the doorway. A torn spider's web would prove it has been opened within the last hour or two. And look at the rock. There might be drag marks, or nail scratches."

"And it wouldn't do any harm to cast an eye over those boats tied up alongside the quays, in passing," Phipps suggested.

"Yes, of course. Somebody may have loaded that gear aboard before going home for tea . . . in readiness for setting tonight," Bun encouraged them.

"What about a quick peep in that shed?"

"Absolutely not, Debbie!"

"Goodness me," Phipps added, "that would be worse than sneaking over in the middle of the night."

"Can't see why," her nephew muttered sulkily.

"Because the whole village would know, that's why, Mister Addle-Brain!" Bun exploded with exasperation. "And Debbie: make sure you put yourself in a position which enables you to keep an eye on those neighbouring cottages, while your brother is performing his Nosey Parker act."

"Look out for twitching curtains, dear,"

"What happens when I see one, Auntie Phil? Do I give it a wave . . . or sidle over to Timmie and whisper 'nudge, nudge' out the corner of my mouth?"

Phipps thought neither nephew nor niece was taking the matter as seriously as they should be. After all: the ginger-haired man may have been murdered. Surely they could realise they were putting themselves at risk? But she wisely abstained from further comment.

Timothy and his sister finished drinking their coffee, then rushed upstairs. They collected coats and scarves before hurrying off in the direction of Roman Bridge and Fish Quay.

Once they had put a few yards between themselves and Crago's Cubbyhole, Timothy said that was the only trouble with maiden aunts . . . some of them could be a bit of a Droopy Drawers at times.

"Our dearly beloved Aunt Anthea being the current case in point."

"You're only saying that because she didn't want you going into the tarred shed. Personally . . . I think she's marvelous. Fancy thinking of broken spider-webs! A proper wise old bird."

"Can be a bit abrupt, though. I think I prefer Aunt Phil. She's a nippy little number. More fun. Like one of us."

Debbie suggested they had to make due allowance for a retired one-time school teacher, but still defended their older relative by drawing attention to Bun's very dry sense of humour.

"A bit like the Scots. One has to think more if one is to get the point. I'll bet they were a scream when they were nurses."

Timothy said he could well imagine Auntie Phil running about with bedpans . . . but not Aunt Anthea.

They continued discussing the merits, or otherwise, of their two maiden aunts as they walked past Sam Puckey's Shell House, then turned down towards the quays. There was no sign of that honeymoon couple. The boy and girl carried on up a short slipway, behind cottages built on Old Quay, to inspect the door of the tarred shed for signs of damaged cobwebs.

Timothy drew his sister's attention to the fact that - although provided with a stout hasp and staple - this was secured by nothing more formidable than a wooden peg.

"God! What a temptation, Debs."

"Don't even think about it, you idiot!"

Timothy gave a quick glance round. "Nobody out and about."

"But if you could see this place so well from one of the bedroom windows . . . so can Aunt Anthea!"

Her brother acknowledged the wisdom of this caution. "She's probably watching at this very moment . . . and wishing she'd learned to lip-read!"

Debbie moved closer to the door.

"Well she's right about spiders' webs, Tims. There's a very disgruntled specimen out with the darning needle, making repairs, up at the top right hand corner."

"Marks on the ground, too," her brother observed, pointing towards glazed crescent-shaped scoring at his feet.

"Probably a bit of seaweed trapped under those crab pots when they were dragged into the shed."

"All the more reason for taking a squint inside."

Debbie insisted it would be safer to go for a nice long walk and perhaps come over again on the following night . . . whilst their aunts were busy talking over old times with Colonel Pickford. "It will be dark long before they come home."

"Hmmm. Not much in the way of street lighting either, Debs," her brother said after looking up at one rickety lamp, not very securely fastened to the corner of a nearby cottage wall.

Well: it was a lovely evening, he thought to himself. And there was still warmth in the land, although the sun had just set. Idyllic, really, for enjoying a quiet stroll. Not a breath of wind to disturb the sea and smoke from cottage chimneys going straight up in the air, to hang above the village like a very fine evening mist. Peaceful. Even the gulls were silent.

Timothy patted his sister's shoulder.

"OK. You win. Let's explore the cliff path."

Conversation lapsed as soon as they began climbing Chapel Steps, for narrowness prevented two people walking side by side, as did the footpath beyond.

"No wonder everyone looks old, down in that village," Debbie murmured as they leaned on a fence, just above the tarred shed, to catch their breath. "People must wear themselves out climbing all these Cornish hills. Do you know: I counted thirty-seven steps on our way up . . . and that's the only path to those cottages behind us, or the big house on the headland."

Timothy reminded his sister there appeared to be a shelter out there. Perhaps they could sit down for a while. He led the way along a path, which skirted the long garden of Bay View House, to where an open-fronted slate and stone shelter had been built against its boundary wall. This was unoccupied, faced the open sea and was lined with wooden benches.

Debbie brushed past her brother to flop down with a sigh of relief. He looked to his right, where the path continued uphill, passing behind cliff top allotments growing Cornish new potatoes. There were two people walking towards Polperro from the direction of Lansallos Cliff. A man and a woman.

He appeared to be empty handed.

She carried a bulging shopping bag and something else.

Behind Timothy, his sister was saying that their aunt had certainly been right about watching cottage windows. She had noticed old net curtains fluttering in two homes which overlooked that path leading towards the tarred shed.

The boy went into the shelter to drop down beside Debbie as she said, "I can't believe the remains of our ginger-haired man are in that shed. I mean to say . . . if local residents rush to their windows as we pass by, imagine their eagerness to spread the word, when a dead body is involved."

"Could have been a fight."

"But the neighbours would have heard."

"All right. Perhaps Mister Ginger was dead on arrival."

"So how did he get inside the shed?"

"Wheeled there on a fish barrow?"

"Don't be daft! Those things have wooden wheels with iron bands. Wheeling one of them across Fish Quay in the middle of the night would have woken half the village!"

Timothy pointed out one could make the same journey at midday without arousing any interest whatsoever. "A tarpaulin covering the load. If challenged, our man could simply say he was taking some nets up to his store."

Debbie said her brother had been seeing too many films of the wrong sort . . . and was obviously under the influence of Chinamen who kidnapped people by rolling them up in carpets, then carrying them off in laundry baskets.

"Well how about this: the body was rowed ashore at night. Low tide - which meant that sandy beach in front of Willy Wilcock's Hole was uncovered - then the chap who owns the shed walked round there in a perfectly normal manner . . . and hauled up his grisly load on the end of a rope."

"Why was the body dead . . . in the first place?"

"Hell! How should I know? Maybe he ran out of puff while running up Chapel Steps."

"Then it was a natural death. Why not simply tell the proper authorities: such as the village bobby?"

"Because our shed owner was short of crab pot bait and brought up on the maxim of 'waste not, want not'," Timothy replied with an irritable shrug.

By then, the two people whom he had seen earlier were drawing abreast of the shelter. The man was wearing a clerical collar. The woman was holding a professional-sized butterfly net in one hand, while her other arm was stretched full length with the strain of carrying a heavy, large blue-grey shopping bag.

After they had passed out of earshot, Timothy said he thought he heard the clink of bottles. His sister supposed the vicar and his wife were returning home from a picnic. They could therefore presume the shopping bag contained empty lemonade bottles.

"Rubbish! Those bottles were full. The clinking sound was all wrong for empties. Too dull and muted. Empties would have made a sharper noise. Anyway: it's a bit late to be coming back from a picnic. I wonder if they were carting home the weekly supply of best French brandy?"

Debbie gazed out to sea in thoughtful silence for a few moments, then asked her brother why he didn't get up and follow his suspected smugglers.

"Too obvious. Put 'em on their guard. In any case: there's no fun in discovering where they live . . . we need to head in the other direction."

"Meaning: if we can find out where they land the stuff we ought to be able to snitch a few bottles for ourselves?"

"Re-labelled A Present From Polperro . . . ?"

" . . . for presentation to our grateful parents when we get home to Lewes," Debbie suggested with a laugh. "And I dare say the aunts would be equally appreciative."

Timothy thought they might be persuaded into actually helping secure supplies. "I mean to say: Auntie Phil was showing a very definite interest in smuggling history, as we were coming down here, wasn't she?"

Brother and sister continued to sit talking until the light finally began to fail, and cooler night air caused them to shiver.

But just as they agreed to return to their holiday cottage, the young honeymoon couple came up from the village.

Getting to his feet, Timothy called, "Come on in. Only my sister and I in residence . . . and we're just about to make tracks down below." Then, without knowing what he was talking about, but determined to start a conversation, he asked the man if either of them had seen a big, burly fisherman, wearing a stained blue yachting cap, whilst sitting on the breakwater, earlier.

This ruse worked, for the young man replied they had the place to themselves. This was hardly surprising, because it was then round about local people's tea-time.

However, his young wife recalled seeing somebody come out of a shed, built against the cliff above Willy Wilcock's Hole. This man had gone into a nearby cottage.

"But he wasn't what I'd call 'burly'. More like old and scraggy. Didn't stay long . . . before coming out again, carrying a small brown leather overnight case."

"Oh that's right, Ethel," the young man joined in. "He went off with that tall bloke. Remember: I said he reminded me of a plain clothes policeman, what with the height, his neat brown suit and trilby hat?"

Ethel did remember.

Timothy cheerfully changed the subject.

Conversation then proceeded along the usual lines for holidaymakers meeting far from home.

"Wasn't it nice down here?"

"Yes very, we're from Kilburn . . . where do you come from?"

"Lewes, Sussex . . . and are you staying long?"

"Got another week, before we're due back," and so on.

Timothy let things run their course, making an excuse to leave during a lull, then setting off for the village. He stopped after passing the entrance to Bay View House. Leaning on the fence, above a steeply sloping plot of overgrown tussocky grass, he nodded towards his left.

"That's the cottage our newlyweds spoke of, Debs. This bank's too steep to climb down without a rope. Break your neck in trying, but one could roll a dead body below . . . "

" . . . and then carry it those few yards into the tarred shed, on our right," Debbie murmured. "But what about this pair of semi-detached houses, a bit further along the path from where we're standing? Bit chancy, surely? One might be seen."

"Not on a pitch dark night. Very feasible, I'd say."

Debbie accepted this, but said she was getting colder by the minute and dying for a mug of hot cocoa . . . then bed. Her brother agreed they'd done enough for one evening and they set off once again.

At the bottom of Chapel Steps, Debbie asked her brother if he really believed the man from the end cottage had been taken away by the police. Timothy replied it was most unlikely because there would have been a terrific hullabaloo if anyone had found the remainder of Mister Ginger's body.

"An ambulance, or something, to cart it away; bobbies questioning the immediate neighbours . . . and half the villagers standing about so's they wouldn't miss anything."

"I suppose it could have been the old fellow's son or nephew, come to take him on a family visit elsewhere," Debbie allowed.

Her brother said they would get a second opinion, by asking the aunts over supper.

When they did so, Phipps agreed with the family visit theory. Bun thought not, pointing out that fishermen were notoriously poor. It therefore followed no one would miss this fine weather by going away when he could be out in his boat.

Timothy then changed the subject by mentioning the lady with the butterfly net and heavy shopping bag.

Bun pulled a local map off the small bookshelf, opened it and gestured towards the coastline. "There's a footpath all the way back to Polperro from this place: Lansallos. I suggest we hire a car to take us out - complete with picnic food - then we can have a slow stroll home, keeping our eyes open for signs of activity in the coves: such as odd shaped buoys close inshore, marks in the sand where boats have been landed or . . . if we're very lucky: perhaps a broken bottle bearing a French label."

"And what about checking up on this fellow who may have been taken away by the police?" Timothy asked.

"Walk round the harbour, first thing tomorrow morning, stopping to admire the view when you get within earshot of fishermen mending their nets. Haven't you noticed?" Bun asked, "They chatter like magpies. Must be saying something of interest. Bound to mention anything as sensational as police business. Go out before breakfast. Give it a try."

Chapter Six

Next morning dawned bright and clear. All four Hydes were out of bed and eating an early breakfast shortly after eight o'clock, though Bun and Phipps were doing so in their dressing-gowns. This was an accepted routine when home in their cottage on Tozers Quay, in Topsham. Bun saw no reason to change such a comfortable habit just because their present dining-room window looked straight out onto The Warren, despite Phipps pointing to a lack of garden between themselves and local residents, passing to and fro a few feet away.

Phipps, who sat facing the window, had only just regained her chair after serving plates of bacon and eggs. She was about to start eating when she stared out, exclaiming, "There she goes again!" and rushed across the room to crane her neck, trying to look further up the narrow thoroughfare.

"Who is it? Anyone we know?" drawled Timothy, regardless of this being such an improbability when so far from Lewes.

"Only some old village woman," his sister told him.

Phipps said this was the fifth time she had seen the same woman, always carrying two covered plates and a shopping bag.

Bun observed that other people's idiosyncratic eating habits were nothing to do with them.

Timothy suggested the local woman probably kept a mad son locked up in her back garden coal shed, so that he wouldn't be taken away to the loony bin.

Debbie said it was far more likely to be an illigitimate child whose presence was being kept from the neighbours. "Country folk can be quite strait-laced about that sort of thing . . . very probably still believe in death-by-stoning for a woman taken in adultery," she added in matter of fact tones before stuffing more bacon and egg into her mouth.

Bun suggested a change of subject.

Phipps returned to her seat, saying she was intrigued.

"But it's not quite so exciting as dead bodies and bottles of brandy is it, Auntie Phil?" Debbie said gently.

Phipps replied that she did not - as a general rule - make it her business to mind that of others, but this constant carriage of food along a public roadway was an activity quite new to her. She was surprised her companions displayed such marked indifference. She ate the rest of her breakfast in a huffy silence.

Timothy rose from the table as soon as he had cleared his plate, saying he was off to find the local church . . . and see if last night's clerical gentleman was the incumbent.

The boy walked briskly down The Warren, continuing straight on through Talland Street into Fore Street, where he turned left just before the bakery. He hurried through Big Green - where no grass grew - and up Saxon Bridge to its junction with Landaviddy Lane and Lansallos Street.

An arrow, high up on a cottage wall, pointed towards St John's Church. Timothy reasoned the vicar would come this way, down Little Laney, when he had seen his parishioners out of the building at the conclusion of the early morning service, and propped himself against a convenient wall.

The boy took a local guide-book from his coat pocket, and made a pretence of orientating himself by comparing the map inside with his actual locality.

Five minutes later, a small group of mainly elderly people walked slowly down Little Laney, murmuring quietly amongst themselves. Their vicar followed a few minutes after, robes folded carelessly over his left arm, humming a reprise of that morning's final hymn.

Timothy pursed his lips, nodding to himself with satisfaction. Just what he had expected: the same man who had accompanied the woman with the butterfly net and heavy shopping bag on the previous evening.

The boy closed his book and began retracing his steps along Lansallos Street, heading for the harbour quays.

A small half-dressed child wandered out in front of him from an open cottage doorway. Its mother hurriedly followed, giving the poor child a thorough shaking as she dragged it, frantically screaming, back indoors. Timothy wondered if she ever dislocated the child's arm, as he continued on his way.

There were sounds of raised voices further on, down the road. The boy paused to re-tie a perfectly satisfactory shoelace, soon concluding - from what he could hear - that the housewife was berating her husband for spending so much time in the Ship Inn.

The smell of frying kippers drifted across his path, as he continued towards the waterfront. This mingled with the flavour of bacon and eggs when he passed a neighbouring doorway, where cheap - and very cracked - linoleum displayed a degree of polished shine far in excess of its present market value.

Two doors down, a large ginger cat waylaid Timothy by stepping purposefully in front of the boy, then laying over to roll on its back in an abandoned manner.

Timothy bent to rub his hand gently across the animal's stomach. Instantly, four legs and a mouthful of needle-sharp teeth set about his unprotected flesh. The boy withdrew, muttering that anyone would think the cat hadn't been fed for a month . . . which was in direct contradiction to evidence afforded by a glance at the animal's bulging abdomen.

A dairyman was making door to door deliveries at one of the last cottages. Timothy, mindful of his aunt's advice to eavesdrop where the locals were talking, took out his guide-book and stopped while pretending to read it.

Straining his ears, he heard the housewife complain of the man being late again.

"What's the matter, this time, Jacko? Forget to put the milk in the water an' 'ave to go back for it?"

"Aw you've no need to worry your 'ead 'bout things like that, Miz Hocken. You always gets yourn out o' the good churn. I keeps that there watery ole stuff for 'im on the quay. 'Ee wants a ha'penny off the pint for takin' quantity . . . so I puts a drop of tap water in 'is milk to balance things up, like."

"Oh I dunno, Jacko. You'm turning into a proper ole crook!"

"But I doan't make no more money, m'dear," Jacko protested. "It's just that the cafe do get a little less milk!"

Timothy nodded judiciously. That sounded fair enough, even if it wasn't strictly legal. He closed his book and went on his way.

Two old men stood gazing down on a fish box, halfway along the first quay. Timothy strolled over to stand within earshot.

The man with the pipe was murmuring about a poor catch.

His companion tapped the edge of the box with his walking stick, saying they caught all the good fish when they were young.

The pipe smoker agreed.

"Ess! Getaway: I mind the times when I've crewed my cousin Mervin West's lugger - over to Looe - for a night with the longlines, down off The Lizard. Us caught bass so heavy the gut'd cut yer fingers right down to the bone when you wuz pullin' the beggars up over the side," he said with obvious pride.

Timothy shuddered and moved over to the top of steps where a small blue crabber was tied up. Three younger fishermen, all dressed in the 'regulation' flat cloth cap, guernsey and serge trousers tucked into turned-down thigh boots, stood on the edge of the quay, idly watching the owner trying to start his engine without much success.

"Denzil wants to git a Kelvin. Ah told 'im so time an' agin'."

"Won't 'ave none of it, will 'ee, Amos? Daft beggar!"

"Can't tell the likes of 'ee nothing, boy. Gits it from the mother. Ah knew 'er when we wuz still at school. Proper know-it-all, wuz Bessie Tripconey."

"Denzil there, sticks to that lil' ole Stuart Turner year in, year out, an' spends more time trying to start the danged thing than 'ee ever does in goin' fishin'. Tell 'ee boy: 'er's wore right out!"

"Reminds me of ole' Vicky Vague, George."

"An' 'ee were so mean 'ee wouldn't give a crippled crab a crutch!" Timothy heard George reply with a loud laugh.

The boy moved away . . . resolved to fit Kelvin engines to his motor yacht - if he ever owned one - and be kind to crippled crabs.

There were men at work, mending a net, outside one of the cottages on Old Quay. Timothy edged close . . . to discover their conversation appeared to be centred upon conger eels.

One young fisherman was saying he wouldn't never have one in his boat, after that time old Charlie Collins got bitten in the ankle. "The damn'd thing 'ad bin lyin' in the sun for ages. Us both thought 'im dead. Then poor old Charlie goes to step over the body and the fish ups an' got 'im . . . just like that!"

"Never touch a conger 'til you've cut off 'is 'ead, Janner!"

Timothy felt this to be rather useless information for a solicitor's son who lived several miles from the Sussex coast, and mooched away in the general direction of the breakwater.

He paused to look longingly at the tarred shed's closed door. Could there be the remains of a man's body inside? Perhaps now reduced to bare bones after all edible flesh had been cut off and used to bait those missing crab pots?

And what would he feel like . . . confronted by a skeleton which still had gobbets of human flesh adhering to it? I wonder if it will smell awful? But no . . . because if that were the case, we should have smelt something when we were looking at that door, yesterday. However: it might be a good idea to pop the odd clothes peg in my pocket, he decided, and a nice clean handkerchief for stuffing in my mouth, too.

Timothy found three groups of men out on the breakwater. Some were mending crab pots, others splicing ropes, while their elders sat on a wooden bench. Sheltered by a masonry wall, they were keeping an eye on harbour activities, when not discussing local fishing boats and the characters who ran them.

The boy gave up and made his way back to Crago's Cubbyhole in time for morning coffee.

He found his aunts seated in one of the front bedrooms so that they could enjoy an unobstructed view of the opposite waterfront. Bun poured coffee and Phipps offered a plate of garibaldi biscuits.

Before Timothy had a chance to moan about his wasted morning, Debbie returned, running upstairs to join them.

"Hello Tims. How d'you get on? Amongst the Old Men of The Sea?"

"Wasted effort! Sweet Fanny Adams! Though I did hear of an amusing expression for personal meanness."

"Do tell!" demanded his sister.

"But only if it's fit for mixed company, young man," Bun cautioned.

He repeated the comment concerning crutches being withheld from crippled crabs, feeling gratified when Auntie Phil and his sister burst out laughing . . . but somewhat chagrined to hear Aunt Anthea advance her own opinion that the expression did not sound very 'Cornish'.

"The chap who said it was a proper 'Janner'."

"Yes . . . but fishing boats come down to these small ports from as far afield as Aberdeen," Bun nodded her head as if quite making up her mind. "I think you'll find that expression originated North of the Border . . . it travels well, though."

"So what happened - down on the quays - did everybody clam-up when you sidled over?" Debbie asked.

"Huh! They had plenty to say, but it was all about fish. I am now a positive mine of information on cuckoo wrass and cod; grey gurnard and red mullet; to say nothing of ling and the lesser spotted dogfish."

"The one that barks when you catch it?"

Timothy ignored his sister's interruption, going on to say that he could also regale them with blood-curdling stories of mortal combat with man-eating conger eels . . . but nothing of any consequence relating to the use of human bait in crab pots.

Debbie shook her head, gulped some coffee and told her brother not to fret . . . it had been just the same in the shops.

"I got endless talk of countless grandchildren, complaints about the price of pasty meat and detailed instructions concerning the marinading of mackerel. Oh yes! And Mr Dyson's car has a dent in one wing!"

The girl looked brightly round her audience before adding, "Anyone happen to know a Mr Dyson?"

Phipps looked across at her sister. "You don't suppose . . . ?"

" . . . he could be one of the Wisborough Green people?" Bun nodded, her lips compressed with obvious distaste.

"There was some sort of scandal, wasn't there, dear?"

"Yes. Too free with the beer during a by-election. Accused of buying votes. Must have been just before The War."

Phipps wrinkled her eyes with concentration before suggesting she thought the Liberals had still been in power - under Mr Asquith - so that would have made it about 1912. "The same year as poor Captain Scott reached the South Pole. I wonder what happened to him . . . George Dyson . . . not Captain Scott."

"I heard he eloped with an under-age heiress, old girl. Married in Scotland - if they married at all - then skulked off to the South of France as soon as War was declared to avoid service in the trenches. Mind you, Phippsie: his card playing earned him a pretty dubious reputation before all that happened."

"But he was never actually caught cheating, surely?"

"No . . . but let's just say that he was always the last person to be asked to make up a foursome!"

Timothy, becoming bored with these reminiscences of life before he was born, observed that the Polperro Dyson couldn't be the same man as the aunts were speaking about. "He'd be dead and buried by now. All that was over twenty years ago."

His Aunt Anthea's reply rocked him back on his heels, making him wish he'd kept his thoughts to himself.

"Nonsense! George Dyson wouldn't be more than a few years older than I am . . . and I'm still alive!"

Timothy apologised and offered the plate of garibaldi biscuits.

Bun declined, saying that she disliked them because bits always became stuck between her teeth. They were Phipps' choice.

Everyone lapsed into silence until Timothy, impatient to get on with solving mysteries, asked what they should do next.

Bun thought somebody ought to take a look at the damaged car. "What else did you hear, Debbie?"

"Not much. Only that it hasn't been out of its garage since the accident. But the woman who was doing all the talking didn't seem to know what hit it, or when the damage was done."

Conversation lapsed once again, though it was obvious to Phipps that her sister was deep in thought.

Bun voiced some of these, as soon as she had refilled her coffee cup, by observing that - in general terms - a damaged rear wing could indicate somebody else had run into Dyson's car. "On the other hand: a dent in the front wing is surely evidence that Dyson drove into another vehicle, stray cow or person on foot?"

"You don't suppose, by any chance, that was how our ginger haired gentleman ended up in a crab pot?" Phipps enquired.

"Meaning this chap Dyson paid a local fisherman to get rid of the evidence . . . following a fatal accident?" Timothy suggested.

Bun shrugged her shoulders.

"It has been my experience that black sheep do not change the colour of their wool with advancing age. If the George Dyson I knew had been involved in something which could lead to a charge of manslaughter, I wouldn't put it past him to find a way of dodging the issue."

"In which case: perhaps we should try and discover where he garages the car dear," Phipps proposed.

"Then we could check for bloodstains and human hairs," Debbie suggested.

Bun asked Timothy if he had passed a public telephone box.

"Yes. End of Fish Quay."

"Then have a walk over there . . . now!"

"To give him a ring?"

"No. Of course not!" Bun grumbled, giving her nephew a sharp glance. "To find out where he lives. Look in the directory. Shouldn't take long. Can't be many people named Dyson living around these parts. It comes from the Greek. Not a Celtic word."

Timothy stood up, ready to leave immediately.

"Half a tick! I'll come too," his sister called as she swallowed her last mouthful of coffee and rushed across the room.

Once outside their cottage, and hurrying down The Warren, Debbie said their aunt's car accident idea seemed a pretty sound explanation of the crab pot mystery.

Her brother replied that he hoped not.

"Why? Think we were on to a cold-blooded murder?"

"Not necessarily. Don't know what to think until I've had a poke around inside that tarred shed. But a car accident's going to turn our mystery into a dreadful anti-climax, don't you think?"

"Terribly ordinary," Debbie agreed, then nodded to herself, as she pointed out this must be a very likely explanation. "It was the way that woman spoke about Dyson . . . "

"Saying the car hasn't been on the road, since the accident?"

"Yes! I'll bet he's too scared to drive it. Sure sign of a guilty conscience!"

Timothy shrugged. "Probably our rotten luck to find out the car was kicked by a horse that doesn't like motors . . . and Dyson has left it in his garage for the simple reason that he's been in bed with a bad cold, or a touch of food poisoning."

They crossed Fish Quay in thoughtful silence to find the telephone kiosk occupied by a young woman wearing a cheap wrap-around print pinafore over a sleeveless brown cotton frock. Carpet slippers on otherwise bare feet indicated she lived in a nearby cottage. Curler rags, tied in her obviously dyed blonde hair, had Timothy scowling with distaste.

Her mannerisms, whilst speaking on the 'phone, gave his sister an attack of the giggles.

The woman was chatting garrulously: one minute laughing at the kiosk roof, next moment looking down at her feet and going all coy.

Timothy suggested strolling as far as the breakwater and back again, by way of passing the time. "You can stay on the line as long as you like for tuppence, if it's a local call," he reminded Debbie, "and, judging by her performance over the past few minutes, I'd say she's out to get full value for her money."

"Probably regards the 'phone as being put there especially for her use, Tims."

"And isn't going to be cut short out of consideration for a couple of passing holidaymakers like ourselves, chum."

Walking behind Old Quay, Debbie observed this was really only an excuse for having another look at the tarred shed.

"Can't help it, Debs. Boys are naturally curious."

"Like stray dogs and Tom cats? Mind you don't get a bowl of cold water thrown over yourself, one dark night!"

But, to their surprise, the brother and sister found a carpenter at work on the end cottage, when they reached the path sloping upwards towards the tarred shed. Timothy led the way, with Debbie close behind, each sneaking a sideways glance at man and cottage in passing, then stopping to lean on an iron rail and gaze down into Willy Wilcock's Hole.

"Something's up!" Timothy murmured.

"There's a new padlock on the shed door."

"And that carpenter's fixing a Yale lock to the front door."

"Perhaps your old fisherman's left. Gone for good. Never to return again," Debbie suggested.

Timothy admitted his youthful optimism had just taken a very severe downturn. "At this rate: we'll never get to the bottom of things," he grumbled, turning back for the telephone kiosk.

They found the bottle-blonde had gone and it took only a matter of moments to look up Mr Dyson's address. Timothy grinned when he rejoined his sister.

"Guess what?"

"Not on the 'phone?"

"Living just across The Warren from Crago's Cubbyhole. Probably on the water's edge. A place called: 'Rowett's Cellars'."

Debbie said she remembered passing the name on an iron gate. Steps led downwards to a building with a new roof and lots of small square-paned, cottage-style windows.

"It must have cost a fortune to renovate . . . if it was once a fish cellar," she observed. Turning to look out across the narrow harbour, the girl nudged her brother's shoulder. "There you are. The one with that little terrace at the seaward end."

"Low roof, single story, with a bit of a balcony. Wish we were staying there. Look: it's even got a ladder down to the water. One could land one's mackerel right alongside the kitchen door!"

"Might even find a fish on your hook - dropped overnight from the bedroom window - if it was high tide," Debbie suggested.

"Grow new potatoes in the window boxes - instead of all those geraniums - and one could live for nothing, Debs."

His sister agreed with all these flights of fancy, but brought her brother back to earth by pointing out none of the waterside properties possessed garages.

Timothy saw no reason why this should cause any difficulty.

"In a village as small as Polperro, it surely won't take long for us to check up on most of the out-buildings capable of bedding-down a motor? I propose a quiet stroll up Fore Street and past those shops in The Coombes, as far as Crumplehorn Mill, after lunch. Pity we don't know the make, though."

Debbie said that was unnecessary, on the grounds that they were unlikely to find more than one car with a dented wing. In fact, on reflection, she did not suppose there would be many cars in the entire village. Fishermen tended to put their money into bigger boats and larger nets . . . so they could earn more.

"From what I've seen, I don't think your average fishing family even owns a push-bike."

This proved to be the case when they peered through cobweb begrimed windows of suitable premises, after a luncheon of fresh lobster salad, followed by strawberries and Cornish cream.

They found upright mangles, tin baths hanging from nails on walls, copper boilers lurking in dark corners beneath piles of old nets, and countless tea chests filled with mouldering ropes, but few bicycles or motor cars.

Then Debbie remembered seeing several garages cut into the roadside, as one looked up Talland Hill from near the corner grocer and newsagent's shop.

Struggling up this incredibly steep hill - once the main road into Polperro - they eventually found a two-seater sports car, finished in light cream cellulose. It was standing in an open garage, large enough to take three vehicles, and its front off-side wing was badly dented.

On walking inside for a closer inspection, Timothy found traces of soil and vegetation around the damaged area and also sticking to the wheel nut. He examined the R.A.C. badge, fixed to a chrome bar beneath two wire-screened headlamps, then rejoined his sister.

"Looks as if our much-respected Aunt Anthea is right, once again, Debs. That car's grazed a hedge on what would have been the wrong side of the road."

"Which means the driver swerved to avoid something? But went too far and ploughed into the Cornish scenery?"

"More or less . . . but he didn't miss the man in the road! I found some hairs trapped beneath that member's badge. Difficult to say for certain - because it was a bit dark inside there - but I reckon they're a very light brown . . . or could be ginger!"

Chapter Seven

Bun agreed with her nephew's interpretation of the evidence found on the car, when Timothy and his sister returned for afternoon tea. "However: wouldn't it have been a good idea to bring back a few of those hairs in an envelope?"

Timothy replied that he had not been carrying envelopes at the time. In fact, he didn't believe he had ever taken envelopes out walking. "The odd penknife and length of string, when I think of it, but not much else . . . except for the regulation clean handkerchief."

Debbie, anxious to stick up for her brother, reminded her aunt that they no longer possessed the original specimen - taken from the crab pot at Talland - so they couldn't run any sort of comparison test.

Timothy added that he had thought it best to come away from the vehicle, once its identity was established, in case he was caught in the garage. "Didn't want to draw attention towards us. Better to return during the late evening."

"When everyone's safely shut up beside their cottage fires, toasting their toes," Debbie added.

"By the way: the car's a Riley Imp, if you're interested."

Phipps smiled to herself as her sister informed their nephew she had been brought up during the latter days of the governess cart, which his grandmother had used when making calls around the parish. She had never been vibrantly interested in cars.

"And when we were older," Phipps joined in, "we used to think it quite dashing to be invited for a ride in a young man's curricle."

"So you see Tim: we're really still horse and carriage people," Bun explained. "Nothing like the sound of jingling harness - as one jogs along country lanes - and the delicious smell of horse."

Phipps, recalling what the horse left behind, steaming in the road, hoped Timothy would not make indelicate remarks.

She had been toasting tea-cakes beneath the kitchen grill, because Bun and herself always considered they made tea so much more civilised, while her sister set out plates, jam and cream on a tray. All this was carried through to the dining-room, where Phipps was shocked to see Debbie promptly spread her buttered tea-cake with a thick layer of Cornish cream.

Once they had finished eating, Bun said she must remember to mention Dyson's name during the evening, when they were up at the Pickfords home. "The Colonel told me he'd been living down here for several years so he's sure to have heard of George Dyson, even if they don't mix socially."

Timothy reminded her to see what she could find out about the chap who used to live in the cottage with the tarred shed.

Phipps was secretly amused when her niece enjoined both her aunts to employ devious stratagems and low cunning when raising either subject. "We don't want to let everyone know what we're up to. Might get back to the Interested Parties!"

Bun assured the girl all approaches would be the soul of tact.

In return, nephew and niece were enjoined to keep out of trouble . . . and tarred sheds.

"Just think of Proverbs 1:10, dear," Phipps suggested with what she fondly believed to be a winning smile. "'My son, if sinners entice thee, consent thou not'."

"'For wrath bringeth the punishments of the sword'," Bun cautioned. "Wise words from the Book of Job. See you pay due heed, Master Timothy."

The boy shook his head sadly, observing that - as it was written in Chapter Eight of Mica - 'truly: the most upright is sharper than a thorn hedge'.

Bun sniffed disdainfully, pointed out there were only seven chapters in the Book of Mica, then went upstairs to change.

However, when the aunts reached Colonel Pickford's home, they found circumspection unnecessary because everyone was talking about the old fisherman who had been living just above Willy Wilcock's Hole.

"One of the coastguards, years ago . . . !"

"Name of Penaluna. Jack Penaluna."

"Committed to prison for six months!"

"Lucky it wasn't a twelvemonth. That's what he would have got from a judge, at Quarter Sessions!"

"Can't understand what got into the fellow," Colonel Pickford told everyone. "A lifetime's service to The Crown, then does a stupid thing like that."

"Goodness me. Whatever has he been up to?" Phipps asked.

Sybil Pickford explained that the silly man had been convicted of stealing a War Pensions payment book. "But no one can understand how he came by it. It wasn't stolen from a local person. We'd have the whole story, if that were the case."

The vicar, James Tremain, smiled indulgently. "The news would have been round the village quicker than that of Jesus casting out the unclean spirit from a man in the synagogue at Capernaum."

Colonel Pickford, nodding in his wife's direction, said Sybil had been the first to tell him about it. "Found some small paragraph in the Western Morning News. Case was tried before the Liskeard Magistrates. Dirty business . . . making off with some poor fellow's disability cash."

The Reverend James Tremain explained to Bun and Phipps that War Pensions were only paid to ex-servicemen who had been so severely wounded that they wouldn't be able to go back to the job they had been doing before The War. From the weekly sum involved in the present case, it could be inferred the rightful owner of the pension book was pretty badly crippled.

"Probably missing an arm or leg," the Colonel called over his shoulder as he replenished sherry glasses. "You can tell by the amount being paid. Our country is glad enough of its soldiers when there's wars to be won . . . but leaves us to starve in between conflicts. I know! Been a half-pay colonel for years. But I'll be wanted when the next lot comes."

Phipps said - given those facts - she was surprised anyone could manage to steal a pension book at all.

"From what you've just said, one could presume the real owner to be a man existing in most straightened circumstances."

"Living in abject poverty," Hilda Tremain, the vicar's wife, cut in as she crossed the room.

Phipps agreed, saying that when they all lived at Warningfield, their late father's parish, one noticed the poorest people - usually the sick and elderly - were most careful with what little money they had. "A pension book would be terribly important to its owner. His only way to obtain money for food."

Hilda Tremain took the view that Jack Penaluna had probably found the book . . . perhaps lying on a pavement, where it had fallen from the owner's pocket.

Sybil Pickford pointed out that Jack hardly ever went far from the village. "Might have taken the bus to Looe, once in a blue moon, but why would he ever go all the way to Liskeard?"

"Nothing to interest a seaman," the vicar explained to Bun and Phipps. "It's the local market town . . . with most of the shops mainly concerned with serving the farming community."

Bun suggested Penaluna might have found the book in Looe, but taken it to Liskeard when he wanted to draw cash, because he wouldn't have been known up there.

The Colonel broke in, saying Penaluna would have been forced to go to Liskeard, if he wanted to try drawing cash, because pensions were always paid through a named post office.

"LISKEARD would have been printed on the cover," Sybil added by way of confirmation.

Hilda Tremain suggested this made everything clear as daylight. A Liskeard pensioner had visited Polperro, where he had lost his payment book. Jack Penaluna had found it, then hurried off to the market town . . . where he got himself caught whilst trying to make a fraudulent withdrawal.

"That's why I say the fellow's a born fool," Colonel Pickford responded. "Should have realised the owner would report his loss which, in its turn, meant the post office clerks at Liskeard being warned to make no further payments."

"But what if the pensioner had dropped dead? Penaluna would then think he was safe enough for a few days . . . ?"

" . . . or even a couple of weeks," Phipps suggested.

The vicar said no strangers had dropped dead in Polperro, or he would have heard about it. "My job to bury 'em!"

"But how does one find out about sudden deaths in other places: such as Looe, Liskeard or villages in between?" Phipps enquired generally.

Sybil Pickford told her there were weekly newspapers with very comprehensive hatched, matched and dispatched columns.

"Cornish Times in Liskeard and the Cornish Guardian at Bodmin," the Colonel added. "But you'll be wasting your time, if you're thinking of playing at detectives. Whatever the pensioner's status - alive or dead - it's obvious the post office had been told to stop further payments on that book . . . or otherwise Jack Penaluna wouldn't have found himself headed for Exeter gaol."

"So that's all we know, at present?" Bun asked, looking about the room.

Sybil Pickford rooted about under cushions, produced her copy of the Western Morning News, turned to an inside page, found a small paragraph and passed it across to Bun and Phipps.

"Nothing more than the charge, defendant's particulars and sentence. Probably more details in the weekly newspapers."

Having talked themselves round in a circle - as far as Jack Penaluna's story was concerned - the diners changed their subject matter by mutual consent, discussing more mundane events over their meal . . . such as the quality of this year's Channel Island new potatoes, what that fellow Hitler was getting up to - over in Germany - and the high cost of fish in a fishing port.

Sybil Pickford gave it as her opinion that the local fishermen must all have sacks full of sovereigns, tucked away beneath their mattresses, because village poverty was in direct contradiction to the obvious profits which could be made from spending a few hours afloat with nets and crab pots.

Hilda Tremain assured her hostess the poverty was real enough.

Her husband advised Sybil to count the number of children in each fisherman's cottage.

"Young families eat all the profits as they grow . . . while quite a few of the older men unfortunately drink their profits in the local pubs," the vicar ended with a resigned sigh.

When the party eventually broke up, Hilda Tremain invited everyone to join them for tea at the vicarage, "Day after tomorrow. Nothing formal . . . or to do with parish affairs. Just a chance for us to get together with a few personal friends." Turning directly towards Bun and Phipps, she continued, "Give you a chance to meet some of our more interesting residents."

The village streets were quite deserted of humans, when Bun and Phipps walked back to their holiday cottage. Local folk were having supper behind lamp-lit windows, whilst publicans cleaned their bars with doors and windows open wide to dispel the evening's tobacco smoke.

However, small, dark, slowly moving shadows crossed their path with increasing frequency as the sisters approached the narrower part of Talland Street, just before The House on Props.

"It would appear the local cats all head for Fish Quay, once everything's gone quiet," Bun suggested.

"I know, dear. Just seen one slink around that corner, closely followed by another," Phipps agreed.

"First stop: Roman Bridge to make sure the coast's clear . . . "

"Then a quick shake of the tail, at the top of that slipway opposite the Three Pilchards, before quartering the ground to see what the gulls have missed during the day."

Bun said it was a surprise to her that seagulls ever found time to eat . . . they seemed to spend so many hours screeching at one another from the tenuous security of the nearest telegraph post.

Phipps expressed the hope that these feline prowlers would behave more silently than the gulls.

"A chorus of caterwauling could ruin all prospects for a sound night's rest, dear"

"They only make that particular noise when they're on heat, Phippsie," Bun explained as they crossed into The Warren.

"Ah . . . rather disregarding First Corinthians."

"How so?"

"That bit about one's body not being for fornication, but for the Lord."

Bun dismissed this example of her sister's scholarship, pointing out she'd yet to see a cat reading a copy of the Holy Bible.

The sisters walked on in pensive silence, until Phipps raised the question of whether they had pressed too avidly for details about local deaths, when that Jack Penaluna business was under discussion.

"Shouldn't think so, old girl. In any case, those other four were all talking nineteen to the dozen. Don't think they'd have noticed our own interest particularly."

"I suppose - like me - you feel this could be one more link between the ginger-haired man and Timmie's crab pot?"

Bun agreed, saying that a reasonable sequence of events could have commenced with George Dyson killing the one-legged man with his car; then getting Penaluna to dispose of the body.

"At which point, poor Jack goes through the victim's pockets, finds the pension book and decides to draw what he could while the going was good," Phipps suggested.

"Knowing full well that nobody was going to report the book missing because the body would not be found . . . at least: not in one, easily recognisable, piece."

"'For wheresoever the carcase is, there will the eagles be gathered together'," Phipps intoned thoughtfully, quoting from the Gospel according to St Mark. She shook her head. "But we haven't seen as much as a swarm of Cornish blow-flies. Curious!"

"Yes . . . because even if all the flesh has been cut off, and used as bait in the crab pots, there must be bones lying about."

"Some of them quite distinctively long," Phipps added, thinking of a man's lower legs.

"And if that body was cut up in the tarred shed we know it would be impossible to bury the remains beneath the floor . . ."

"Because that shed's built on rock, dear."

Bun tightened her lips, nodded and said, "In which case: it's time we permitted young Timothy to break into the shed!"

Chapter Eight

To Phipps' amazement, her nephew declared that there was now little point to breaking and entering the tarred shed.

After listening most patiently while Bun recounted what she had heard at Colonel Pickford's small dinner party - followed by the aunts' presumption that Dyson had killed the Ginger Man and persuaded the retired coastguard to get rid of the mortal remains - Timothy produced a counter-argument . . . reminding them of that new padlock, recently fitted to the shed door.

Bun, smouldering with exasperation, said she failed to understand how anyone - so ready and willing to break the law with complete disregard for all consequences one minute - could now be telling her that he had changed his mind.

Their nephew replied circumstances had changed the outcome.

"I fail to follow!"

"Well . . . I've been thinking. Yesterday: we all believed there might be a body in the shed. Today: we saw a man working at Penaluna's cottage. He must have looked inside that shed, before putting a new lock on the door. If he'd found anything gruesome, the news would have gone twice round the village by now. But all is strangely silent . . . "

"There could be bones," Phipps suggested hopefully.

"And other clues too," Bun added. "If Penaluna took the dead man's pension book he may have removed other personal items."

"If only to help establish the victim's name and address," Phipps said.

Timothy told her Penaluna would already know this, from reading the front cover of the pension book.

"Oh stop prevaricating, Tims!" Debbie shouted, wildly waving her hands in the air. "Let's go up there and have a look in the shed anyway . . . unless you're too scared."

To Phipps' amusement, this taunt did the trick.

"When d'you want to start?" he asked truculently.

Bun proposed they wait until midnight - not so far away - and fill in the time by having a substantial supper.

Since Phipps was well aware that the way to any growing boy's heart was by way of his empty stomach, she couldn't prevent a cynical smile fluttering across her face. This was immediately disguised by pointing out to her nephew that he should look for clues which could give them an idea of why the dead man had come to Polperro. Then they could possibly establish some sort of a connection with George Dyson.

"Blackmail!" Debbie suggested. "If Mr Dyson's reputation is still as bad as we all suppose . . . given his past life."

"Perhaps both men were part of a smuggling gang?" Phipps said, her head tilted quizzically to one side.

Over supper - in Timothy's case: two fried egg sandwiches - he asked his aunts what they had found out, regarding Mr Dyson's period of residence in Polperro.

"Nothing dear," Phipps replied. "Everyone was so full of this Jack Penaluna story that we couldn't get a word in edgeways."

"But it doesn't matter," Bun added. "Phipps and I have been invited to the vicarage in a couple of days time."

"Tea dear," Phipps explained, "and there are going to be several other people present. I shouldn't be a bit surprised if we don't hear something useful during the afternoon."

Timothy observed the aunts might have already learned something of help, if they had only managed to raise the subject of Mr Dyson's sports car.

Debbie told her brother to shut up, and stop trying to find fault then, after a short pause, they all began discussing the forthcoming break-in above Willy Wilcock's Hole.

Upon being reminded that the shed door was only secured with a hasp and staple, Bun told her nephew not to worry about the new padlock. "All you'll need is the screwdriver blade of your boy scout clasp knife. The base of the hasp will be held in place by three or four screws. Remove them and you can get into the shed . . . but remember to replace the screws when you leave!"

Timothy said they should approach by the top path, to avoid being seen from neighbouring cottages on the waterfront, but reach there by way of an inland lane.

"According to what I could make out, when looking over my map, earlier this morning, it doubles back towards the sea from a tarmac road . . . just after one leaves the village."

"Quite close to Landaviddy Manor," Debbie added. "Sounds exciting. I wonder if the squire's head of our local smugglers?"

Ignoring his sister, Timothy explained how this lane would bring them out above Chapel Cliff - where they had sat in that shelter on the previous evening - then they could walk back towards Polperro, only having to pass one house instead of half the village. Gulping down the remainder of his coffee, the boy jumped up, "Going to change into darker clothing. Debs! Slip out the back and borrow the clothes-line."

Phipps, feeling quite startled, asked why?

"Because I'll have to slide down the cliff. Need something to steady myself. There's plenty of long grass and it's not exactly vertical . . . but I shouldn't care go down in the dark without some means of support."

"And how will you get up, afterwards?"

"Shan't bother, Auntie Phil. Easier to run home across the quays. But I don't want to go in that way, in case I'm seen and followed. I'd look pretty silly if the local bobby crept up behind me . . . just as I was busily unscrewing this thingummy-bob on the shed door."

Once ready, the party set out, walking quickly through the sleeping village without speaking. Darkness of the night was offset by starlight from a clear sky, so they could find their way easily enough until they turned off into the unmade track.

They discovered this was surrounded by overhanging trees, with narrow paths occasionally leading off towards houses or modern bungalows which were almost hidden from sight. At one point, a gap provided them with a view down the valley to the silvery waters of Polperro harbour. But most of the way, Phipps thought it probably similar to walking through a black tunnel.

Desultory barking indicated their passage was being noted by dogs living nearby, whilst a higher-pitched duet came to her ears from more distant cats: presumably locked in sexual union.

Screech-owls called a warning to each other, as they swooped unseen amongst the treetops, then there was a shout - followed by the sound of a pail clattering across cobbles - and the cats went silent.

Phipps thought their track was becoming rougher and more pot-holed, then they were stopped by a couple of motor cars, parked across the end of the lane. Torches revealed the path continued to one side, now skirting a much more densely planted woodland, and the Hydes formed a single file.

Suddenly there were screams and thumping sounds. Phipps and Debbie clung to each other in fright as Timothy shone his torch upon the wooden doors of an almost derelict stone barn.

"Pigs!" he muttered laconically.

Shortly afterwards, they found a flight of stone steps curving downwards, then a house showed up as a dark outline. The Hydes crouched low beneath its boundary wall as they scuttled past. Then there were more steps, this time cut into the slate surface of natural rock. This brought them to the junction of another path and Timothy pointed out a cupola below them, where it showed against the night sky.

"St John's Church - our lot - not much further now."

Perhaps not . . . but could one trust those Cornish mapmakers? Phipps wondered doubtfully to herself, following their leader up some dangerously small steps and out onto an extremely rough path. Outcrops of natural slate made this the worst part of their entire journey.

Debbie was first to fall. Phipps, who had been relying upon her niece for support, stumbled over on top of the girl. Then Bun - quite unable to see anything in such Stygian darkness - fell across the two of them.

Timothy, pausing to flash his torch back, asked sotto voce if they would care to be roped together . . . after the fashion prevalent amongst Swiss mountaineers when climbing the Matterhorn.

Bun pointed out that the first time it was climbed, the rope broke and four members of the seven-strong team were killed. She, at least, would continue unassisted, on her own two feet.

They struggled upwards, over this ankle-twisting slate, originally thrown up and skewed sideways by geological upheavals of long ago, until a gap in surrounding trees revealed they had reached a crest . . . with the boundary wall of Bay View House below and to their left.

All around there was only the silence of a starlit night, except for distant sounds of wavelets rippling along the shoreline, far below where they stood. Phipps thought she heard the slow beat of a single cylinder marine engine far out to sea, and concluded one of the fishing boats was heading in towards Looe.

A sickly-sweet perfume of some scented shrub wafted around them, combining with acrid woodsmoke which drifted upwards from a villager's cottage chimney. Suddenly, Phipps saw a light flare briefly, down on the much lower cliff path, followed by a smaller, pulsating red glow.

Somebody lighting a cigarette!

The Hydes ducked down behind bracken and long grass, hiding themselves from view, until this other person had passed by.

Phipps assumed the figure to be that of a woman, because a man's coat wouldn't have swirled about so much as a skirt. Who ever she was, the walker disappeared to their right as if setting out for Lansallos Cliff.

"Probably the vicar's wife," Timothy muttered, "nipping out to collect a few more bottles of best French cognac!"

When the woman was out of sight, he led them down and around the shelter where he and Debbie had first seen the lady with the butterfly net and large shopping bag. The Hydes passed beneath the lower boundary hedge of Bay View House, finally stopping above the back of Jack Penaluna's cottage.

Debbie uncoiled the clothes-line, throwing one end down the steeply sloping grass cliff. Her brother checked the top end, now held by several turns round a wooden fence post, then dodged between the wires to begin descending.

He had almost reached the bottom when Phipps saw the outline of a man in a raincoat and peaked cap approaching from the direction of the headland.

She whispered to Debbie . . . who immediately let go of her end of the rope. A brief rustling sound reached their ears . . . to be followed by a faint cry and then a 'thump'.

"Whatever was that, dear?"

"Probably a seagull fallen from its nest, Auntie Phil," Debbie replied with what sounded like a most unsympathetic giggle.

She gestured for her aunts to follow her own example and lean over the handrail, as if merely pausing to admire the view.

No further sounds came up from beneath them, so Phipps concluded her nephew had understood the implied message of the suddenly slackened rope and concealed himself in silence.

"Youm out some late, m'dears," the man observed when he drew abreast of the three Hydes. "Won't see much at this time o' night! Stars is all right . . . but you needs a bit o' moon if youm goin' ter admire the view."

"Oh hello," said Debbie. "Actually: we're not admiring the view. We're out looking for Lampyris Noctiluca . . . wingless females, of course," Phipps heard her explaining, in what sounded like Debbie's best imitation of a public school accent.

There was a pause while the man tried to understand all this. He appeared to give up, asking, "Think you'll find many?"

"Don't really know. Might not be the right month."

"Ah! Got a special time 'ave 'em . . . like mackerel?"

"Naturally! They only mate once a year!"

"Arr. Like a dark night for doin' that sort o' thing, do 'em?"

"Really couldn't say . . . but it's easier to find them."

"That a fact? 'Ow d'y'make that out then?"

"Well: all the females have luminous organs beneath the abdomen . . . for attracting the males. One simply looks for a greenish-blue light amongst the bushes."

"Ah!" There was a long pause before the man stated - rather than asked - "Down 'ere on 'oliday? I just met another of your mates. Ole Miz Accle. She comes down a couple o' times every year. Interested in leopards." He shook his head. "I told 'er straight: you won't find any o' they creatures round these parts."

Phipps began to think they had been waylaid by the local village idiot. And she couldn't fail to notice that Debbie had been rendered temporarily speechless too. However, her niece rallied round within a few moments to say that she supposed the speaker had misheard what Miss Accle said.

"Don't think so, m'dear."

"Oh yes," Debbie replied firmly. "She probably said 'Lepidoptera' . . . that's moths and butterflies. Tell me: what are you doing, out so late?"

"D'you read books? 'Cos if you do, you'll 'ave 'eard of Riding Officers. Well . . . I'm doin' the same sort o' job, without the 'orse."

This took their conversation away from the esoteric world of would-be glow-worm hunters, as Bun and Phipps joined in to discuss the activities of smugglers and excise men. They learned that contraband running still went on, though now mainly practised as a form of sport by people who were fairly well-off.

"Mostly young gents with nothing to do. They comes down to Cornwall, thinking to make a fool of us. But we knows who they are! We knows who to keep an eye on, you can depend on that."

The man turned to stare up at the darkened shape of Bay View House muttering, "'An that pair o' young rips are goin' to get a bit of a shock before they'm very much older, I can tell you. But don't go spreading that about, all over Polperro!"

And with this caution, the coastguard went on his way, saying he had to get as far as Talland before he finished his night patrol.

Once they had the path to themselves, Phipps congratulated Debbie on her presence of mind in thinking of glow-worms. Bun made the dry comment that her niece had surprised them all. Debbie freely admitted she never dreamt one of her dreary old biology lessons would have ever proved to be so very useful.

Phipps murmured about rubies and the price of wisdom.

Bun asked if her sister was 'at it again', making up spurious biblical quotations to suit the mood of the moment.

Phipps replied no, she had been thinking of five verses from the Book of Job where wisdom is put above the price of gold.

Bun made a 'humphing' noise, turned to Debbie and said she had noticed her brother exhibiting similar symptoms.

"Well if you mean that bit about 'the sleep of the labouring man', I must admit he usually manages to raise a laugh. But his real interest - being a boy - is finding all the juicy bits. You know: whoredoms and fornications. The older boys at his school used to run a term competition for the Alternative Scripture Prize . . . presented by a senior prefect in the lavatories."

"To the boy who discovered the greatest number of references to lewdness and adultery?" Bun asked. "But surely: they used an expurgated version of the bible in scripture classes?"

Debbie agreed, explaining that there was a standard version on the chapel lectern. "And - I mean to say - no master was going to criticise a boy for showing a religious interest. Not in a Church of England school . . . where most of the pupils were sons of the clergy! Tims was telling me one boy found a super piece . . . all about foreskins. But he wouldn't tell me any more. Do you know what foreskins are, Auntie?"

Phipps had to cram her handkerchief into her mouth, to avoid laughing aloud, at the hurried way in which her older sister changed the subject by saying she hoped Timothy would find some 'juicy bits' when he got into the tarred shed.

Bun threw a tiny pebble down upon the shed roof.

Timothy came out of the shadows to hiss: "Quiet!"

Bun told the boy they were going to make their way back to the cottage, in a whisper so loud that Phipps was reminded of steam escaping from a railway engine. But their nephew appeared to understand and waved, before returning to the shed. Debbie retrieved their clothes-line, coiling it round her waist and beneath her coat, in case they met any more midnight walkers. Then the three of them made off in the direction of Chapel Steps and the head of Fish Quay.

Where Debbie barked her shins against an empty fish barrow.

Bun nearly fell over a heap of broken fish boxes.

And Phipps stepped on something so squishy that she had to leave her shoes in the back yard overnight.

Timothy returned more than half an hour later . . . also without shoes or socks, which were too wet to bring inside.

"Ended up by being followed . . . by the village policeman!"

"Did he see you come out of that shed?" Debbie squeaked.

"No. The blighter was lurking in shadows at Old Quay. Probably having a quiet smoke . . . when he should have been protecting us from thieves, knaves and other sundry rapscallions."

"And he followed you back here?" Bun demanded.

"No. Of cource not. I saw him behind me. Waited 'til I'd crossed Fish Quay, then ran down that bit of a slip opposite the Three Pilchards pub, ducked under Roman Bridge and ran up the river behind The House on Props."

"With your shoes on?" Debbie asked.

"Couldn't stop to take 'em off, could I? Nitwit!"

Phipps handed Timothy a freshly made mug of Horlicks, together with a plate of chocolate digestive biscuits. He gulped at the hot drink, then added that it was a good job he had kept his shoes on, or he would have probably cut his feet.

"But how did you know where you were going," Phipps asked.

"Remembered from looking at the village map. I was going to climb out beside Couch's House, at Saxon Bridge. But I noticed an opeway between the backs of other buildings, just before, and got out there."

"In somebody's back garden?" Bun enquired drily.

"No. A sort of square, shaped like a letter 'Y'. Narrow roads with cottages all round. The tail of the 'Y' leads down to the river; left hand branch goes out through Big Green into Fore Street; while the right hand exit comes out near that baker's shop at the bottom of Talland Hill."

"Your 'Y' roads are called Little Green," Bun explained. "The famous John Wesley preached there in 1762."

Timothy observed that it was a good job there wasn't a prayer meeting being held on the present night.

"Fortunately, I didn't see a living soul. Scooted along Talland Street back into The Warren as if Old Nick was trying to get his hands on m' coat tails!"

"Well it's a relief to know you dodged the bobby, young man," Bun commented, "but did you find anything in that shed?"

"Sure thing!" Timothy replied with a self-satisfied grin, as he reached into his jacket pocket.

Chapter Nine

Phipps jumped up from her chair to move closer.

Debbie ran round the dining table to do the same.

Bun, carefully controlling her own demonstration of interest, placed both hands on the arms of her chair, stretched her neck and turned her head so that her eyes looked directly at her nephew's hands.

Timothy produced a brown, once-stout manilla envelope which was now soiled, with many creases, dog-eared corners and an illegible address. A printed frank and words indicated it had originally been sent on His Majesty's Service. A return address, on the back, included the word 'Pensions'.

Phipps watched as her sister took it and reached inside to withdraw a thin card of the same colour. This had been creased and folded many times, so that it looked as if it might split into several parts at any moment. Bun managed to straighten it out. She carefully scanned the page of print and handwritten notes.

"It's a release certificate for a Private Alfred Jackett. Apparently he enlisted for military service on the tenth of July, in nineteen fifteen . . . and was discharged on August the twenty-second of the following year."

"Before the end of the war?" Phipps queried.

"Yes . . . but I see this has been signed by the Officer Commanding No 8 Convalescence Depot, for other ranks, which was located somewhere near Clacton-on-Sea."

Bun looked across at the others. "Means he was badly wounded and unfit for further duty. That was the only way a ranker could escape the bloodshed in Flanders before they signed The Armistice."

She passed the tattered document to Phipps who saw that Private Jackett had been considered hard-working and conscientious, with sober habits and a smart appearance. His military conducted was stated as being Very Good.

Phipps handed the form on to Debbie who glanced over it then said, "What a swizz. No home address. Does this mean a trip to Clacton-on-Sea by any chance?"

Phipps explained that wouldn't be much use, so long after the war had ended, because the convalescence depot had probably only been a field of wooden huts . . . long since chopped up for somebody's firewood.

"Or converted into a chicken farm by some retired naval officer with more foolish optimism than sound common sense," Bun added with a shake of the head.

Phipps suggested the dates could be a helpful indication of the man's age. "If he volunteered . . . and didn't enlist until near the middle of July, we might suppose he did so shortly after his eighteenth birthday."

"Which would make him about thirty-seven, by now, old girl, and pushing thirty-eight."

Debbie asked who cared?

Phipps pointed out that - in the seemingly unlikely event they should find a body - prior knowledge of the victim's age would help establish identity.

Debbie gave it as her opinion that there were probably very few dead bodies awaiting discovery in this part of Cornwall, so identification could hardly be considered of supreme importance.

Phipps glanced across at Timothy, expecting him to come out with some choice wisecrack, but was surprised to find her nephew remaining thoughtfully silent. Almost as if he was watching Bun and herself to gauge their reactions.

When further discussion over Timothy's discovery tailed off, Bun looked at her watch, then suggested they may as well make a night of it.

"D'you feel up to taking another look around that Riley Imp?"

"Could do. Pick off a few hairs . . . and that sort of thing?"

Debbie clapped her hands, saying she could send some of the samples up to her old biology teacher, in Lewes, for microscopic examination.

"I remember she once said all hairs are different. I can tell her something has been at the chickens and we found our hairs caught in the fencing wire. Can she tell us whether the intruder was a fox, ferret or stray dog?"

"But she'll tell us what we know already," Phipps said, "It's a man . . . with ginger hair."

"Not necessarily, Auntie Phil. For all we know, that car might have run into a stray cow."

Bun seized upon this point, saying they were taking too much for granted; seeing what they wished to see, rather than what was really before them. "Faulty interpretation, combined with wishful thinking, rather than impartial valuation of established facts."

Timothy, about to go upstairs for clean socks and dry shoes, was heard to mutter something about the philosophy of the wet blanket. On his return, Bun produced some clean envelopes and Debbie ran out to fetch her nail scissors . . . all of which Timothy accepted with what Phipps thought a somewhat supercilious smile.

She pressed a spare torch upon him, with instructions to examine the car's boot because - according to a lot of detective stories - that was where the criminal put the body . . . when he wasn't dropping it off in somebody else's library.

Once Timothy had been seen out, Bun said she fancied a decent cup of tea. The others agreed so she went off to fill the kettle and set it to boil.

Debbie gave the release certificate one more glance before tucking it between a couple of books on a nearby shelf. Then asked Phipps how they were going to find out any more details about Private Jackett.

Bun heard this, as she brought in a tray of cups, saucers, milk and sugar. She said they would have to go up to Liskeard.

"Need to have a word at the newspaper office. Their reporter would have taken a shorthand note of Penaluna's court case."

When her sister returned to the kitchen, Phipps shook her head, giving Debbie a regretful smile.

"That's your Aunt Anthea, all over: a quiet-living, law-abiding citizen until she gets her teeth into a mystery . . . and then she's like a runaway horse! No stopping her at all! I wonder what explanation she's going to offer the editor of the Cornish Times?"

"She could say she's the pensioner's long lost mother."

"No Debbie. She can't say that. She's not old enough."

But Bun had obviously been giving much thought to this question. For when she returned with the teapot she told them they would march into the newspaper office saying they were up-country cousins of the missing pensioner - on his mother's side of the family - who had mislaid his address but wanted to pay him a visit whilst down here, on holiday.

"A story which is at least half true, so you shouldn't get confused, Phippsie."

"What about me?" Debbie asked excitedly. "Can I come too?"

Phipps, who always wore her late mother's wedding ring, moved it to the third finger of her left hand. "You can be my daughter. Lost your father when his ship went down in a typhoon off the South China coast while you were only a babe in arms."

Bun, an amazed expression on her well-rounded face, demanded to know what this was all about.

"Newspaper editors like a good sob story, dear. It will make him feel sorry for us . . . then he'll probably be more helpful."

Bun turned towards their niece, shaking her head. "That's the trouble with your Aunt Phil. Loses control of her vivid imagination so easily. Comes of reading too many penny dreadfuls but don't worry . . . she'll have forgotten all about that typhoon by the time we reach Liskeard."

They continued discussing their day out in Liskeard until Timothy's return. This time, there had been no wandering policemen to frighten him. In fact, he hadn't seen as much as a stray cat out in the streets, leave alone any people.

"Thought you'd be all right. If your bobby was working the usual nightshift hours, that's when he would have been tucked away somewhere to have his meal break."

Debbie was surprised by her aunt's self-assurance.

"How did you know?" she asked.

"Worked it out when we lived in Brighton. Used to notice a lot of coming and going at the local police station round about two in the afternoon, and again at ten o'clock in the evening. So I assumed this was when they changed shifts. They would have a meal break in the middle of their duty . . . and from there it's easy enough to calculate what happens in the middle of the night."

Debbie turned to her brother, asking if he had got a decent hair sample. He replied: better than that. He had collected three.

"Some from the badge bar - at the front - more from round a wheel nut, and then I found some caught beneath a chrome trim strip, further back along the edge of the front mudguard, close to the door. Oh yes! A damned great Old English Sheepdog crept up behind me, as I worked. Didn't bark or anything. Just sat down to watch. Suppose he just wanted a bit of company. Anyway: I snipped off a canine kiss-curl for good measure."

Asked if he had found anything else, the boy produced a time-worn army jack-knife. He passed it to Bun, drawing her attention to initials scratched on the handle.

"A.J. 1915. Obviously issued when Private Jackett joined the colours. Anything else, Timmie?"

"Yes. But it's a bit mucky. I left it in the back yard.

"Dear God! You haven't brought back a dead body, have you?"

"Or is it only an arm . . . or leg?" Debbie asked.

Phipps thought Timothy was giving them a rather pitying look, as he turned away to lead them out into the cobbled yard. When they got there, she saw a large bundle - big enough to wrap round a body - of rough brown hessian.

Bun prodded it gingerly with the toe of her shoe.

Debbie, obviously not keen for such personal contact, broke a twig from the hedge and used that to stir things around a bit.

Phipps stood back and let them get on with it.

Timothy watched, with what his younger aunt thought to be an expression of sardonic amusement, before telling them there was nothing to be afraid of within the sacking.

"Exactly what it appears to be . . . however, I did find it in the boot of Mr Dyson's car . . ."

"So it could have been used to wrap up a body . . .?"

"That's what I thought . . . so I brought it home as evidence."

Bun said she didn't much care for the look of the bundle, no matter what its place in the scheme of things.

Phipps asked if there were other clues: such as a name.

"As it happens . . . yes!" Timothy bent down, seized a tattered corner and gave it a jerk.

The other three Hydes started back to avoid any dirt.

The hessian unrolled in a cloud of blackish-brown dust.

"Must have been dumped in the coal-house at some time," the boy observed as he finished shaking the material out flat, then pointed to a label.

"West Somerset Peat Company?" Phipps read aloud. "I shouldn't think our body has come from up there, surely?"

"Quite agree, Auntie Phil, but read on . . . "

Phipps could only just make out the handwritten words.

"A. J. Ackroyd, Bay View House, Polperro, via GWR to Looe."

"That's the end house . . . above and behind the footpath near Willy Wilcock's Hole and Timmie's tarred shed," Debbie said.

"My guess," her brother told them, as they all went back into the cottage, "is that this chap Ackroyd killed the ex-soldier, then sneaked across the village at dead of night and left the body in Dyson's Riley Imp."

Bun pointed out there was at least one other possible explanation: that Ackroyd and Dyson were bosom pals. The former gave the latter part of a bale of peat . . . which was carried home in its original hessian.

"Or Mr Dyson could have killed the man - by running him down with his car - then dumped the body in Bay View's coal-shed because he didn't like Mr Ackroyd," Debbie suggested.

"And so we could go on all night," Bun said abruptly. "You've done a good job, Timothy, but let's leave further speculation 'til after breakfast. It's nearly three o'clock. I'm going to bed!"

"And what about Liskeard?" Phipps asked, climbing the stairs.

"Depends upon what time we wake up, old girl," Bun replied.

However, to everyone's disgust, they were awakened four hours later by a runaway fish barrow toppling over the edge of the quay, to land in a crabber moored beneath.

No damage was done but tempers flared though - with Church and Chapel still ruling people's lives - as it did in those days in most Cornish villages, contestants in the shouting match which followed the accident restricted their choice of phrase to 'silly beggar', 'dang'd girt fool' and 'blinkin' know-nothing'.

Phipps heard the contest end with everyone telling everybody else to go to Hell, sighed with exasperation at her loss of sleep, got out of bed and went downstairs to make a pot of tea.

The rest of the holiday party joined her before the kettle had time to boil, all grumbling about the noisy fishermen, then making plans for the day ahead.

Bun observed there would be plenty of time for them to get ready and catch the local motor bus for Looe railway station. They would therefore call upon the editor of the Liskeard newspaper, to see what could be found out about the Penaluna court case.

Timothy begged off this excursion, saying he wanted to walk out along the lane they had used, to reach Chapel Cliff, during the previous evening. In daylight, he might be able to get some idea of how Ackroyd reached Bay View House.

This was agreed and everyone went their separate ways after breakfast.

On arrival at Liskeard station, Bun and Phipps discovered they had a three-quarter mile walk to reach the town centre. Debbie heaved a sigh and looked glum at this prospect. Phipps linked arms with her niece and told her to put her best foot forward, then the other was sure to follow.

As they strolled slowly up Station Road, Phipps could not avoid noticing two young men who drove past in an MG sports car . . . with its passenger looking back at the three Hydes.

Debbie said it seemed like one of the cars, parked in that back lane, when they walked out to Chapel Cliff last night.

Chapter Ten

Ronald Ackroyd, just turned nineteen and recently rusticated by his Oxford college, after being reported for strolling through the grounds of a women's college . . . stark naked, on the night of the full moon, for a half-crown bet, swivelled round in the car's passenger seat.

His brother Richard - just turned twenty - was driving the MG. He too, had suffered rustication after being caught by the proctors, whilst lurking in shadow, outside the walls of the same women's college . . . carrying a spare pair of trousers, shirt, jacket and necktie.

The Powers That Be declared it was perfectly obvious Richard Ackroyd was aiding and abetting Ronald Ackroyd whilst he was committing an offensive exhibition of himself, which could only result in creating yet more difficulties between the new colleges and those of more ancient lineage.

"These women are here to stay, boy. And we all have to make the best of a bad job. Take the next train home . . . and don't show your face in Oxford until Michaelmas!" had been the sentence.

Fortunately for the young Ackroyds, their father - a wealthy Northcountry industrialist - had purchased Bay View House for use as the family's holiday residence some years before, and would not be using it until August. The brothers arranged with Oxford friends to have their mail sent down to Cornwall . . . and replies to be posted in the city so that they would bear an Oxford cancellation stamp, then drove down to Polperro for an extended holiday without another care in the world.

Not that they intended to sit in idleness for several months. The family five-tonner was available for trips across The Channel and, when at home in Polperro, they both took a very close interest in the lives of those around them.

But their's was far from being a benignly charitable activity.

Having been brought up in a household where money problems - if any - were confined to the factory boardroom, Richard and Ronald had enjoyed a singularly carefree existence.

The normal anxieties of more ordinary folk had never touched their privileged lives and, in their innocence, it never occurred to either brother that practical jokes were neither practised nor well received by the majority of the village population.

Richard had read somewhere that a certain amount of strain was good for the human system. He thought the permanent residents of Polperro were enjoying a little too much ease and contentment for their own good.

As he had pointed out to Ronald, nothing of great moment happened from one year's end to the next. "We shall have to liven things up!" he told his brother after they had finished settling in at Bay View House.

Hence this morning's journey which brought them through Station Road, Liskeard, just as the Hydes were setting out to find the editorial offices of the local weekly newspaper.

Not that the two brothers were intending to stop for long in this ancient Cornish market town. Richard drew off the main road, as soon as he reached its centre, to park in a vacant space before the Fountain Hotel. Leaving Ronald in the open car - to sit and watch the girls go by - Richard called at their bank to draw some ready cash. Once this was done, he rejoined his brother and immediately drove on towards Plymouth.

Their main objective was the purchase of a second-hand typewriter . . . with which to write a few poison pen letters.

Not that there was a scrap of real malice in their make-up.

Just a case of the Devil finding use for idle hands.

"Been thinking," Ronald said as his brother roared around a tricky double bend near the parish church and headed out into open countryside, "why don't we make those two old maids - in Crago's Cubbyhole - our first victims of a nasty letter?"

"That holiday cottage, with the ridiculous name?"

"Yes. Terribly quaint . . . owned by some American woman."

"That explains everything," Richard groaned.

His younger brother continued, "Had an idea. Sitting in the car. Waiting for you."

"Do tell. I'm all ears."

"Well: we've got an invite from our noble vicar: tea, tomorrow afternoon. Now . . . the thought crossed my mind that since he dined at Pickford's place yesterday - along with our two old maids - he would have issued invitations to all those present."

"Don't quite see . . . "

" . . . what I'm thinking about?"

"No. D'y'mind elaborating, Ronnie?"

"Thought we might drop a note in, at the vicarage, tonight."

"Something to cause mild shock?"

"Yes. Nothing heart-stopping, of course."

"Just enough to start up a slight case of nervous twitters?"

"A few telling phrases concerning our old maids' previous bad character, Richie."

"But how shall we find out anything in the time?"

Ronald said he had no intention of playing at private detectives. All the best poison pen mail was the product of a creative mind. One used imagination . . . rather than bare facts.

"So we're thinking of personal immorality, are we?"

"Calling them ladies of easy virtue, now living in respectable retirement. How's that strike you?"

"Too Victorian!"

"OK . . . let's just say they're a pair of lesbians."

Richard pointed out that - in these modern times of the mid-1930s - intelligent people accepted That Sort Of Thing with neither comment nor sideways glance. Whilst lesser mortals had yet to learn the meaning of the word.

By now, their car was running down the slight hill approaching Trerulefoot junction. Richard asked his brother if he had any preference which road they took. Left for the Saltash car ferry, or straight on for the one at Torpoint. Ronald voted for Torpoint because the riverside road between Polbathic and Wacker Lake was so much more attractive at this time of the year, with all the trees coming into leaf.

They waved to the signalman, leaning out of his box where road and Great Western Railway ran parallel for a few hundred yards, then roared on downhill to receive a salute from the Automobile Association scout. He was standing outside the AA box, just after they passed the East Looe turn-off.

Ronald's next suggestion was: that their vicar should be informed the two old maids were recruiting agents for a group of White Slavers . . . who made regular exports to the Argentine.

"I wouldn't go that far. Might bring the police into things. Don't want the bobbies on our tail," Richard cautioned.

This exhausted Ronald's ideas. He said they may as well give up on this one. But Richard wouldn't allow that either. "Those two old dears look so infinitely respectable, and possess such blameless characters, that we must do something terrible!"

72

"Well that's how I feel," Ronald exclaimed. "I was watching them through my binoculars, as they sat on one of those public benches overlooking the inner harbour. I thought how much they reminded me of a couple of cashiers in one of those small - but very exclusive - Soho restaurants, up in Town."

Richard thumped the steering wheel.

"That's it, Ronnie!"

"I don't follow . . . ?"

"For 'restaurant' read 'brothel'!"

"Retired Madams?"

"Absolutely!"

And with this problem behind him, Richard Ackroyd began humming Lullaby of Broadway, a tune which he had recently danced to, in the Carfax Assembly Rooms, up at Oxford.

Ronald sat in silence, fragmentary passages for inclusion in his letter to the vicar of Polperro running through his mind. And thanked his lucky stars that he would be able to type this one. That first effort, made during the previous summer, had necessitated a few very tedious hours with Gloy, scissors and pages torn from the previous week's Cornish Guardian.

He couldn't supress a reminiscent giggle.

The results had been spectacular.

The brothers had spent their last ten summer holidays in Polperro, which meant they knew many of the local people by name. Old Bill, a jobbing builder, was a celebrated local lay-preacher, noted for his rigid teetotalism, who everlastingly warned his flock to beware the dangers of Demon Drink.

The young Ackroyds had decided to show that he was the worst of all . . . a secret drinker!

Richard - dressed in dark clothes and wearing plimsolls - had waited until the early hours of one morning, then slipped silently down into the village, where he entered the back yard of their nearest public house. He had filled an old sack with empty beer bottles, then flitted across to where Old Bill parked his car and placed them in its boot. All easily done because the lid was only secured with a piece of bent wire.

Meanwhile - back in his bedroom at Bay View House - Ronald had created a short, but most informative letter which was then slipped beneath Snarling Aggie's front door.

The same fearsome lady who was a trustee of the local chapel.

Ronald giggled again.

Rattling a stick in a wasps nest could not have produced a more dramatic reaction on the following morning.

The Ackroyd brothers had stationed themselves on a vantage point - easily done in a village such as Polperro which is surrounded by hills on all sides - and taken turns to keep a pair of high powered binoculars levelled in the direction of Snarling Aggie's cottage door.

Ronald's face broke into an ear to ear grin at the memory.

Shortly after cock-crow, the chapel trustee had opened her door and peered out, first to the right and then to the left. Popping back inside - as suddenly as a wooden cuckoo retreats into its Swiss chalet after sounding the hour, on one of those popular wall clocks - she had slammed the door.

There was a short intermission.

Then old Aggie reappeared, steaming like a kettle on the boil, wearing her best coat and Sunday-go-to-meeting hat.

Richard and Ronald had watched her buzz round to a neighbour's cottage, more like a hornet wasp in search of a honey thief than a motherly old soul of seventy summers paying a fellow trustee a friendly visit.

Bert 'Bumblegums' opened his door as soon as she knocked.

A spirited discussion took place, Bert only pausing to put in his false teeth, then the two trustees scurried across to Eddystone View - from where it was quite impossible to see the famous lighthouse - and beat a frantic tattoo on Busty Bella's door, because she was known to be a trifle deaf.

The third chapel trustee stepped outside, obviously demanding to know who wanted whom, and why, at this time in the morning.

Following a brief altercation, Bella withdrew for a few moments, before rejoining the other two in her best coat, and a hat quite suitable for Ascot Week. She locked her door, pocketed the key and all three proceeded in the direction of Old Bill's home, shoulders hunched, stooping forward with the urgency of the moment . . . and looking neither to right nor left.

When Old Bill emerged - in shirtsleeves and showing his braces - hands were soon waving in the air, fingers being pointed to emphasise conflicting opinions, and heads shaken. Then shoulders were shrugged to indicate the absolute impossibility of one party believing what the other party had just said.

Finally, Old Bill had gone over to his car, undone the retaining wire on its boot, lifted the lid and waved an open hand, obviously inviting the other three to look inside.

They bent to their task as one person.

Then all straightened up . . . brandishing empty beer bottles!

Old Bill feebly waved his arms about, rendered speechless.

74

Ronald scowled, recalling the eventually serious result.

Poor Old Bill had been suspended from preaching.

Stupid people, the younger Ackroyd thought to himself as his brother rushed through the outskirts of Antony village, then past the triangular entrance to the drive for Antony House, before descending through Torpoint's shopping streets. He pulled up at the bottom of the hill, joining a short queue waiting for the ferry.

Richard switched off the engine, stretched his arms above his head, leaned back on the driving seat and twisted each foot round in a circle to ease any cramp, then jumped out and strolled down to the water's edge.

Ronald followed suit, without quite so much stretching. They stood in silence, looking across at battle-cruisers moored alongside the Royal Dockyard, whilst numerous small steam pinnaces criss-crossed the sluggish Hamoaze between ships and shore bases on the Cornish side of the river.

"Shouldn't much care to live in Plymouth," Richard observed.

"Shouldn't much care to live in any large town," his brother agreed. "I mean to say . . . think of Oxford."

Richard turned towards Ronald, a supercilious smile on his face.

"Grand old college buildings, noble towers, gleaming spires, the bustle of undergraduates as they move between tutorials and lecture halls, then back to their rooms for tea and toasted crumpets . . . by way of ancient streets now often ankle deep in animal excrement! Good job when we finally get rid of all that horsedrawn traffic. We need to go over to the motor lorry. Far and away a cleaner proposition than the horse and cart. Ah! Our ferry's just pulling out from the Devonport side. Back to the car, Ronnie!"

Once seated in their MG, Ronald let his thoughts wander back to those two old maids. "I wonder where our proposed victims are, at the moment?"

Richard glanced at the dashboard clock.

"Drinking tea in The Blue Geranium cafe, I dare say, after an exhausting morning traipsing round the parish church and admiring ye ancient Pipe Well."

Chapter Eleven

Bun, Phipps and Debbie were certainly drinking tea - and eating petit beurre biscuits too - but in The Liskeard Tea-rooms rather than The Blue Geranium cafe, because Bun had thought the latter too crowded for comfort on such a warm spring day.

Oblivious of the young Ackroyds' interest, the Hydes were also unaware of the unsettling effect their visit had caused in the editorial offices of the Cornish Times, earlier that morning.

They had marshalled the known facts, adding in just a soupçon of supposition where necessary, whilst walking up Station Road.

Once past the newspaper's filter system - a painfully thin, adenoidal young woman with protruding front teeth, whose breath suggested to Phipps that the poor creature was unlikely to ever be troubled with would-be suitors . . . or even rapists for that matter - the Hydes had been invited into the editor's jumbled office. They had been offered seats on a form, which reminded Phipps of one she used to sit on in their schoolroom, when a girl in her father's Sussex vicarage.

Bun put their case with commendable brevity.

She said they were visitors to Cornwall, who wished to look up a disabled cousin whose address had been mislaid.

"Lost a leg on the Western Front," Phipps added.

"Ginger hair, if that's any help," Debbie explained.

Bun told the editor their cousin's last commanding officer had described him as being a sober man of smart appearance. "He was given a very good reference on his discharge."

"In a convalescence camp near Clacton-on-Sea," Phipps said.

"Somewhere in his late thirties," Debbie chimed in so's not to be left out of things.

The editor of the Cornish Times, when he could get a word in, told the Hydes that he couldn't recall having seen any one-legged ex-soldiers - with ginger hair - wandering about Liskeard's streets during recent months, and asked their cousin's name.

'Jackett' failed to jog his memory, though he did mention having seen that particular surname on tombstones.

"Pelynt - pronounced 'Plint' - a village between Lanreath and West Looe. Pretty little churchyard. Well worth visiting, if you go out in that direction to make enquiries. One of our folk heroes buried there too . . . Bishop Trelawny. Died in 1720, though I enjoyed reading the obituary of an earlier member of the family when I looked around the church." The editor closed his eyes to aid concentration, then recited:

" 'Here lies an honest lawyer, wot ye what
      A thing for all the world to wonder at.' "

Phipps said in that case they must certainly go there.

Her sister, still with her mind on the purpose of their visit to Liskeard, suggested the editor must surely have come across Jackett during the past fortnight. "A man living in Polperro, called Penaluna, was up before the Borough Magistrates for attempting to draw money from our Alfred's war pension book."

To Phipps' surprise, this had brought no response.

Her sister had continued by saying the case had been reported in the Western Morning News.

"That's why we've come to see you," Debbie explained.

"Thought you could give us Alfred's address . . . because it would have come out when he gave evidence of ownership," Bun added in a hopeful tone of voice.

The editor excused himself for a few minutes while he went out to check with one of his reporters. On returning, Phipps had thought his attitude somewhat distant. He had resumed his seat and said shortly that the police had not called any witnesses because Penaluna had pleaded guilty. He was therefore quite unable to help in the matter of an address.

Back in the street, Phipps had voiced her disappointment.

Bun had expressed mystification.

"Frankly, old girl, I don't believe the editor. Remember that nasty business with the maid - caught stealing the children's pocket money during my last year at Miss Crawford's prep school? Before we left Brighton?"

"Yes dear. She pleaded guilty, didn't she?"

"My very point! They still read out names and addresses in court . . . though I grant you they weren't printed in the Argus. The Liskeard court reporter would have heard all the relevant names in this case . . . "

"Yet the editor said he couldn't help," Phipps said thoughtfully. "I wonder why?"

Back in the reporters room of the Cornish Times, their editor was in conference with his senior man. Both were wondering just how much of the Hydes obvious cock and bull story was based upon true fact.

"You're sure you didn't get your notes muddled up . . . like you did at last year's pony gymkhana, John?"

"When I reported the principal winner as coming second, sir?"

The editor shrugged, saying these things happened. It was sometimes the only remaining proof that they were human beings.

"Fallible I may be . . . but Penaluna was up before a special court," the reporter replied firmly. "Only one defendant."

"And the magistrates' clerk definitely read out the name of this fellow who owned the pension book as being Armstrong?"

The reporter glanced down at his shorthand notes.

"James William Armstrong . . . can't possibly confuse that with Alfred Jackett." The man looked up to add, "Three words instead of two . . . even if I couldn't read my squiggles."

The editor shook his head in puzzlement.

"One leg . . . ginger hair . . . they even gave his age!"

"Some sort of a hoax, sir?"

"No. Over-elaborate. Confidence tricksters keep it simple."

"Definitely up-country folk?"

"Tell that from their voices, John." The editor shrugged again and turned to leave the room. "Oh well: best get on, I suppose. Hurry up with your auction prices. I want to get that page down to the printers before lunch."

However, back in Liskeard's Fore Street, Miss Anthea Eulalia Hyde was not prepared to let the matter drop quite so easily. Firmly believing she had right on her side, Bun had sent Phipps and Debbie off to do any necessary shopping whilst she made her way around to the local police station.

She received no help there either.

The elderly desk sergeant stated that it was not official policy to give out particulars of either witnesses or complainants. "I mean ter say: 'ow do I know you ain't the village busy-body, goin' in fer a bit o' tit fer tat?"

The elder Miss Hyde had stiffly assured him her intentions had not been motivated by malicious desire, then stalked out to rejoin her companions.

The sergeant immediately telephoned the Cornish Times, with a view to warning its editor he might soon receive a call from a middle-aged woman, concerning the Penaluna case.

"Above average height . . . somewhat matronly?"

"Make a good figurehead for a battleship, sir."

"Certainly got enough bust for the job, sergeant."

"So she went to you first, Mr Reynolds?"

"Yes. A load of old flim-flam, we thought."

"Didn't tell her nothing, I 'opes?"

"No. Shan't be printing much, either."

The sergeant said that was a good job. He'd had quite a bit of experience with this sort of thing. In his opinion: the woman could have been trying to find a missing husband . . . who preferred to remain missing, if the editor got his meaning.

"So you think she might have been trying to find this chap so's she could have him up before the Bench and slap a maintenance order on him?"

"That's about the size of it, from where I'm sitting, sir. Good job you kept mum!"

Bun took an opposite view when she rejoined Phipps and Debbie, being vociferous in her condemnation of both tight-lipped policemen and newspaper editors.

Debbie told her not to get upset. "Those silly old policemen will laugh on the other side of their faces when we present them with Private Jackett's mortal remains. Come on, let's find a nice cafe and have a pot of tea."

Bun returned to the subject of finding Alfred Jackett once she was seated in The Liskeard Tea-rooms, reminding her companions of the editor's suggestion to visit Pelynt. Where there were dead Jacketts there could well be a few live survivors, such as church flower ladies, parochial church councillors, vicar's wardens or just honest sons of the soil.

"But is it worth all that trouble?" Debbie asked.

"I believe so. If we can talk to relatives we'll get to know something of our victim's character and this - in its turn - might show us why he was killed."

"But we can't be sure he was murdered. It might have been an ordinary accident," Debbie cautioned.

"Even so, dear, everyone looks for a motive," Phipps observed.

"And motive leads to the killer," Bun explained.

Debbie contended they knew who dunnit: George Dyson.

Bun reminded her of the hessian with that Bay View label. "Seems to me we've got at least two possible killers. Maybe we should find out more about the Ackroyd family . . . though Timothy may have been doing that whilst we've been wasting our time up here, in Liskeard."

Once rested and refreshed, the party did as Richard Ackroyd had supposed they would. First, they walked to the end of Fore Street, then doubled back behind the last shop to look at the town's ancient Pipe Well . . . with its discreet notice advising that this water was no longer fit to drink.

Then they wandered up narrow back streets to look around the 15th century parish church and admire its eight windows depicting scenes from the life and death of Dorcas . . . of whom Debbie had never heard. Was she a Cornish woman?"

"Acts of the Apostles. Greek translation of Tabitha. Lived in Aramaea. North-east of Palestine. Worked herself to death by doing too many good deeds," Bun explained.

"Then Peter, who had just cured a man - sick of the palsy, came over to Joppa and raised her from the dead," Phipps added. "Towards the end of Chapter Eight, if you want to know more, dear."

"Nine, Phippsie! Nine, old girl!"

"Are you sure?"

"Positive!" Bun told her sister in a voice which brooked no further argument. "A renowned needlewoman. Made clothes for the poor."

The Hydes took a taxi back to the railway station after this, where they were fortunate in catching the next train for Looe.

Bun had expressed determination that they should eat lunch whilst enjoying a sea view, so they walked down through the narrow shopping streets - running parallel to the river - only pausing briefly to admire the ancient Guildhall, as they made their way towards the sea front.

Delicious fresh crab salads were followed by strawberries and Cornish cream inside a weatherboard cafe, sited within feet of the beach, but coffee was taken outside.

Then Bun and Phipps strolled along the sea front, out to the end of Banjo Pier, where they sat in warm afternoon sunshine to wait for Debbie. She had taken a ferry boat across the river, saying she wanted to walk around Hannafore Point - where all those new hotels had been built - to get a closer look at St George's Island, which lay a half a mile offshore.

Their niece returned bearing gifts - three sixpenny ice-cream cornets - over an hour later. Once these were consumed, the three Hydes got up to look around the town, where Phipps bought herself a useful guide book for this part of the coastline.

Over the inevitable Cornish cream tea, she amused her sister and niece with folk stories of local smuggling activities.

Bun said she supposed St George's Island must have seen some activity in that line, since it was so entirely cut off from the mainland . . . where the excise men would be billeted.

"Oh yes. There's a tale about Fyn, his sister who was always known as Black Joan and a murdered negro. I don't wish to be disgusting at the meal table, so I shall merely mention Mr Fyn's signal station. According to my book - if it can be believed - this was maintained on top of the hill for the sole benefit of local smuggling craft."

Debbie pestered her Aunt Phil to tell them about the disgusting bit.

Bun told her sister to go ahead and satisfy the girl, or they would have no peace.

Phipps screwed up her face with distaste.

"I don't suppose it's true for one moment."

Debbie said they should be given the evidence and allowed to judge for themselves.

"Tradition has it that the brother and sister cleared their island of its entire rat population . . . by eating them!"

"Oh fancy that," said Debbie, appearing quite unmoved at such a thought. "Just like our history teacher told us about the poor people of Paris . . . when they were starving. Perhaps that's where Black Joan got the idea in the first place. Anything else?"

Phipps, feeling distinctly let-down by this lack of reaction on the part of the younger generation, replied that the negro's ghost was supposed to haunt the beach.

"Bit difficult to see him on a moonless night, Phippsie."

"Oh I don't know," Debbie joined in. "His skin would reflect the ethereal light of the stars. I mean to say: Paul Robeson shows up all right, in Hollywood films."

Bun said the make-up department probably swabbed their film star down with a glycerine mixture to obtain that glossy effect, and asked her sister if she had found out anything about Polperro in the guide book.

"Only just reached that part, dear. But I did notice something about there being a smuggler's cave out on the cliffs. We must try and find it, while we're staying there."

Bun observed this would make a change from trying to find a dead body which appeared to prefer playing hide-and-seek, rather than give itself up for a decent christian burial.

Timothy agreed, when the subject was being discussed around the kitchen table as dinner was prepared.

"I spent the morning prowling round Bay View House."

"Hope you didn't draw attention to yourself," Bun said.

"Lord no. Simply walked up that hill beside the church, then took a very slow stroll out to Chapel Point. There are three gateways to that big house on the end."

"One near the front door . . . opening off that path from Chapel Steps, " Debbie agreed. "But where are the other two?"

"One's near that shelter, a bit overgrown with new season bracken, but still usable. The other opens onto that path we used, at the back of the property. I watched the servants going in and out through there. Two of them, probably a maid and cook. Came out while I was pretending an interest in local hedgerow plants. I heard the magic words: 'look forward to an easy time if that pair push off to France'."

Debbie mentioned seeing one of the cars in Liskeard, which had been parked there on the previous night, and supposed the two young men in it were those being referred to by the women.

Bun asked her nephew what he had in mind.

"There's several small outbuildings clustered together at the back of the house. If our body was dumped in one of them, I might find some odd clue about Private Jackett's present whereabouts."

"What about other members of the family?"

"Had a bit of luck, Auntie Phil. Met the postman. Asked if Bay View was empty 'cos I never saw anyone about. He said: 'only a couple of Oxford undergraduates down at present'. Sons of the A J Ackroyd mentioned on our Somerset peat label!"

"And the two women?"

"Obviously live in the village. Both carrying baskets when I saw them. Time: five past twelve . . . so I reckon they work mornings only. I bought crab sandwiches and a couple of slices of fruit cake from that cafe behind Fish Quay, then dined alfresco, right on top of a huge rock above the harbour entrance. Possible to look right into Bay View's garden; and their end windows too."

"No sign of anyone else moving around?" Bun enquired.

"Not a whisker. I stayed up there. Spent most of the afternoon watching one of our cruisers doing speed trials. I noticed the marker posts - with triangles on top - up in fields above Talland churchyard. They indicate a distance of one sea mile."

"So that's why the warship kept steaming up and down," Debbie exclaimed. "I saw it when I was out at Hannafore Point, looking across at the island . . . where they once reared a particularly edible species of rat, if Auntie Phil's guide book can be believed," she ended with a laugh.

Shortly afterwards, Bun cleared them out of the kitchen to give herself more room. Debbie went upstairs to write a letter to Miss Halford, her biology mistress.

The girl decided against mentioning chickens, having now thought of a more plausible story. She wrote that a joint of beef had mysteriously disappeared from their larder. Hairs had been found caught round a projecting nail and were enclosed, together with a sample clipped from the principal suspect.

She'll love this, Debbie told herself, just like something straight out of Girls Own Annual for 1900!

The letter was posted after dinner, as brother and sister strolled round the harbour, watching zephyrs of sea mist form over the water, indicating continued fine weather.

On their return to Crago's Cubbyhole, they found Bun knitting while Phipps was lost in stories about the Quillers, Rowetts, Langmaids and Clements, said to have been engaged in smuggling at Polperro during the Eighteenth Century, according to her guide book.

Later, over a supper of Horlicks and chocolate digestive biscuits, Bun reminded everyone about their tea invitation at the vicarage on the coming afternoon, and suggested a restful morning.

Timothy suggested his aunts put a few loaded questions to the vicar, or his wife, in the hopes that they would let something slip concerning their late evening walks, from the direction of Lansallos Cliff, with such a heavily laden shopping bag.

Debbie reminded her aunts to find out something about Mr George Dyson . . . and perhaps the Ackroyd family, too.

Then the Hydes retired for the night.

And Ronald Ackroyd came out to play.

Wearing plimsolls, and a navy blue roll neck sweater above dark trousers, he flitted through the deserted village streets like a Will-o'-the-wisp . . . heading towards the vicarage, where he made a special delivery to the Reverend James Tremain and his lady wife.

Ronald was not particularly proud of his first cack-handed attempt to use a typewriter . . . but consoled himself with the happy thought that this letter's phraseology could have won him prizes for being the epitome of informative brevity.

Chapter Twelve

Hilda Tremain was first to rise at the vicarage, on the following morning, her head full of thoughts concerning the afternoon tea. This meant an early start in the kitchen, since there would be more baking than usual. But scones and Victoria sandwiches took second place, halfway through reading a brief typewritten letter which she had picked up from the door mat.

The vicar's wife returned to her husband and passed across this single sheet of notepaper. Sitting up in bed to read it, the Reverend James observed mildly that he would have rather received a cup of tea.

After taking in the content of the first paragraph, he said it was indeed heartening to receive such praise and recognition for his christian qualities.

"Read on!"

James Tremain did so . . . and said, "Oh my goodness!"

"Quite!"

"Well of course . . . this last bit is from Revelations, chapter seventeen unless I'm very much mistaken. But the writer's got it all wrong. Should be: 'kings of the earth have committed fornication,' not . . . "

"Never mind textual errors! What about the subject matter?"

"Hopefully untrue. Such nice gentle souls, those Hyde sisters. Pickford told me they were daughters of a retired Susex vicar when he first made their acquaintance. One wouldn't imagine them running a . . . "

Hilda Tremain reminded her husband that many of the former Upper Classes had come down to earning their own living, since the end of The War.

"But surely not as a pair of . . . "

"Well of course . . . never having met anyone in that particular branch of the entertainment professions . . . "

" . . . or visited a house of . . . "

Hilda Tremain cut her husband short with a withering stare.

James continued on another tack, quoting from the Beatitudes: "'Blessed are ye, when men shall revile you, and persecute you, and shall say all manner of evil against you falsely . . .'"

"Oh for goodness sake! My dear man . . . you're not in your pulpit now! These women are coming here . . . to tea . . . today!"

Her husband said it was hardly likely they would be touting for custom . . . even if accusations contained in the letter were true.

Hilda glared. "Even I do not suppose they would be that crass!"

"Well then . . . ?"

"How do we handle it?"

Her husband's eyes twinkled.

"Offer to keep mum . . . providing they pay us a decent commission on all orders taken beneath the vicarage roof?"

Hilda Tremain looked daggers.

Her husband hastened to add that he was thinking in terms of compulsory donations to the Parish Poor Box . . . not lining his own pockets with silver tainted by sins of the flesh.

His wife replied that he was being deliberately obtuse. Should she cancel their invitations to tea? Plead a sick headache, sudden death or shotgun wedding?

James Tremain suggested that - bearing in mind the writer's obvious high regard for his christian charity - they should put evil thoughts to one side and accept the Hyde sisters in a true spirit of forgiveness.

"Ah! So you think there's something to forgive, do you?"

"Not exactly, my dear. I simply said the first thing which came into my head. Though I suppose . . . "

"No smoke without fire?"

"Well: you could be right. After all . . . "

"Stranger things have happened!"

"But you'll notice the writer gives a Brighton address for these business premises. How would anyone, living in Polperro, know where to find a house of ill repute located in Brighton?"

"Colonel Pickford!"

"Oh surely not? The poor chap was in a convalescence home!"

"Ah! But: what about when he got back on his feet? How do we know he didn't stray from the straight and narrow?"

"Well of course . . . "

"If Sybil found out . . . ?"

"This letter could be an act of vengeance. I suppose the Hyde sisters could have joined the VADs for 'business purposes'?"

"You mean: soliciting for custom amongst the ambulatory patients?"

"The letter writer did mention the Hydes were running a very respectable establishment . . . for officers only."

"And Pickford would have been in a . . . "

" . . . a convalescence home for officers only! Hmmmm."

After a few moments silent thought, the vicar persuaded his wife to bring him a cup of tea, promising to put a few leading questions to Sybil Pickford during the course of the afternoon.

Privately, he decided to do the same to the Miss Hydes.

Hilda Tremain returned to the kitchen, shaking her head at what she considered to be her husband's ineptitude. Questioning Sybil would be a waste of time, either way.

If the colonel's wife knew anything - and had written that letter - she would be on her guard. Wouldn't say a thing. Probably run a mile if James as much as mentioned 'Brighton'.

And if she was innocent she couldn't tell anything anyway.

No! The way to address this problem was to throw a few carefully chosen remarks at one of those Hyde sisters, by way of seeking to provoke reminiscences of their life in Sussex.

Neither of the Hydes know about our letter so they can't possibly realise that we are aware of their murky past.

Therefore - if our informant has got the facts right - the Hydes will arrive this afternoon, secure in the belief that we all think them to be perfectly respectable . . . rather than knowing all about their previous 'business experiences'.

"Oh bother it all! Now look what I've done," Hilda stormed and stamped her foot. "Put the milk in the tea-pot! Anonymous letter-writers really are the giddy limit. There ought to be a law against them!" she grumbled, rinsing her tea-pot . . . then standing stock still.

The Law! Now why didn't James think of that? Fat lot of use, having a man about the house, when his wife has to do all his thinking in times of stress. She raised this matter when she took up the tea, suggesting James call the village bobby immediately.

James Tremain refused. He had already considered that approach, but rejected it. "I prefer to get to the bottom of this in my own way, without causing possible harm to innocent people. Which means: playing one's cards rather close to the old surplice. Not a word to anyone outside this room!"

Hilda left, walked to the head of the stairs, had a sudden thought, then returned.

"James: do you know if the Pickfords own a typewriter?"

James admitted ignorance, but instantly came up with a plan to find out. Hilda's cousin Doris always typed her letters, having learned during The War, when she had worked as a government clerk in one of the Whitehall offices.

Hilda must write to Doris, asking her to copy-type a letter and post it to the Pickford's home.

"You must make up something along the lines of: 'looking for a holiday cottage in Polperro. You have been given Sybil's address by a friend, who met her whilst on holiday in the village a couple of years ago, and wonder if she can now help you find suitable premises'. Give Doris a stamped and addressed envelope to make certain she gets a reply, then instruct your cousin to send Sybil's letter down here by the next post."

"You want Dorrie to make the enquiry in her own name?"

"Naturally, dear. And use her own address too. Somewhere in Dulwich, isn't it?"

"Yes. Upland Road . . . the better end. Quite respectable."

"Good. Sybil won't suspect a connection with us . . . "

"And if we receive a typewritten reply . . . "

"We can compare it with this morning's missive."

"Hmmm. Clever old thing when you want to be, aren't you?"

James admitted he felt complete confidence in his scheme, and quiet pride at being able to devise it, because after all was said and done . . . this was outside the usual routine for a Doctor of Divinity.

Hilda observed that it was fortunate he liked reading detective novels, then went downstairs.

As she laboured between mixing bowls, hot oven and kitchen sink, to produce the necessary pile of scones and several Victoria sponges . . . which all sank in the middle . . . she told herself they would get to the bottom of this unpleasant poison pen business, even if it took the rest of the year.

But she hoped Sybil would not prove to be the writer. Hilda was very fond of the colonel's wife.

"Oh well, hungry mouths to feed," she sighed, going over to her breadboard and beginning to make the cucumber sandwiches.

Chapter Thirteen

Nigel Barclay was the first guest to put in an appearance at the vicarage. Short, round and aggressive, he had been Something in the City. Since retiring to Polperro, he spent most of his waking hours in sea-fishing . . . for sport, not profit. Some days his bulging silhouette could be seen standing on a rocky ledge, patent leather shoes splashed by rogue waves, but he much preferred being out in his motor-boat whenever wind and tide permitted.

In keeping with his earlier life as a business tycoon - though nobody had ever found out exactly what he did - Nigel Barclay liked to say he could trace his ancestry right back to Roger de Berchelai . . . first mentioned in the Domesday Book.

George Dyson - who really was a direct descendant of Richard Dysun, first mentioned in records dated 1275 - asserted that their 'gentleman sea angler' was more likely to be the distant relative of an escaped Gloucestershire sheep-stealer, who once lived in the village of Berkeley, and had preserved his life by always keeping one step ahead of the hangman.

Acquaintances who knew both men were unanimous in their opinion that - of the present generations - George Dyson would make the better sheep-stealer. Furthermore: he could be relied upon to accomplish the act with considerable panache.

The young Ackroyds were next to arrive. Richard, who had recently visited Germany, was monopolised by Barclay. The retired businessman paid income tax and resented the loss of every last penny, on the grounds that it was only helping to keep the unemployed in luxurious idleness.

He suggested 'that Hitler fellow' had the right idea.

Richard agreed there were fewer men propping up German street corners - than one saw in English towns - but expressed the opinion that labour camps, as a solution, were too drastic.

"Don't you believe it! I admire Hitler. He's got the right idea!"

"Turning Germany into an armed camp, you know," Richard said. "Frankly: I came away with a much diminished respect for the Jerries. The younger ones can't wait to get into a brown shirt and gird on their leather belt, with that stupid buckle motto of 'Gott mit uns' . . . whilst the elders glue their ears to the wireless whenever their beloved Fuhrer is due to speak."

"Ah . . . but there you are! Herr Hitler will get Germany back on her feet. He knows how to stir things up."

"I thought he was just spouting a load of old rot. Meaningless ranting and raving . . . with countless brass bands playing Deutschland Uber Alles or Die Fahne Hoch. He'll end up being locked away in one of his own lunatic asylums!"

"Ah, but we need somebody like Hitler - a man with fire in his belly - instead of tired old men such as Stanley Baldwin and Ramsay MacDonald."

Richard pointed out that at least they did not take all the buses off the roads when they intended speaking to the electorate. "D'you know: we went to a big, open air, Nazi rally one evening - just to see what happened - and when we came out we had to walk all the way home. Herr Hitler had ordered the buses to stop running! Apparently the idea was: we should march home fired with enthusiasm and singing warlike songs."

Nigel Barclay said he couldn't see much wrong with that.

"Well the Jerries did . . . displayed minimal joy, I can tell you. The people were there right enough . . . but the streets remained strangely silent."

At this point, to Richard Ackroyd's relief, George Dyson and his wife, Beatrice, turned up.

Dyson, noted for his thorough dislike of Barclay's humourless pretensions, went into an immediate attack by bawling across the room, "Hello Nigel. Got yourself married, since we last met?"

On receipt of a surly answer in the negative he pressed on with, "About time you made an honest woman of your poor old housekeeper. People are beginning to talk, you know!"

Nigel Barclay walked away, saying that he had to speak to their vicar about something.

George Dyson strolled across to Richard, jerked his head at the older man's retreating back and declared, "Calls himself a rod-and-line man . . . but I've seen him come ashore carrying a nice fresh lobster more than once. Don't catch them with a garden worm wriggling about on a bent pin! Probably dipped his thieving hands into one of the commercial fishermen's crab pots."

Richard changed the subject by asking after Dyson's car.

The man's shark-like grin changed to a scowl. "Having a spot of difficulty with the insurance company, at the moment; that silly business when I dented a front wing. By the way: apropos my mechanical steed . . . you don't know of any garages to rent, I suppose? I'm on the lookout for a more secure stable."

"Thought you had one, part-way up Talland Hill?"

"So I have, but I'm after one with doors which close and lock. Found a flea-bitten mongrel sleeping in the Imp one evening."

Richard said he would grab any decent garage for his own use, if one ever became available. "Got to leave our MG at the end of that back lane. Gets covered in bits and pieces falling from the trees whenever we have a gale . . . and it's not uncommon to discover screwed up sandwich papers, or empty lemonade bottles on the seat, if the hood's left down for long."

Dyson nodded, "Same here. Never know what I'm going to find . . . or lose. Your father gave me an old peat wrapping, to put over the engine in frosty weather. Gone! One day: a half dozen milk bottles turned up. Next day: a sackful of garden rubbish. Leastways, I suppose that's what it was. Didn't bother to look inside. Could have been a dead body, for all I know.

"What did you do with it?"

"Picked it up - bit heavy actually - and passed it on for somebody else to worry about."

As they drifted apart, Richard overheard Beatrice Dyson ask her husband what he meant when he spoke of bodies in sacks. George replied that he had been speaking metaphorically . . . but Richard Ackroyd began to wonder. One never knew with Dyson. A man of mystery, if ever there was.

To his delight, he saw the Pickfords turn up with those two old maids from the holiday cottage shortly afterwards. Richard watched Miss Hyde the elder being cornered by their vicar, then wandered closer to hear what they were chatting about. He smiled as Ronnie eased himself across to lurk nearby.

Following an opening gambit, observing that they were having wonderful weather for the time of year, James Tremain went smoothly into the attack by asking Bun if she missed Brighton. This was followed by seemingly casual questions about the house where they had lived.

"A fairly large place, was it?" James Tremain enquired, just as Richard noticed Miss Accle arrive in the open doorway.

"Oh yes. A very good seafront location. Six bedrooms, with two reception, in addition to breakfast and dining-rooms. And only the two of us left after our parents died in that flu epidemic."

"So you sold-up and moved down to Devon?"

"Oh no. We stayed on for something like fifteen years. Filled the house with women."

Good God, Richard thought to himself, I do believe our silly joke is going to turn out to be true! Who'd have thought it?

He heard the Reverend James Tremain ask to be told more.

The man echoes my thoughts to perfection, Richard decided, edging marginally closer so that he shouldn't miss a single word.

"Turned the old family home into a small, but very secluded business. We used to advertise in the Brighton Argus."

Richard shook his head. Got to hand it to these old girls, he decided, they had a nerve. The vicar obviously thought so too.

"But were you not taking a terrible risk?"

"Not at all. We were very selective. One has to be, when starting up any business," Bun replied.

Richard Ackroyd glanced across at his younger brother. Ronnie's eyes were almost out on stalks . . . indicating that he could hear everything too.

The vicar asked what criteria they used.

"Age, first and foremost. Didn't want anyone on her last legs."

"No. I suppose not. So all your er, 'guests', were quite young?"

"Yes . . . we tended to favour war widows, or ladies of good family who had come down to living in reduced circumstances."

God! She's so matter of fact about the whole thing, Richard thought with a shock . . . but there you are . . . as the lady said: they were running a business. I wonder what the vicar will ask next?

"Obviously trying to maintain the right tone," James Tremain observed with an understanding nod.

"Oh yes. One had to consider the neighbours. After all: we were living in a very good class property."

"And they knew what you were doing?"

Hah! Even the vicar is sounding shocked now, Richard told himself with a secret smile.

"Well: of course! One can't keep that sort of thing concealed from the people living next door . . . too many comings and goings. Though, curiously enough: the council never rated us as a business premises. Regarded the place as being a private house."

"And your neighbours? They did not object to these activities?"

"Far from it. A couple of times they actually recommended young women who had fallen on hard times, when they thought they might be suitable and accommodate themselves to our own way of doing things."

"How very co-operative."

Richard asked himself whether it was his imagination, or was their vicar's voice beginning to sound faint?

"But what about the police?" James Tremain continued. "I mean to say . . . they must have known what you were doing."

"Never troubled us. Why should they? The same sort of thing was happening all over Brighton in those days."

What a delightful den of iniquity, Richard thought with envy. Wish I'd spent a few summer holidays there . . . instead of always coming down to Polperro.

"You must have done very well . . . to retire so early in life?"

Richard heard Bun explain that the house had not provided such a very generous annual income. "A lot of expenses with that sort of business, you know. The beds tended to wear out quickly."

Richard almost laughed out loud as the vicar blenched.

Miss Hyde - apparently oblivious of the impression she was creating, explained most of their present capital originated through a general increase in property prices. "Oddly enough: quite a lot of people, running our sort of business, gave up and sold out at the same time. All those lovely old family homes converted into small hotels by now."

Richard felt terribly disappointed when further conversation made it quite clear that the Hyde sisters had been renting bed sitting-rooms in a perfectly respectable manner. Observing the vicar's changing expression, Richard concluded the Reverend James Tremain had previously been thinking along the same lines as himself. Glancing across to the other side of the room, he saw the younger Miss Hyde deep in conversation with Hilda Tremain and wondered what they were discussing.

The initial pattern of Hilda's remarks to Phipps, had taken the same course as her husband's had done with Bun. Then Phipps, remembering her nephew's suspicions about the vicar's wife collecting smuggled brandy when it was nearly dark, had begun questioning Hilda about her cliff path walks.

Did she particularly like the coastline at dusk?

But wasn't she afraid of twisting an ankle in a rabbit hole?

And . . . so much to carry. Quite a strain on the wrists surely?

Hilda Tremain replied that she rarely had either time or inclination to go tramping about their cliff paths . . . and never took a picnic bag. It would make her feel like a summer visitor!

"But you were seen, one night recently. At least: my nephew said it was you: passing in front of a stone shelter, above Chapel Cliff?" Phipps asked in quizzical tones. " You and your husband?"

Phipps studied Hilda Tremain's face. She was obviously thinking back a couple of days, then her expression lightened.

"That must have been the evening James went for a stroll, but I remained at home. He met our Miss Accle. She'd been chasing about, all over the place, catching butterflies or moths. The light was fading by then, so she packed up her killing bottles and walked back to the village with my husband."

Hilda smiled at Phipps.

"Your nephew must have taken it for granted that a respectable vicar could only be out with his wife at such a time, whereas in reality he was very much out with another woman!"

Hilda pulled a face.

"Sounds dreadful, doesn't it?"

"Never mind, dear. All quite innocent when one hears the whole story," Phipps reassured her. "But I expect you know what today's youngsters are like . . . "

"Pick up half a story . . . put two and two together and make half a dozen before you can say 'knife'! As the vicar's wife, I encounter quite a lot of that sort of thing. 'He said this' and 'she said that' . . . and 'what should I do now, Mrs Tremain?' There are times when I've wished I had married a bus conductor. Life would have been so much simpler!"

Phipps murmured words of sympathy, mentioning that Bun and herself were vicar's daughters, so knew something of the trials and tribulations of a clergyman's wife.

Hilda glanced at her watch, then said she must slip out to the kitchen and begin organising tea for the multitude.

"Come and chat, while I work."

Phipps was only too delighted to agree. After all: one could not make searching enquiries about a fellow guest while standing only a few feet away from the subject, in the same room.

Once within the privacy of the otherwise empty kitchen, she put a few tentative questions concerning George Dyson.

"James feels constrained by his christian teachings and tries not to express uncharitable thoughts . . . but others . . . "

"Call the kettle black?"

"Nothing impossibly frightful. Just little things such as: he's too flashy, or his finances are a bit of a mystery." Hilda smiled wryly. "When people can't see where one's money comes from they tend to imagine a dishonest scource."

"How about his card playing, nowadays?"

"Never touches the pasteboards. Why d'you ask?"

"He had a dubious reputation by the time he went abroad."

Chapter Fourteen

Hilda Tremain and Phipps returned to the drawing-room as soon as the tea was made, without the younger Miss Hyde learning anything further concerning George Dyson's current mode of life.

Passing close to Richard Ackroyd and Colonel Pickford, she caught the words 'our five tonner' and paused to listen, whilst pretending an interest in nearby pot plants.

She heard the two men discussing details of a cruise to France.

Where the brandy came from, Phipps thought to herself as she strained her ears without - hopefully - appearing to crane her neck.

She heard Pickford observe that the weather seemed to be set fair, according to what he'd read in this morning's Times. Richard agreed, but said he would ring up the Plymouth Met Office tomorrow. If they could be certain of four days fair weather he, and his brother Ronnie, would drive up and get away on the outgoing morning tide.

It all sounded a bit of a hurried job, to Phipps way of thinking. She remembered that remark by the coastguard, when they were caught on the cliff path. He had gestured towards Bay View House, saying that the pair of young men who lived there were going to get a shock before they were much older. Did he suspect them of smuggling-for-fun? And was this what they were planning for the following four days? A quick there-and-back trip, with enough contraband to pay expenses?

She heard the Colonel ask where Richard kept their yacht.

"Mashfords Yard, this side of the Tamar. A little place called Cremyll - three cottages and a pub - just round the corner from Mount Edgecumbe."

"Thought your father used to keep her at Looe?"

"He did. But the river dries out for hours. One is too restricted by the tides, whereas we've got deep water all day, off Cremyll."

Handy for those sort of people who want to come and go as they please, Phipps told herself as she thoughtfully stroked the leaves of the pot plant . . . to which she was ostensibly giving her undivided attention. Especially useful for yachts returning to their moorings after dark!

To her disappointment, this seemed all that was going to be said on matters maritime, because Richard Ackroyd changed the subject by asking if the Colonel knew of anyone with a vacant garage. Their MG was being used as a corporation litter bin, now that they had to leave it out in all weathers, at the end of their back lane.

Phipps moved further into the room, before she wore out the leaf of her convenient pot plant, intending to join her sister. Bun was chatting with Miss Accle in a window alcove. Beatrice Dyson looked on . . . looking bored.

She broke away as Phipps approached murmuring, "Why on earth do people like the Rosie Accles of this world, who wouldn't know a Paris 'model' from an East End copy, always insist on talking 'clothes' at these chummy little get-togethers?"

"But I thought she was only interested in catching butterflies?"

"Yes . . . well I suppose chatting about the latest Paris fashions makes a change from endless reminiscences apropos where she caught her very first Purple Hairstreak, Silver Spotted Skipper, or listening to some college professor giving a learned discourse concerning the mating problems of the Camberwell Beauty."

Phipps said this was news to her because she was not aware that Camberwell Beauties experienced those sort of difficulties.

"It's their rarity, my dear! The poor creatures spend all their time looking for a member of the opposite sex . . . generally without success. You're not down here to indulge in nature studies, are you?"

"No. I wouldn't know a Painted Lady from a Scarlet Woman!"

"My dear . . . that's easy! The one in the Coco Chanel 'original' is your Scarlet Woman," Beatrice replied languidly, as she moved away in the direction of the cucumber sandwiches.

Phipps heard Miss Accle's voice rise as she declared she would never shop at Selfridges. "The man's an American - came from Chicago - probably sent over by Al Capone and his bootleggers!"

Bun replied that the new store was proving popular with the masses. Some people spent an entire day in the Oxford Street premises, "And one couldn't do that in Harrods."

Miss Accle said she really would not know. "Jumped up grocers! I prefer Fortnum and Mason."

Phipps remained where she was just long enough to hear her sister agree that - compared with Fortnum and Mason - Harrods were only Johnny-come-latelys, dating from the middle of the last century . . . as opposed to the other firm's origins which were to be found back in the early seventeen hundreds; then wandered further around the room.

As might have been expected, George Dyson was talking cars with James Tremain and the younger Ackroyd.

"Had an Austro-Daimler ADM3 in the late 1920s. Good for a hundred miles an hour. Ideal for those continental roads."

"Designed by that fellow Porsche?" Tremain asked.

Phipps learned he had left the firm by then, and a gentleman named Karl Rabe was responsible for the twin-carburettor sports editions which were raced so successfully in the latter part of the nineteen twenties.

Just a perfectly normal men's subject of conversation. Nothing to be learned about dead bodies or smuggled brandy.

Phipps saw Richard Ackroyd move away from Colonel Pickford, to chat with Beatrice Dyson, and crossed the carpet to take his place.

She brought their conversation round to Jack Penaluna's personality, as soon as possible, by asking if he had been a hard sort of man, or relatively easy-going.

"Relaxed sort of a chap: mild mannered . . . but that's what you'd expect from a sailor who'd spent a lifetime living amongst the men with whom he worked. I won't say he wasn't hardened, but that was due to what happened back in The War. He once told me he'd been at the Battle of Jutland."

Phipps admitted they had lost a lot of ships in that action and enquired if Penaluna had ended up swimming in the North Sea.

"No. Might have been easier for him, if he had done so. Jack was sent onto one of their big guns . . . after a German shell burst had wiped out the original crew. Told me there were arms and legs all over the place!"

"How dreadful."

"Yes . . . a fellow has to have a pretty strong stomach to do his job in those sort of conditions." Pickford shook his head. "Different for us army chaps. One's mortal remains got blown all over the surrounding landscape if a minenwerfer got your range. Not contained in one place, as happens on a warship."

Phipps remarked that she had been told - when nursing - the human body contained as much as nine pints of blood.

The Colonel said he could quite believe it.

"And there'd be at least a half a dozen men on one of those naval guns . . . fifty-four pints of 'claret' . . . over five kitchen pails full to the brim! Imagine that much sloshing about steel plates . . . or dripping from the overhead deck beams!"

Phipps gulped, felt herself going pale, said she'd rather not think about it, then made her excuses on the grounds that she had promised to help Hilda Tremain. Passing round a plate of cucumber sandwiches was infinitely preferable to hearing any more of the Colonel's graphic descriptions concerning naval warfare . . . though it clearly indicated Jack Penaluna could have been a man capable of cutting up a human body.

Out of the corner of her eye, she caught sight of the younger Ackroyd sinking his teeth into a slice of Victoria sponge. Bright red raspberry jam oozed out. Phipps shuddered and moved across to where Hilda Tremain was refilling teacups, wishing she had used apricot . . . or anything other than a red jam.

"My dear! You're looking quite ill."

Putting on a brave face, Phipps assured her hostess she was fit as a flea, but accepted a cup of tea with secret gratitude.

"Tell me: how well did you know the Pickfords, when you lived in Brighton?" Hilda asked quietly.

"No better than a hundred others. Mother and Father were still alive . . . so they ran the house, leaving Bun and myself free to help where needed. I became paid companion to a very pleasant lady who had been invalided home from India and Bun went to one of the town's many prep schools as an assistant."

"But I thought, from what the Colonel said, you both nursed?"

"Only part-time, as VADs. Father suggested we bring some of our 'boys' home for Sunday tea . . . and Colonel Pickford, then only a captain, began visiting us at Brunswick Terrace."

"Was he married, at the time?"

"Oh yes. We used to put Sybil up from Friday to Monday, on occasions."

"Nothing particularly close though?"

Phipps shook her head.

She thought Hilda Tremain was looking extremely pensive.

Following a long, silent pause, she asked Phipps to come into the kitchen. "There's something I wish to discuss privately."

Once seated round a corner of the table, with a pot of freshly made tea for refreshment, the vicar's wife told Phipps that James wouldn't bless her for what she was about to do . . . then recounted most of their early morning conversation concerning the totally unexpected receipt of that poison pen letter.

Phipps said 'Good Heavens' and 'How awful for you, dear' at appropriate moments.

Hilda went on to explain her husband's plan for checking whether either of the Pickfords owned a typewriter.

"As you must realise: all perfectly pointless! Of course, when we read the letter, we thought you might have been living on your own . . . "

"Thereby giving grounds for the writer's revelations?"

"Quite." Hilda thought for a moment, then shook her head. "We must have been awfully stupid . . . thinking the Pickfords had anything to do with it. After all: why should they invite you to dine one evening . . . "

"And accuse us of running a disorderly house, next day?"

Hilda said she must be excused, it had been very early in the morning, and they hadn't even had a cup of tea.

"Our brains were simply not working, my dear."

Phipps admitted she was much the same at that time of day, before her first cup of tea, then asked to see the letter . . . if only for its novelty value, because she had never received one.

"Sorry. No can do. James locked it away in case one of the maids found it. But it was very ordinary: civil, even flattering where my husband's christian principles were mentioned, and this wild accusation about you and your sister was suitably brief. Oh yes! There was a misquotation from Revelations: something about 'the kings of the earth' and their sexual habits."

"Promiscuity?"

"I believe so . . . certainly fornication."

Phipps made a mental note to look it up when she returned home to Tozers Quay, at Topsham. Then, recalling there were twenty-two chapters in the Book of Revelations and realising she didn't have the reference, decided to forget the idea.

She was about to get up when a more practical thought crossed her mind.

"Tell me dear: what happened to the envelope?"

"Thrown into the waste bin."

"Then I could have it . . . for comparison, if we should happen to receive anything like that at the holiday cottage?"

Hilda delved into the rubbish bin, produced a crumpled, egg-stained envelope and offered it to her companion.

Phipps glanced at the address, decided it must have been typed by a very old machine because many of the characters were out of true, with hollows in the 'R's, 'e's and 'a's filled in solid black, then sponged it off in the kitchen sink.

Bun was standing near the door, as Hilda led the way back into her sitting-room. Turning to face the vicar's wife, she demanded to know if Hilda had been satisfying her sister's curiosity concerning the mysterious Lady with the Plates.

Taken so completely by surprise, Hilda could only stand and gape for a few seconds. Phipps described what she had observed from the front window at Crago's Cubbyhole during meal-times.

"Ah yes! The Cornishman's answer to matrimonial aberrations, as practised in some of our more rural parishes. Though I must confess this is the only example of which I have personal knowledge," the vicar's wife answered with a laugh.

Glancing to either side, and making quite certain all the men were otherwise engaged, Hilda lowered her voice to what Phipps recognised as a conspiratorial mutter . . . as favoured by rumour-mongers, scandal-bearers and purveyors of grubby gossip for the girls.

"Jane is married to William . . . but prefers to live with Denzil. Denzil's cottage is quite small, with totally inadequate cooking facilities. William has nobody to cook his meals. So: Jane cooks all the meals in William's kitchen, leaving one third for him and carrying the other two thirds of the food back to her love nest in Denzil's cottage."

"Polperro's version of the ménage a trois!" Bun laughed.

Phipps observed that people living in small villages usually held very strict views about that sort of misconduct.

Hilda disclosed that Jane had received the traditional stoning, as reserved for women taken in adultery . . . but - being hard as nails - threw the stones straight back at her tormentors, which stopped the old biddies in their tracks.

When this trio broke up, Phipps drifted over to speak to Miss Accle. Recalling Beatrice Dyson's remarks, she asked if Rosemary was on the look-out for a Camberwell Beauty.

"Wouldn't be much point. They come over here from northern Europe. First pair seen in Coldharbour Lane, near Camberwell, way back in 1748 . . . hence the name."

Phipps suggested Miss Accle must find butterfly hunting rather exhausting in a county such as Cornwall - with all those hills and valleys - along the Channel coastline.

Rosemary Accle replied that she preferred it to the North coast because one found so many more varieties.

"But . . . so much to carry, dear?"

"Only a killing bottle, specimen case and net. No weight."

"But my nephew saw you quite weighed down, one evening!"

Chapter Fifteen

Was it her hopeful imagination, Phipps wondered, or did Miss Rosie Accle catch her breath for a moment? At any rate, the butterfly hunter certainly made a quick recovery.

"Oh that evening when I met our vicar! Yes. I do get rather loaded down when I'm out all day. I expect I'd been to Lansallos Cove. There's an interesting neck of woodland, running back up the valley of a small stream, towards the parish church. I saw a pair of Marsh Fritillarys there, one year . . . but never again."

When Rosie paused for breath Phipps, thinking of Alfred Jackett, asked if she had seen much of the local vagrant: a middle-aged tramp who walked with a limp. "Said to have lost a leg during The War?" she prompted."A fine head of ginger hair?"

"No. At least: not out on the cliffs. But then: that sort of person usually frequents inhabited places . . . where he can pick up a few pence or a bit of bread and cheese to help keep body and soul together," Miss Accle replied.

Near the doorway leading into the front hall, on the opposite side of the room, Bun had been making similar enquiries of Sybil Pickford, Hilda Tremain and Beatrice Dyson. No one could recall seeing a ginger-haired tramp in recent months. But Sybil mentioned receiving a visit from a beggar with whispy blonde hair who was minus an arm. He had been wearing a long string of campaign medals.

"Good job my husband didn't catch sight of him! He would have probably told the wretch he wasn't entitled to wear half of them!"

Beatrice Dyson declared she kept her door firmly bolted when she knew there was a vagrant in the village; while Hilda told them she received so many callers at the vicarage that she could never remember one from the other.

And, by then, it appeared to Phipps that Rosie Accle had tired of her company, for she drifted away to join the other ladies.

Phipps walked off in the other direction so that she passed close to where Nigel Barclay was deep in conversation with the younger Ackroyd. Dropping her handkerchief, then stooping to pick it up, enabled her to hear such interesting phrases as 'bring a few bottles back in the bilges', followed by a laugh from Ronald Ackroyd as he replied 'got a better place than that, bilges are the first place the customs men look'.

Firm intentions to smuggle wines or spirits? Then again: perhaps it was a load of hot air, wishful thinking to help pass the time.

Phipps had no way of knowing the truth of the matter and made a zig-zag to pass near the vicar and Richard Ackroyd.

The subject matter of their conversation was substantially the same: France and the Ackroyds' intended ports of call.

Finally, Phipps hovered near George Dyson and Colonel Pickford.

One point seven litres was coupled with forty-one brake horsepower; Roesch's accelerating pre-selector was compared to the old crash gearboxes; and when Dyson mentioned a total brake failure just outside Monte Carlo - back in '19 - Phipps heard the Colonel say he still preferred the horse.

"Might take a bit of effort to get some of them started, but I've never yet had any trouble with their braking systems; especially when they reach an obstruction which they consider too high to jump. The beggars slide to a halt so suddenly that they can have an inexperienced rider sailing over their head to land on top of the ruddy hedge!"

The groups began breaking up when Nigel Barclay declared he must be off because he wanted to fish the evening tide. The Ackroyd brothers followed him, explaining there were preparations to make if they were to set sail next morning, and Phipps began moving towards her sister.

Halfway across the room, George Dyson sidled up murmuring, "Rosie Accle loves to cackle. What's the latest on the Red Admirals? Caterpillars fattening nicely? Going to have lots of little brown chrysalises for Christmas?"

Phipps said she was sure she didn't know and passed on. But there you are, she thought, he always appears to take the initiative: makes sure every conversation is about his choice of subject. He might well have given up playing cards, but George Dyson still needed to be watched. Could it be that he really had known there was a body in his car, and was very carefully guiding all discussion away from such a worrying subject

Shortly after this, Phipps watched covertly as George Dyson collected his wife and they left arm in arm . . . with Miss Accle following at a safe distance behind.

There was definitely something suspicious about that man, but what? And why?

Bun and Phipps were next to depart, making use of a lull in conversation to take their leave . . . since neither of them were the least bit interested in the morality of whether it was wrong to add bottled pectin to home-made jams and jellies, when showing the results at the annual horticultural show.

"It may well be a matter of the utmost consequence to Women's Institute members when competing for the Jerusalem Cup, but I'd sooner cheat than have trouble with my setting," Bun commented. "Hear anything exciting, old girl?" she enquired, as they made their way back to the holiday cottage.

Phipps recounted Hilda Tremain's story concerning the poison pen letter, accusing Bun and herself of once keeping a brothel.

"You don't surprise me, Phippsie! The Reverend James asked me a lot of the most peculiarly worded questions, during the earlier part of the afternoon!"

"Goodness me. Such as . . . ?"

"Let's just say I gained the impression that he was quite surprised - and no little disappointed - to hear we had only been running a boarding house, back in Brighton!"

"But he didn't explain what it was all about, dear?"

"Probably too embarrassed. Anyway: Beatrice Dyson and our butterfly lady rather let the cat out of the bag, a bit later on. Mentioned an anonymous letter received by the chapel trustees, some time ago. They took it seriously and suspended one of their number from the lay-preacher's circuit. Accused the poor old man of being a secret drinker whilst publicly advocating total abstinence!"

Phipps said she didn't think too highly of people who could condemn on the basis of such a letter.

"Oh but there was evidence . . . a car-full of empty beer bottles. Not easy to explain away to those who had spent a lifetime railing against The Demon Drink."

Phipps cautioned her sister not to repeat that story to Timothy, in case it inspired him to do something similar. Then a look of horror distorted her face.

She stopped in the centre of the road to stare up at her sister.

"What's the trouble, old girl? Hilda's Victoria sponge making you feel queasy? I noticed they'd all sunk in the centre."

"No dear. I didn't have any. It's what you just said about Timmie. I suddenly wondered if he was the one who wrote the vicar's letter!"

"No typewriter! More likely to be those young Ackroyds. I heard they've both been rusticated from Oxford . . . and you know what a reputation college undergraduates have, for playing practical jokes."

Phipps repeated everything she had heard regarding references to their yacht and smuggling.

"Hmmm! And that horseless riding officer passed some adverse remark about them, the other night. They'll bear watching, especially in view of the fact that Timothy found sacking addressed to their house in Dyson's car."

"But I thought the present craze at Oxford or Cambridge was more towards hair-raising climbs, up some public pinnacle, which is generally crowned with a chamber pot?"

Bun pointed out the dearth of public pinnacles in Polperro.

"So you think Richard and Ronnie have taken to writing poison pen letters instead, dear?"

"It's possible. However, to be on the safe side: we'll keep quiet about the vicar's specimen when Timothy and Debbie are about. Don't want them taking up poison pens! They've got a dead body and live smugglers to hold their interest. That should keep them fully occupied for the duration of our holiday," Bun concluded.

The sisters walked on in companionable silence for a while, then Phipps suggested George Dyson might have written the letter. "He made some very cutting remarks today: 'Rosie Accle likes to cackle' . . . "

" . . . and bawling across the room at Nigel Barclay, telling him to make his housekeeper an honest woman," Bun added. "I heard that from Hilda. It happened just before we arrived. Mr Barclay was not amused!"

"Perhaps, whilst Tim and Debbie are searching for that body, we should be looking for a typewriter," Phipps proposed.

However, when they reached Crago's Cubbyhole, they found the continued search for clues relating to Private Alfred Jackett's final hours would still have to take precedence.

Timothy was standing beside the kitchen sink, watching as his sister industriously scrubbed some small object with the nail-brush.

Debbie stopped when her aunts came over to see what she was doing, flicked water from her hands, dried the unknown article on a towel and held it out saying, "Look what I've found."

Phipps stared down at a bronze star-shaped object. It had three points with the fourth place being occupied by a crown and was obviously meant to be worn, because she could see a small ring at the top. Crossed swords were kept in place by a wreath bearing a capital 'G', surrounding a smaller 'V', at the bottom. The dates 1914-15 appeared on a centre scroll.

She heard her sister ask if it was a brooch, and was it of any value because it didn't look very impressive?

"This was Private Jackett's medal!" Timothy said in clearly shocked tones. "If Debs was to turn it over you could see his name, rank and regimental number impressed on the back."

"And we've checked this against the number on his release certificate," Debbie said. "They're both the same."

Asked where this medal had been found, Timothy explained he had been thinking of George Dyson's car accident and reasoned that - since it was garaged in Talland Hill - the driver might have returned to the village by this route.

"We took a stroll up the hill - intending to go as far as its junction with the main road to West Looe - just past the new cemetery."

"But there was no need to walk that far," Debbie joined in. "We found marks in the hedge, where one turns off to the right, near the top of the hill."

"And, after scraping about in fallen mud, beneath the gouges, Debs let out one of her famous shrieks - normally reserved for when she finds a spider in the bath - then dug this thing out with a piece of broken hazel branch," Timothy continued.

"Then a coastguard came along - said he was walking home from Talland beach - had a look, mumbled something about the War Office having issued nearly two and a half million exactly the same, and went on his way!" Debbie concluded dolefully.

Bun, recalling Sybil Pickford's statement that she had seen a beggar wearing a long string of medals, asked her nephew if this one could have been torn from a man's coat . . . by a car crushing him against the hedge.

"Exactly what I thought!" the boy replied eagerly.

Phipps suggested there should have been a piece of ribbon through the top ring. Was there anything like that nearby?

"No. But it could have been washed away by rain," Debbie pointed out.

Bun observed that ex-soldiers never wore one medal on its own. They were usually found in groups of at least four. Could there be more medals still hidden in the roadside mud?

"Not a chance," Debbie assured her.

"We scoured every inch for at least fifty yards," Timothy confirmed. "I reckon we now have to find that raincoat."

There was something in her nephew's manner which made Phipps wonder if he wasn't secretly laughing at them. But why should he be doing so? No. Impossible. Her silly imagination at work: seeing something which wasn't there.

She listened as Bun said that if they found the remainder of a set of medals - still fastened to the coat - it would surely prove Private Jackett had visited Polperro.

"And that he was knocked down and killed in Talland Hill," Debbie added.

Phipps was watching Timothy. He simply smiled and nodded.

Bun reminded them nobody, at the vicar's tea party, had seen any tramps answering to their imaginary vagrant's description, wandering about in the village. Discovering the medal appeared to confirm this, because it showed Jackett never came any closer than the outskirts, before being knocked down in the hill.

Phipps mentioned what Rosie Accle had told her: that she had never passed any tramps on the cliff paths.

"Which means Our Alfred did not approach Polperro from the direction of either Lansallos or Crumplehorn," Bun said. Turning towards her nephew she suggested, "You'd better go back to Dyson's garage. See if you can find any old raincoats hanging up behind a door, or bundled away in a cupboard."

Phipps reminded her sister of what she had overheard, regarding the Ackroyd brothers' projected yacht voyage to France, pointing out this would surely be an excellent opportunity for Timothy to explore those outhouses at the back of Bay View House.

"They're going to telephone the local meteorological office first thing tomorrow morning . . . so I suggest you do the same from that kiosk on Fish Quay."

"Then station yourself near their back lane - if you receive a good forecast - to be certain of when they leave," Bun added.

"A job for Debs," Timothy stated abruptly. "Then she can keep cave for me, when I go in to snoop around."

Bun cautioned her nephew to keep an open mind. "We don't want you jumping to the most convenient conclusion, thereby making your Aunt Phil and I look like a couple of fools!"

"Oh I wouldn't do a thing like that!" he replied piously.

Phipps almost shook her head at Timothy's attitude. He was obviously having difficulty in suppressing a fit of the giggles.

"Have you got something up your sleeve?" she demanded sharply.

"Only a couple of arms . . . one each side."

"You know what I mean!"

Timothy had the grace to look embarrassed as he admitted being amused by his aunts' eagerness. "I mean to say . . . "

"Schoolboys don't expect a retired lady's companion - or teacher - to take much interest in crime?" Bun enquired haughtily, tilting her face and raising one eyebrow.

"Well . . . you don't strike me as being regular readers of our more lurid Sunday newspapers," Timothy replied in an attempt to justify himself.

"One doesn't have to concern one's self with crude vulgarity," Phipps explained mildly, "in order to read the latest news."

"Quite right, old girl! To us: this is merely an intellectual exercise. Debbie found a slice of pasty steak which obviously had human origins . . . and now we want to find the rest of the body."

"And as for pulling our legs," Phipps joined in, "remember what you told us about the vicar's wife being engaged in collecting smuggled brandy!"

"So she was," Timothy replied.

His sister confirmed this.

"Stuff and nonsense! Miss Accle was the lady with our vicar, walking home after a day's butterfly hunting near Lansallos Cove!" Phipps retorted scathingly.

Timothy said it didn't matter who she was . . . the lady was carrying a large bag, so heavy it was nearly breaking her wrist. She had been up to something . . . and he fully intended to find out the whats and whys. "And while we're on the subject: didn't you say we were going to hire a car and visit Lansallos sometime in the not so distant future?"

Bun told her nephew she was coming to that. Since the editor of the Cornish Times had mentioned those Jackett graves in Pelynt churchyard, she thought it could be helpful if they stopped to take a look at the place.

"It's directly on our route to Lansallos," Phipps told her sister. "I've seen it on our map. We could kill two birds . . . "

"Precisely what I had in mind. We'll have our driver stop on the pretext that we wish to see Bishop Trelawny's relics, then try to engage a local person in conversation."

Timothy reminded his aunts that he would be searching for signs of smuggling, when they got down to the beach, and suggested taking a number of empty carrier bags along.

Bun, somewhat shocked to Phipps' way of thinking, questioned their nephew's intentions, saying they couldn't carry bottles of brandy away . . . because it would be somebody else's property.

"But they couldn't call the police, could they?" Debbie said.

"Finders-keepers!" Timothy asserted.

Phipps, recalling what she had read, concerning Battling Billy, an 18th century landlord of the Halfway House Inn, and his efforts to run contraband in a hearse during a smallpox epidemic, said she hoped his ghost wouldn't be standing guard.

Pressed for more information, she recounted the legend of how Battling Billy had driven the hearse from Talland to Polperro, with a bullet in his neck.

"Witnesses said his head hung down over one shoulder, but he still lashed the horses with his free arm. They rushed through the village streets, across the quay . . . and straight down into the harbour! Polperro folk say it's a good idea to face the wall when Battling Billy's ghost is out and about."

"And how does one know that Billy Boy is coming to town?" Timothy asked with a supercilious smile.

Phipps replied that he was said to drop in when the moon was on the wane.

"Any other signs or portents?"

Phipps told them that naturally there was the sound of horses hooves . . . but first: one heard the low rumble of iron rimmed wheels thundering over cobbles.

"And that's when one screams and runs for cover?"

"You can laugh . . . but local people, unable to get indoors, are said to throw themselves into the nearest ditch and pull their coats over their faces!"

"And what's the All Clear sign, Auntie Phil?" Debbie asked.

"Apparently there is a terrible silence . . . and if you run out into the street immediately afterwards . . . you'll find a strong smell of horses sweat hanging in the cold night air!"

Timothy declared he would still be taking a couple of carrier bags with him, when they visited Lansallos, because everyone knew ghosts never walked abroad during daylight.

"All that haunting, after the clock's struck twelve, apparently takes it out of them. I have it on good authority that no ghost, who puts his back into the job, can get through a decent night's haunting on less than sixteen hours sleep once the sun's risen!"

Bun said, in that case, they may as well go round to the cove tomorrow, since they had all enjoyed such an easy time today.

Chapter Sixteen

Plans were also being made in Bay View House though Richard Ackroyd - as nominal captain of their yacht - found himself in a somewhat cross-purpose discussion with young Ronnie.

Richard was trying to establish their proposed port of call in France. This was necessary before he could work out a suitable course across the English Channel.

Roscoff, on the north coast of Brittany, appeared to be ideal for his purpose. This would give them plenty of land to either side, with several smaller ports as second choices, if they lost their way through falling foul of a sudden sea-fog.

"Then we could do a bit of rock-dodging as far as St Malo. Have a slap-up meal in the Hotel de l'Univers," he suggested.

"OK by me, Richie. And what shall we do about spreading a little more grief amongst the solid citizens of Polperro?"

Richard said he had not given the subject further thought. His mind was presently centred upon navigational problems. Perhaps they should have another look inside the Treguier River. "You know: the one with those high wooded banks . . . similar to the River Dart, between Noss Point and Galmpton Creek."

"Yes. Very nice. I'd like that," Ronnie replied, instantly changing the subject to tell his brother he had recently seen Miss Accle come in from the cliffs, accompanied by their vicar. "I thought we might consider sending Hilda Tremain a short note to warn her the Reverend James was cheating on his marriage vows. What say you?"

"That I should like to keep my mind on one subject at a time! And NO! Leave Rosie Accle alone. I like her. She's got character. Why not have a shot at upsetting Nigel Barclay?"

"Oh yes. Jolly good idea. Pompous old bore, isn't he?"

"Yes . . . very," Richard said, bending over his charts.

"Then again . . . there's that beastly blighter George Dyson."

"Ah! Now there's a challenge worthy of your inventive ingenuity, Ronnie, old lad."

"Really think so? I've come to regard him as a bit of a Great Pretender, always leading one up the garden path. Nobody seems to know where he gets his money from either. I sometimes wonder if he's a retired confidence trickster . . . you know: sort of chap who's keen to sell Tower Bridge to visiting Americans?"

Richard said there was more to George Dyson than met the average eye. "Anyway, he was moaning to me about people throwing rubbish in his car. Muttered something about 'it could have been a body'. The beautiful Beatrice asked what he meant, unfortunately as they drifted out of earshot, so I can't tell you anything else . . . but a dead body should give you a useful starting point."

"I could drop Beatrice a line or two . . . while you're busy scribbling all over our cross-Channel chart, I suppose."

"Good! Off you go! Then we can post the result of your labours as we drive through Looe, tomorrow morning. By the way . . . have we ever visited Triagoz Island?"

"Sounds Spanish, rather than French," Ronnie replied. "Where is it?"

"Between Ile de Bas and Treguier River."

Ronnie said the name didn't ring any bells with him then departed, to type his letter in another room, so that Richard could concentrate on his charts and tide tables.

Both Ackroyds were wide awake almost as soon as the dawn chorus of blackbirds, song thrushes, sparrows and robins started up, on the following morning. Heads looked out of bedroom windows, glancing upwards to see a clear blue sky, nodded in unison and withdrew.

Once dressed, Richard hurried into the kitchen, cooking bacon and eggs while Ronnie 'phoned Plymouth met office. Immediately after putting the phone down, he joined his brother to cut bread and make toast.

"Well . . . how's are chances?"

"Very good," Ronnie said enthusiastically. "Set fair for the next few days. There might be a bit of a northerly wind, once clear of the land, but that'll drop to nothing by nightfall. A period of calm to follow, then we should be able to pick up a freshening south westerly wind to bring us back into Plymouth Sound."

The brothers ate breakfast in record time, heaved their kit-bags outside, then locked the door and put the key under the mat so that their daily cleaning women could gain entry.

When they reached Looe, Richard stopped the car beside a convenient post box - just after crossing the river bridge - and Ronnie slipped Beatrice Dyson's letter into it, then his brother drove up past the railway station, dropped a gear and put his foot to the floorboards.

They were off and away.

Fortunately, it was too early for many visitors to be out and about. The young Ackroyds had the roads almost to themselves, except when meeting the odd workman pedalling to farm or factory on a rusty black sit-up-and-beg bicycle.

Richard wound up the MG's engine to maximum revs. Sun shone through overhanging treetops, dappling the road ahead, and there was a delicious smell of new-mown hay in the fresh morning air. Ronnie threw his yachting cap into the back of the car, letting the slipstream blow through his hair.

"Beats the Hell out of Oxford, doesn't it?" he yelled.

"But the Old Man will beat the Hell out of us if we don't buckle down and get good degrees," Richard shouted back.

"I know. This could be the last time we ever have so much freedom. Let's make the most of it!"

Shortly before they reached the main road for the Plymouth car ferries, Richard caught sight of a limping figure who looked as if he might be walking from Widegates to Hessenford.

"One of the less fortunate, Ronnie. Shall we give him a lift?"

"Might smell," Ronnie cautioned his brother.

"Shouldn't think it would linger . . . with the hood down. Any noxious odours will blow away in the slipstream."

By this time they were abreast of the walker, who turned out to be a tramp. Richard pulled up and offered the man a lift.

"Ain't much room in that lil' ole car, matey!"

"You'll be all right. Hop up in the back and sit on our kit-bags. Only clothes in there, so you can't do any harm."

"But hang on tight, going round corners," Ronnie warned.

The tramp climbed into the car. Richard was just about to engage gear when he noticed a bit of broomstick, with a funny wooden cup, lying in the grass. Turning to gesture at their passenger, Richard told the tramp he appeared to have dropped something.

"Oh arr," the tramp shrugged as he added, "Shan't want 'ee no more. Leave 'un be. Must 'ave fallen out me knapsack. Me ole wooden leg. I 'ung on to 'im in case me new one let me down, but I reckon 'ee's goin' ter be all right."

"Couldn't we find a use for it?" Ronnie asked his brother.

"It is my carefully considered opinion that no young man should be without one," Richard replied. "I can think of a dozen things to do with that object . . . all most unpleasant."

"In that case: hang on a minute," Ronnie said, climbing swiftly out of the car to pick up the discarded peg-leg.

"Grown a new one?" Richard asked the tramp.

"Nar. 'Ad a metal one given me by the British Legion. Lost me own in Flanders, back in 1916."

"Out looking for work?"

"Nar. Goin' up Plymouth to see me ole mother an' feyther."

Ronnie put the unwanted peg-leg in the back of their car and Richard drove off once again, shouting to the tramp that they were heading for Cremyll. "You can pick up a passenger ferry to Stonehouse, opposite the Edgecumbe Arms."

The Ackroyds stopped at Millbrook, to buy food for their yachting trip in the village shops, then hurried onwards. The road was soon following a low boundary wall, built of local ragstone, which enclosed Mount Edgecumbe deer park.

On their left, the ground fell sharply towards the river, giving them an unobstructed view across the Hamoaze, with its lines of naval warships moored between buoys.

Richard pulled up, gesturing towards the battle cruisers, destroyers, and other vessels lying alongside jetties, in Devonport Dockyard, on the opposite shore.

"I read in the Times that there's a lot of frantic re-fitting taking place, throughout our navy yards."

"Arr. They fools in Whitehall be gettin' ready fer the next lot. Re-arming! Glad I shan't 'ave ter go again. Once is enough, believe me!" The tramp looked earnestly into Richard's eyes. "You take the advice of an Ole Sweat . . . when the next war comes . . . dodge the column an' stay alive, boy!"

Richard assured the man that he and his brother were very adept at avoiding trouble, as a general rule. He drove on to the ferry point, slipped their passenger a half a crown for fares and something to eat, then motored round to a piece of waste ground at the back of Mashfords' Yard, parked and went into the office.

Ronnie heaved out the kit-bags and food, causing the wooden peg-leg to fall on the floor of their car, where it was forgotten.

"The foreman's sending an apprentice to row us out to the yacht," Richard said when he joined his brother.

Another half a crown changed hands once all the Ackroyds' gear was aboard, as Richard asked the yard lad to put a bit of tarpaulin over the MG later, and they set sail within the hour.

Chapter Seventeen

The Hydes, too, had made an early start. But this was more due to expediency than eagerness. The only available car would be required for a village funeral during the latter part of that same morning.

On arriving at Pelynt, their driver parked beneath the shade of a large tree growing in the churchyard wall. The Hydes entered by the north gate as latecomers rushed past, heading in the opposite direction, on their way to the village school.

They found the editor of the Cornish Times had been correct in both respects: the centre of Pelynt was very attractive, with its church standing in a lawned island, separated from surrounding rows of tiny cottages by narrow lanes; and there were Jackett graves beside the path . . . in addition to those occupied by former Truscotts, Philps and Cloggs.

Bun led the way around the church, until they discovered the entrance porch on the south side, near the parish War Memorial.

She found no information of any help.

But Phipps observed that there was a Bettinson mentioned, and she had noticed a carpenter's workshop bearing the same surname, as they were driven past, on their way to the church.

"Then we must have a word with whoever's there. He might have come across Alfred Jackett, if he also joined up."

"And if he turns out to be the father of the Bettinson named here," Debbie suggested, "he may remember his son speaking about Our Alfred, when home on leave."

Bun agreed this was a good idea, but pointed out it may be slightly more tactful if only two of their party made the proposed call. Timothy said that suited him. He and his sister would quarter the churchyard to see if there had been any recent burials featuring a member of the Jackett clan.

Bun and Phipps left by the south gate, and strolled slowly round to the carpenter's shop.

Phipps heard a man's voice singing 'All I do is dream of you, the whole day through', as they drew nearer. This was a popular dance tune which seemed to exhibit a vaguely facetious frame of mind . . . considering the fact that they found the singer screwing handles on a coffin, when they entered the building.

By contrast, his apprentice, on a second bench, was busy rubbing beeswax into the coffin's lid with silent reverence.

The singing journeyman looked across at Phipps and her sister, nodded pleasantly, stopped singing and bid them good-morning. Bun enquired if she was addressing Mr Bettinson.

"No. Boss is out. Won't be back 'til well after two o'clock."

"We're looking for people called Jackett, said to be living in this district. Wondered if you could help . . . since you obviously have dealings with most of the local families, sooner or later."

"Wouldn't know, m'dear, 'cos I comes from outside the parish. Your best bet would be the post office: on the corner, t'other side of the road." Nodding at the coffin, he added conversationally that some folk made one laugh when it came to the Last Rites.

"Mason were in 'ere this mornin'. Told me this ole dear an' 'er ole man used to fight like cat an' dog . . . an' now ee's 'avin 'Sadly missed by her sorrowing husband' put on the 'eadstone!"

The tradesman laughed. "Jack Richards, the mason chap, told me 'ee's picked out a nice bit o' granite for the job; which orter suit 'em fine, 'cos folk always said she 'ad a 'eart of stone!"

Phipps smiled, Bun thanked the man, then they left to try their luck with the village postmaster.

He was found leaning against a time-worn, polished wood counter, at the rear of his shop, noisily franking outgoing letters with a hand stamp. Bun explained their mission - now adding an imaginary cousin Betty to the story - but with no useful result.

"Sorry Missus, but I don't know anyone of that name hereabouts . . . except them up in the churchyard."

As they turned to leave, the man's wife called across from the cigarette counter, where she was weighing cut plug pipe tobacco into one ounce bags, priced at ninepence ha'penny.

"'Course you knows them! Lily - used to live opposite they Hamblys - was a Jackett, 'fore she married poor Tom."

She walked over to add more confidentially, "'Ee 'ad an accident with explosives, up to one o' the quarries. They screwed the lid down on 'is coffin . . . before they brung 'im 'ome. Wouldn't let Lily look inside!" The woman paused in thought. "That were three year ago. She'm gone now, married again."

"Oh that's right, Nora. She'm gone over to Lanreath." The postmaster turned towards Bun. "Stop at the village shop, close by the church. They'll know where you can find her, Missus." He paused awkwardly, before asking, "About money, is it?"

Bun shook her head.

Phipps explained a Cornishman of that name had married their cousin Betty, during The War, but was now missing from home. It could be loss of memory due to shellshock.

"Ooo yes. I believe Lily did 'ave a brother. Must 'ave been a good bit older than 'er, 'cos I don't remember ever seein' 'im."

"Nora's right, Missus. He hasn't been around Pelynt since we come to live here. Best try over to Lanreath."

Bun and Phipps returned to their car, Debbie and her brother joining them, as arrangements were being made to go on to the next village.

They discovered Lanreath to be straggling outwards from either side of a 'Y' road junction. Once again, their driver parked beside the parish churchyard . . . where gravestones stood several feet higher than the county council tarmacadam.

When the Hydes went up there, they found this gave them a good view over the cart sheds of Court Farm, to one side, and a short row of fairly derelict-looking thatched cottages on the opposite side of the road. Timothy and his sister elected to wander round the church.

Phipps, spotting a carter harnessing his horse to an empty hay wagon, walked down to the yard and enquired about Lily, a woman who was said to have married and come to live in this village a few years ago. She was directed to another row of cottages, just round the corner and part-way up a slight rise.

"A couple o' doors along from the pub. Ask fer Missus Bunney."

Phipps returned to her sister, thinking perhaps it would be better if only one of them called on the woman, since it would be less intimidating. Bun agreed, left her sister to join nephew and niece in the church, and set out for the Bunney cottage.

From the moment she first saw Mrs Lily Bunney, the older Miss Hyde realised her concern for this woman's finer feelings had been ridiculously misplaced.

She was grossly over-weight, with thighs so large that their girth forced her legs permanently apart, causing her to waddle when moving from one place to another. A shock of poisonously reddish-blonde hair hung down in washed out curls over a pudgy face . . . and red, rat-like eyes squinted from puffily hooded lids.

Bun was invited inside the cottage, but realised this could only have been to prevent any conversation from being overheard by neighbours, for no welcoming cup of tea was offered.

No sooner had they sat down to either side of a grubby, egg and gravy-stained, once-white deal table, still displaying unwashed breakfast plates, than Lily Bunney asked Miss Hyde where she had come from.

This was most disconcerting. Bun felt that she was there to question Lily. Not the other way round. She explained about being on holiday in Polperro, her imaginary cousin Betty's wartime marriage to a wounded Cornish soldier named Alfred Jackett in the Clacton area, and her own hope of paying these people a visit whilst in the county.

Lily offered no information, merely asking where Bun lived when she was home. Bun mentioned Tozers Quay, in Topsham, just down the river from Exeter . . . to be told she did not speak with a Devonshire accent.

"Come from London, do 'ee?"

"No. Sussex. Tell me: when was the last time you spoke to your brother, or received a letter from him?"

"What's that to do with you, Missus?"

Bun patiently explained that a letter would have an address, which would then enable her to visit Lily's brother and his wife, to whom Bun was related because their late mothers had been sisters. "Tell me: have you seen Alfred at all, since the end of The War?"

"Yes. 'Course I 'ave. What were you doin' in them days?"

Bun mentioned her work with the VADs near Brighton and asked if Alfred had returned to live in Cornwall.

"'Ee comes and goes. This 'ere cousin Betty: were she in they there VDs?"

Bun didn't know whether to blush or laugh, as she answered 'Yes' for simplicity's sake. "Did Alfred mention where he was living, last time you met?"

"Didn't say. Here! 'Ow d'you know 'ee were wounded?"

Bun, by now thoroughly exasperated, pointed out that her cousin had told her, thanked Lily for her help - whilst reflecting that this wretched woman had been no help whatsoever - and said she must now leave because her hired car was needed back in Polperro for an eleven o'clock funeral.

Predictably, Lily asked, "Whose funeral would that be?"

Bun, pausing with one hand on the now open front door, said she did not wish to appear unfeeling, but neither knew nor cared.

Chapter Eighteen

Phipps, who had just stepped out from the church doorway, saw her sister approaching with a face like thunder. She decided any artist, commissioned to paint Bun at this moment, would have surely drawn steam coming out of her ears.

"What's the matter, dear? Natives unfriendly?"

"Stubborn and cantankerous! But one has to remind one's self that one is a christian. The poor soul is quite obviously not long for this world. I'm no doctor . . . but anyone can see our Mrs Bunney is an advanced case of dropsy."

"Oh dear, filling up . . . ?"

"Almost full to the brim, old girl! The water's certainly reached her brain . . . if indeed she ever possessed one. I diagnosed the little grey cells as being completely awash."

Bun led the way back to their car, asking Phipps if the church had been worth a visit, to be told there were some very nice seats with carved poppyheads; the rood screen had been tastefully renovated and there was a huge, elaborately carved wood monument, to a family named Grylls: mother and father, their chaplain and steward, "Watched by eight little Grylls."

Once seated in the hired car, Bun instructed their driver to carry on for Lansallos, because the sooner she saw the back of Lanreath, the better she would be pleased.

And, at number five, Tresidder's Row, Mrs Lily Bunney wondered what she should do for the best. That woman who had just called - Miss Hyde - was a real 'lady'. Any fool could tell. A bit like the old squire's unmarried daughter, Miss Wetherhead, who spent all her time in training dogs or riding horses.

Mrs Bunney shook her head. Chasing foxes when she should have been looking round the neighbouring parishes, trying to catch herself a man. Ended up an old maid, like Miss Hyde.

And that was an unlikely tale: her cousin marrying Alfred! In Lily's experience, fine ladies did not marry Cornish labourers!

Lily picked her nose thoughtfully, wiped her finger on a corner of her filthy apron and shook her head again. One only had to look at that there Miss Hyde to see she'd got money. Smart, but a bit on the dowdy side when compared to most people of her class. Quality rather than high fashion . . . and that cost money too! No. Her Alfred couldn't have got hold of anyone so obviously related to the County families.

But then again: you never knew, especially in wartime. People behaved differently when away from home. She'd heard some of the village men talking, after it was all over. According to them: some young women from the Upper Crust had gone completely off the rails . . . believed they ought to give the boys something worth fighting for, and all That Sort of Thing!

Felt it didn't matter what happened . . . so long as the recipients of these maidenly favours went across to France and got themselves killed in a decent, proper manner. But they weren't supposed to return and cause embarrassment once the Armistice had been declared! Oh my dear life and soul, no. That would never do, would it?

Lily Bunney closed her eyes, the better to concentrate upon what she had learned from questioning Miss Hyde. She had mentioned Clacton . . . and said her family came from Sussex. All a long way from Cornwall. Who knows? Perhaps Alfie had pulled off the hat trick and persuaded some girl from a monied family to marry him. One of they there natural wallflowers: with buck teeth, a hare-lip and a body which was all skin and bone.

"One like that'd be glad to git herself a man, regardless of his background and any unpleasant future consequences," she murmured.

Of course, Alfred had never said anything to her. Just turned up on the doorstep from time to time, in old clothes which looked as if they'd been taken from some farmer's scarecrow, saying he was 'on the road'. But that could have been his way of putting her off the scent, couldn't it? To stop her asking for a hand out, as he knew she would have done if she'd found out he was married to a wife who had money in her own right.

At this point Lily Bunney realised that if her brother had been lucky enough to marry well, that was that. He'd finally got fed up visiting her and she wouldn't see him no more. But this raised the question of why had this Hyde woman turned up, looking for him? Sixteen years after The War ended?

"Looks like he's gorn missing," she ruminated. "Perhaps some workhouse tramp heard about the cash and killed our Alfie!"

She coughed up some phlegm, lifted the lid of the teapot and spat into it. No one to see her . . . and it saved getting up. All be washed out later.

Nodding to herself, she became more and more convinced that her brother had been killed. Them there ex-soldiers - usually missing an arm or leg - who tramped around the countryside saying they was looking for work were a crafty old lot. Easy to chum up with somebody who had a bit of money, spend the night together in some farmer's haystack, kill the other chap, go through his pockets and then disappear.

Lily Bunney compressed her pudgy lips.

It was the only possible explanation for this morning's visitor.

Why only t'other day she'd seen that there report in the Western Morning News about some chap called Penaluna, said to be living in Polperro, who had been caught trying to cash somebody else's war pension book!

For all she knew, it might have been her Alfred's! She knew he received a disability pension . . . and that newspaper hadn't printed the real owner's name.

Reluctantly, she concluded she would have to get in touch with the police. But there again: a fat lot of good that might do. All the details of that Brighton Trunk Murder were still fresh in her memory because she had only recently read the latest comments on that case . . . and they still hadn't found out who killed those two women!

Dismembered bodies packed into trunks, one lot being left at a main line railway station. Why, the police hadn't even found out the identity of the younger victim . . . said to be 'a well-nourished 25-year-old, from a good family background, who had obviously been in the habit of caring for her appearance'.

And those remains had come to light over a year ago!

The Daily Express was offering a reward of five hundred pounds for any new information, yet these poor women's deaths still remained an unsolved mystery.

Lily shook her head, sniffled and wiped her nose on the edge of her apron. What did it matter? She'd be washing it next week, or the week after.

"Can't get away from it: the police ain't goin' to bother their heads much over a missing tramp," she grumbled sullenly.

Then a fresh line of thought crept into her mind and she broke out into a fit of sudden trembling. That Miss Hyde had spoken of visiting her cousin Betty and her husband!

"My Gorr! 'Ave our Alfie done 'er in?"

Until then, Lily had only been concerned with her brother's whereabouts but now . . . well it stood to reason, didn't it? If that there Miss Hyde, with all her money, couldn't find her own cousin, this here Betty had to be missing too!

What if Alf . . . but no, he couldn't have . . . or could he? After all: men were like that. Discarded their unwanted women just as spoilt children threw away a broken clockwork toy.

There had been that case of Patrick Mahon, the Bloomsbury sales manager, who killed one of his firm's shorthand typists in a rented bungalow at Pevensey Bay, near Eastbourne!

Lily nodded to herself. That were in Sussex . . . not far from Brighton. Must be something in the air, up them parts. Anyways: Mahon got caught and they hanged him.

Then blow me if some businessmen hadn't taken over the lease of the bungalow and opened it up to visitors. Charged a shilling a head and packed 'em in by the coachload! She remembered reading all about it, some ten years back along. The Mahon bungalow had been one of the top visitor attractions, in Sussex, for the summer of 1924!

Well she didn't want her Alfie ending up on the gallows.

If her brother had done something wrong, it must be between him and his conscience. She wasn't going to start no police hunt. Alfie was the only living blood relative she'd got in the whole wide world . . . and she wasn't going to be the cause of no harm coming to the poor chap.

In any case: she had to think of herself, too.

The disgrace, when the story came out!

She'd have to move and where would she go?

More to the point . . . who would want her?

Lily realised it behoved her to think most carefully before committing herself to any action which she might live to regret. A cup of tea should help clear her head. She struggled to her feet, started to cross the room, then set her face with renewed resolution. If a woman didn't know her own brother well . . . who did? Alfred wouldn't hurt a fly!

This settled all doubts. She would ask the police to find him.

Lily took out two pennies, from the Oxo tin she kept on the mantelpiece, and waddled across the road to the telephone kiosk beside the churchyard wall muttering, "Our Alfie's got rights, same as anyone else. If he's come to harm, the police should do something about it. No good them telling me they ain't interested, just 'cos he's an ex-soldier, who nobody wants!"

Chapter Nineteen

The Hydes were nearing Lansallos by this time, after being driven through more than three miles of narrow winding lanes, where no more than an occasional stunted oak tree broke the overhanging roof of hazel branches.

Phipps was disappointed to find the Cornish hedges so high, a lot of the time, that their journey had been similar to passing along the bottom of a dark trench. Admittedly there had been glimpses of scenery through field gateways, but most of this part of the trip had turned out to be extremely boring.

She was relieved when their car rounded yet another corner, and there was the sea! Miles and miles of clear blue water stretching far away beyond the Gribbin Head - which she knew from her guide book lay between the entrance of the River Fowey and Mevagissey - to Dodman Point, south of Mevagissey.

Halfway down a perilously steep hill, after negotiating another couple of hairpin bends, she saw the top of a church tower nestling between trees in the valley below.

Just before reaching it, their car passed a range of stone-built barns, stabling, cow and cart sheds to the right; then low pig sties fronted a narrow stream on her left. Two tiny cottages stood beside this brook, looking out onto bramble-grown gardens. Phipps thought their slate-hung fronts - with the rows all higgledy-piggledy - gave them a quaintness which their squalor utterly refuted. She wondered if the pigs lived in the greater comfort, as their driver pulled up at the entrance to Lansallos churchyard.

The man drove off for his funeral booking as soon as the Hydes had removed their picnic bags from his car. Bun, who had remained silent during their short journey from Lanreath, then told the others of her unfortunate interview with Mrs Bunney.

Phipps, leading them towards the church, suggested it could be worth a visit before they walked down to the beach.

A few steps along the path, they paused to read a verse on John Perry's headstone. He had been a mariner, unfortunately hit by a cannon ball which was fired by an unknown person in 1799 . . . killing poor John at the age of 24 years.

> I, by a shot, which rapid flew,
> Was instantly struck dead,
> Lord pardon the offender who
> My precious blood did shed.

"Gosh! Bet he was a smuggler," Debbie exclaimed.

"Killed by a gunner on the revenue cutter," Timothy added.

Phipps observed that the poor man must have been almost cut in two, if it was a very large cannon ball. Bun corrected nephew and niece by reminding them Britain had been at war with France since the preceding year. "Probably a Johnny Frenchman."

Several more Perry graves lined the church path, but none indicated anything other than natural death. Once inside the building, the party spent a short time admiring the 15th Century wagon roofs with their carved oak beams, wall-plates and bosses, before turning their attention towards ancient bench ends in the nave: all finely carved and well preserved. Then Timothy led the way out, reminding everyone of their main objective: by saying it was high time they found a footpath leading to the beach.

Phipps discovered this followed the curve of a dry stone wall, with its top three courses laid in a neat herring-bone pattern. She walked past a wide gateway to the old rectory's entrance drive, and turned to stare as rooks called a warning from tall trees nearby. Then she found herself entering a narrow lane shaded by mature ash and sycamores. The ground was very rough earth and stone, but wide enough for a horse and cart, and Phipps could hear a stream gurgling below, somewhere to her left.

"All too terribly thrilling, isn't it?" Debbie asked.

Phipps momentarily closed her eyes - the better to imagine midnight wagon wheels creaking - as smugglers brought their contraband ashore to hide in the nearby rectory or parish church.

"One can only hope the descendants of those original families, up in the churchyard, are still carrying on the traditional calling," Timothy shouted over his shoulder, from a few yards ahead.

Debbie agreed, saying that if the search for Private Alfred Jackett's mortal remains petered out they would be hard up for amusement, without a bit of smuggling to investigate.

Phipps smiled at the abrupt way in which her sister replied the Jackett mystery had only suffered a slight set-back. "If one avenue fails to lead in the right direction, we shall try another!"

Phipps was happy enough simply exploring this fascinating way to the beach. A stream bubbled through a hole in the hedge to run down a deep channel, obviously cut in the underlying slate by centuries of erosion, but soon disappeared again into the adjacent hillside.

She shivered, remarking on the sudden coldness of the air at this point . . . voicing the hope that they were not about to come face to face with ghostly carters or ethereal pack-horses loaded down with tubs of brandy.

Timothy hastened to reassure his aunt, shouting that there was no trace of horses' sweat hanging about in the still, dank air.

"You can laugh, but Zephaniah Job - a Polperro banker - used to organise smuggling runs . . . according to what I've been reading," Phipps called back.

"Sounds like somebody straight out of the Old Testament!"

"You're wrong there, Debbie. Actually, he was a steward to the local gentry. Apparently a family named Carpenter owned the manor of Lansallos, at that time, and Zephaniah used to supply them with contraband wines and spirits."

"But how do we know it's true, Auntie Phil?"

"Because somebody's found the old letters and account books."

Further conversation had to be postponed, for the party had reached a place where seepage of water from higher ground had made the path very muddy. Everyone had to walk in single file. Shortly after negotiating this mess, they came to a rough wooden bridge thrown across a deep gully. Then there was an even steeper length of track, where centuries of rain water had washed away all traces of grass or soil. Phipps found herself stepping gingerly down smoothly rounded bedrock, hoping she would not fall and break a leg.

"Must have been a hard job for horses to pull the smugglers' carts up here," Debbie grumbled.

Bun suggested the men would have pushed from behind.

"With many an 18th Century curse!" Timothy added.

"Hard luck on them if the parson turned up to help," Bun observed drily. "Unable to curse, the men would have only been able to work at half-strength."

Soon after this dangerous area had been left behind, they found themselves at a gate leading into a small field. Signposted footpaths curved upwards on both hillsides: one to Polruan, at the entrance of the River Fowey, on their right; and the other, to Polperro, on the left. Directly below, two huge fingers of rock protected a narrow cove from the waters of Lantivet Bay.

Phipps was surprised to see patches of grass growing on the tops of each rock, surely indicating they were never scoured by even the roughest seas. A solitary rowing-boat was pulled up on the otherwise deserted shingle beach, just beneath a gap where their valley stream created a minature waterfall, as it left the land and headed towards the sea.

Timothy ran down to the edge of a low cliff, where he could obtain a better view of the cove. Phipps experienced a frisson of inner tension when she saw their nephew wave his hand, palm down, indicating the others should remain where they were.

When he rejoined them, he said there was another boat, upside down, and well above the high tide marks. A man was messing about beneath it!

Bun led them down to a vantage point, partly shielded by gorse bushes, from where they could clearly see the man either digging or covering something up. When he straightened his back Phipps caught her breath in astonishment. "Isn't that . . . ?"

"Hmmm. Yes," Bun murmured thoughtfully, "Nigel Barclay."

"I wonder what he's doing?" Phipps said, then realised it was one of her more pointless remarks because everyone else would be thinking the same.

Timothy asked who he was. Bun explained by repeating personal details she had heard mentioned at the vicar's tea party.

Phipps began frantically rummaging in her picnic bag, for all the world like an industrious female mouse building a nest from torn newspapers, then let out a gasp of delight as she dragged out their birdwatching binoculars.

She tilted the brim of her sun hat upwards and began watching Nigel Barclay. "How very odd! He appears to be digging up some shingle." She paused and adjusted the focus to see more clearly. "Good Heavens! I was wrong. He's trying to bury something! Pulling stones over and pushing them under the boat."

"Well put those glasses down," Bun told her. "We don't want to arouse his suspicions. Let's get out the Thermos flasks and have a cup of tea."

"Good idea," Debbie agreed. "Pretend we're a harmless family party having a perfectly ordinary picnic."

Timothy said he was always ready for tea and biscuits, after any long walk . . . "But I can't wait for your Mr Barclay to shove off."

Debbie asked why.

"Dead keen to shake up that shingle!" her brother replied.

Chapter Twenty

When everyone had tea and biscuits conveniently to hand, Phipps heard Timothy ask her sister what she meant, back in the lane, when she spoke about fresh avenues to explore regards Private Alfred Jackett.

"Bones, Timmie! Bones! What's happened to the bones? Then there's still a possibility of turning up the remainder of his medals . . . perhaps in the Ackroyd coal-sheds. Always army records, too. Might find out something from the War Office. And we must talk to the tramps!"

Coming from straight-laced Bun, Phipps found this suggestion a trifle unexpected . . . regardless of the fact that she, personally, felt not the least desire to hold a long conversation with some moth-eaten vagrant who would doubtlessly be smelling of sweat. Briefly, she wondered about the state of their socks, then shook her head . . . deciding that was a subject which definitely did not bear thinking about.

Debbie was also in the dark and asked, "Why tramps?"

"Because they meet in parish workhouses, when they are bound to enquire after others whom they have met previously. Next time I am asked for a couple of coppers to buy a cup of tea, I shall take out a shilling and ask a few questions germane to the issue."

Debbie pointed out they ought to question Jack Penaluna.

"Good idea Debs!" Timothy laughed. "We elect you. Drop into Exeter gaol and ask to see your dear old Grandad."

His sister commented that she didn't think that funny.

"Not very intelligent, either," Bun added. "I gather, from films, that those warders listen in to prisoners' conversations on visiting days. Can't risk drawing attention to ourselves in that manner!"

"Might find one's self being arrested on suspicion of being an accessory after the fact," Timothy added by way of explanation.

Debbie said she was content to leave prison to the prisoners.

Timothy jerked his head towards Barclay and the derelict boat.

"Wouldn't it be a strange coincidence, Aunt Anthea, if we find your gentleman sea-fisherman has been busy burying a bleached skull - boiled free of its more perishable contents - which will display a depressed fracture of the cranium, upon examination?"

"Wishful thinking. Just as likely to be French brandy or . . . "

" . . . his left-overs from an early picnic lunch?" Phipps suggested tentatively.

Debbie said that could be a bit of an anticlimax.

Her brother stoutly maintained it would be most unlikely. The man was obviously hiding something of value . . . otherwise why go to all the trouble of scratching about so near that boat? "I mean to say: there's enough beach available, out in the open."

When he had finished whatever he was doing, Nigel Barclay crossed to the other boat, dragged it down into the water, stepped onboard and pushed off. The Hydes watched him row a couple of hundred yards out from the rocks, then he appeared to pay out a fishing line before turning back towards Polperro and rowing slowly homewards.

Bun held her impatient nephew in check until Barclay's boat passed out of sight beyond the rugged outcrops of Lansallos Cliff, then they all made their way into the deserted cove.

Timothy and Debbie ran on ahead, scrambling down a rough set of steps cut into the earth near the little waterfall, to hurry across the shingle towards the derelict upturned boat.

Bun waited until they were out of earshot, then said thoughtfully, "You know . . . we could go to prison, old girl."

"But whatever for?" Phipps asked in a sudden state of panic. "We haven't done anything wrong . . . have we?"

Her sister shook her head, patiently explaining that she was not thinking of playing the part of female convicts so much as semi-official Prison Visitors.

"To speak to Penaluna, dear?"

"Why not? We're members of the Church of England. We could say we are members of the Ladies' Welfare Committee, calling to see if there was anything we could do to help one of our flock - a Mr Jack Penaluna - who has temporarily strayed from the straight and narrow path of honesty and righteousness."

"But what happens if the poor man's a Methodist?"

"Then we shall have to think of something else." Bun glared at her younger sister. "As Timothy has been heard to remark to Debbie: Don't be such an old Droopy Drawers."

"Can't say that of me. I always buy best quality elastic, dear."

They walked along the top of a slight cliff, crossing the stream by means of a convenient row of stepping-stones, where they came upon a slipway leading down towards the shingle.

Phipps looked at channels cut into the rock floor on either side of this passageway, which appeared to have been hacked out of the cliff with hammers and chisels. "Wheel ruts . . . worn into the slate over the passage of years."

"Doubt it, old girl. More likely to be guides - acting like tram lines - to keep the carts in the centre, so's they don't scrape against the rocky sides."

Phipps walked across - heel to toe - discovering there were approximately five feet between the wheel channels.

Bun stood in the centre, arms outstretched, to see if it was possible to touch both sides of the slipway and almost succeeded. Then she set off towards the boat at the head of the cove.

Phipps remained in the slipway for a few moments, eyes closed, trying to visualise what must have surely taken place on moonless nights of previous centuries, before following in her sister's footsteps.

As she drew nearer to the upturned boat, Timothy called excitedly that Barclay was definitely burying something, because they had found a box.

Further feverish excavation revealed the top of a wooden packing case, which gave off hollow sounds when struck with a stone, proving there was a cavity beneath.

Because her three companions were crowded around the box, leaving little room for another spectator, Phipps turned away, staring out across the wind-rippled waters of Lantivet bay.

From the corner of one eye - on her right - she thought she saw a tiny bungalow tucked away high above the sea. It appeared to be painted white and completely surrounded by gorse and scrub. Phipps dragged out the binoculars to look closer.

She saw a flagstaff complete with flag. In front of this, stood a man wearing a peaked cap and blue uniform. He was staring straight back at her from the other end of a big brass telescope!

"I don't think you ought to be doing that," she said to Timothy.

"Why not, Auntie Phil?"

"Because there's a coastguard watching us."

"Well don't just stand there, Phippsie!" Bun exclaimed irritably. Distract his attention! Take your shoes and stockings off. Go down into the water and paddle your feet."

"Show him the hem of your petticoat," Debbie suggested with a girlish giggle.

"Better still: a bit of leg!" Timothy encouraged.

Phipps did as she was asked, thinking it would take more than that to distract a hardened sailor in the mid-1930s . . . though it might have worked quite well in Victorian times.

As the minutes ticked away she heard squeals and shouts echoing down the beach. Yes! It is a box. Sounds empty. What a swizz: it is empty. How about that crumpled old envelope? Just a bit of rubbish. Never mind. Give it to me. I want to see inside.

"Gosh!"

Soon after this - and a short silence - Bun came down to the water's edge and asked Phipps what she thought of the contents. They had found a handwritten letter and quantity of French francs. Glancing at the note, and trying to remember what that French governess had been trying to teach her all those years ago, back in the vicarage schoolroom, Phipps said, "I can't see anything concerning the pen of my aunt . . . or closing windows on a train. Looks more like a shopping list, wines and spirits, with enquiries about a friend's wife and family. I should think somebody in Polperro has come to a private arrangement with those Breton fishermen we see anchored offshore at night."

Bun thought it surprising that anyone would seek to land contraband goods less than a mile away from the Watch House. Phipps was quick to point out no coastguard would be able to see what was coming ashore on a moonless night . . . with or without his big brass telescope.

Timothy joined them, wanting to replace the envelope, box top and shingle, then keep watch. When the Frenchman made his delivery, they could dash down and make off with the goods.

"And what happens when you come face to face with the rightful owner?" Bun enquired drily.

The boy gave his aunt a sunny smile, saying he would drop the goods and run away faster than a streak of greased lightning.

"No need to worry about Tims, Auntie," Debbie confirmed, "He's won prizes at school sports for his hundred yards sprint."

Bun reminded nephew and niece it was three miles, by cliff path, to the top of Chapel Steps, Polperro. One needed to be a marathon runner - not a sprinter. "You'd end up as crab pot bait, young man! And how should we explain that to your parents?"

At this point, Phipps noticed Debbie beginning to jump up and down, while making 'Mmmmm-mmm-mm' noises. Did she want to spend a penny?

No. It was just that there was this coastguard man . . . coming down the field above the waterfall.

"It's the Riding Officer!" Timothy hissed.

"The one who does it without a horse!" Debbie squeaked.

"Quick! Cover up that hole. Drape our clothes around it, then set out the things for lunch," Bun directed tersely.

Everyone hurried up the beach and, by the time the coastguard had crossed the stream, to cover the remaining hundred yards across the shingle, Bun and Phipps were seated on towels, their backs leaning against the upturned boat. Debbie busily unpacked picnic bags, while her brother set out plates, cups and saucers on a folded tablecloth.

"'Mornin' m'dears. Thought I recognised you when I looked through me telescope. What's on today, then? Out looking for sand fleas? You'll find plenty of they old things round 'ere!"

"No. Just out for a quiet ramble," Bun answered.

"Thought this would make a nice place for lunch," Phipps said.

"Oh arr. That there's one o' Miz Accle's favourite spots, too. We often sees 'er come down to the cove when we're on watch. Spends hours round 'ere, she do, chasing 'er ole butterflies: they big white 'uns - out looking for some poor beggar's cabbage patch; the Red Adm'rals - off to lay eggs in the stingy nettles; an' they li'l ole brown jobs. They'm all over the cliffs . . . feedin' off honey in them there thistle flowers."

Phipps said it sounded as if he had been taking lessons from the butterfly lady, to be told that he always knew a bit about the subject, having chased butterflies on his way to school, when a boy. Bun gestured towards the Thermos flasks, offering a cup of tea, but this was refused on the grounds that the coastguard had just had one before leaving the Watch House.

Timothy, obviously hoping to make off with some of the next contraband to be landed, asked what happened when people bought goods from the smugglers. "I mean to say: it's not quite the same as running the goods ashore, is it?"

"Oh yes it is, m'dear. It's an offence to bring in, handle OR CONSUME! So we can 'ave you up afore The Bench if we as much as catches you drinking wot's been given to you by the next door neighbour, outa the kindness of 'is 'eart, next Chrissmass!"

Debbie said she couldn't see how anything could be proved.

The coastguard explained that foreign companies used different bottles to British firms . . . so one only had to look at the identification marks to find out where the liquor came from.

Phipps, thinking it was better to change the subject before this man became suspicious of themselves, pointed dramatically towards the stream. "Oh look! There's a dragonfly!"

"Yeller an' black stripes?" asked the man. Receiving a nod from Phipps, he turned as if to leave. "I'm off! Don't like the look of they ole things. Wouldn't like one t'bite me."

Phipps said she didn't think dragonflies did that sort of thing.

"'Fraid so, Auntie Phil," Debbie cut in, anxious to air her knowledge. "The correct name is 'Odonata'. Comes from the Greek: 'odon' . . . meaning tooth! We used to call them 'The Flying Teeth', at school. Very predacious!"

The coastguard pulled a long face, raised a hand in farewell, and tramped off.

Bun passed round the plate of crab and lettuce sandwiches, observing that her nephew had better regard that smugglers' shopping list, and any results, as being a purely academic exercise. "Can't have you appearing before the local magistrates! Your father would never forgive us."

"Solving mysteries should bring reward," Timothy muttered.

Phipps smiled as she heard her sister tell the boy he would have to wait until he reached Heaven.

Debbie said there couldn't be much doubt who put letter and money in the hiding place. If Miss Accle spent so much time here, it must be her shopping list. Bun pointed out it might just as well have been written by Nigel Barclay. Timothy suggested Barclay had probably only seen something while out fishing, then simply come ashore to investigate.

At this point, a tall, thin, clerical gentleman came onto the beach with a large dog of indeterminate species. He introduced himself as 'Canon Prendergast', rector of Lansallos, taking 'Old Joe' for his daily constitutional.

When he had passed on, Debbie whispered, "He's our man! Most clergymen have a college degree in the arts or divinity. So he would know how to write French letters!"

Phipps was puzzled at her nephew's sudden outburst of laughter. Upon recovery - without explanation - Timothy asked: how did anyone obtain French money down here, in Cornwall?

Bun suggested one could go to a bank, say one was about to take a holiday in France, and buy francs with pound notes.

Debbie suggested this helped prove her point: their smuggler was one of the 'nobs'. "Fishermen don't have bank accounts. Usually keep any savings in an old sock, under the bed."

Timothy said: surely the main point was that this money and note were in place . . . so there would be a landing tonight!

Bun said it could come in when it pleased, Master Timothy would not be there to see it, which stopped all further argument.

Chapter Twenty-one

But argument raged loud and long at Rowett's Cellars, following delivery of the afternoon mail.

Beatrice Dyson tore open the envelope with its typewritten name and address groaning, "Oh my God! Not another bill? I thought we'd settled everything at the end of the month!"

Her husband - from behind his Times - murmured words to the effect that any forgotten creditor would have to whistle for his money because there was nothing left in the kitty.

He jumped, on hearing Beatrice let out a sudden shriek.

"What's the matter, old girl? Been over-charged by one of our hard-headed Cornish shopkeepers . . . with the soft-hearted smile?"

"It's not a bill, you fool! It's an anonymous letter!"

"Something to do with a complete lack of moral virtue on the part of your nearest and dearest . . . namely myself?"

"Wrong answer, dear old darling. Guess again."

George laid down his newspaper, stared briefly at the ceiling, then heaved a sigh, saying he supposed the letter had really been addressed to himself . . . and contained words of caution regarding what Beatrice was getting up to, on those alleged shopping trips to Plymouth with their vicar's wife.

Beatrice glared daggers, indicating George's joke was - in her opinion - not the least bit funny. Through lips now tightened with considerable anxiety she said, "The writer wishes to know what you've done with the body!"

"What body? I have none but my own . . . and I pride myself I've kept that in pretty good shape throughout the passage of the years. Don't see any call for spiteful remarks on that score."

Beatrice explained that one assumed the writer was referring to a dead body.

George said sorry . . . he didn't have any in stock.

Beatrice demanded to know if he was hiding something.

"Not that I'm aware. But if you're really worried - and I can see you are - why not pop upstairs? Take a peep under the bed. I may have left the odd body up there and forgotten about it."

Beatrice, now almost spitting fire and hot ashes, told George to put aside his Bertie Wooster act and face the question.

"What question? For God's sake stop playing games, old thing, and get to the point. If we're going out this afternoon, I want to finish reading the Times. You know how I detest looking at a morning paper after six o'clock. Something very passé about it."

Telling her husband to see for himself, Beatrice passed across envelope and notepaper. George looked, shrugged and returned them. His wife stared, then demanded to know what he intended doing . . . surely he wasn't going to just sit there . . . with that stupid grin on his face, for the remainder of the day?

George replied that it seemed a reasonable course of action for a gentleman to adopt, "Unless you feel I should show my totally horrified appreciation of your missive by laying back and uttering raucous cries of shock, horror and general dismay?"

His wife expressed the opinion that he had unfortunately not always mixed with the best type of person, whilst earning his living in the South of France, by playing cards with all and sundry. This sophistication was all very well in its place, but it was a quality which often clouded common sense.

"Beatrice darling . . . I fail to follow."

"If you've got nothing to hide, why not call the police?"

"Oh I say . . . bit unsporting, don't y'think?"

"So if a burglar comes in to rob us, you'd say 'help yourself', rather than spoil his fun?"

George Dyson muttered something about not being so damn'd daft, then expanded in a clearer voice, "Can't you see, old thing? This comes from some silly kid, playing tricks." He shook his head. "Definitely NOT to be taken seriously."

Waving his hand at the letter, he added, "Remove that paltry effort to the kitchen. Then sprinkle with a generous pinch of household salt. No one is ever meant to take that sort of thing seriously. Correct procedure is to give an indulgent smile, before screwing it up and chucking it into the waste paper basket."

Beatrice pointed to the fact that children of Cornish fishing families rarely - if ever - as much as saw a typewriter, leave alone actually played with such a machine.

"You're never saying this was written by an adult?"

"Oh yes I am!" his wife responded with a voice which was rapidly rising to an exasperated screech.

"So what? Can't you take a joke? I'm not complaining!"

"Well: I am! This is a deliberate, mean, malicious and carefully calculated attempt to cause trouble between us!"

George let out a bellow of laughter. "Succeeding, isn't it?"

His wife clenched her hands and stamped her foot.

"Best take a cold shower, old thing. You've got smoke coming out of your nostrils!" George paused for a moment, then corrected himself by suggesting two aspirin tablets were more advisable in cases such as this . . . where the patient was about to turn into a fire-breathing dragon.

Beatrice viciously screwed the anonymous letter into a ball and hurled it at the window.

George shook his head. "If that had been a brick, I should have had to stop your pocket money to pay for the repairs. No sweeties or ice cream for a month!"

"Oh you . . . "

" . . . ravishingly attractive and completely irresistible man?"

"More like: self-centred, inconsiderate egotist!"

George complemented Beatrice on her impressive vocabulary, then bet her a dirty ten bob note she couldn't define 'egotist'.

"That's easy . . . Mr George Dyson!"

"Well let's sort out what we plan to do. How about tit for tat?"

"Could be fun, I suppose . . . but who should we write to? And what could we say? Think back a few days. Have you spoken about dead bodies to anyone living in the village?" Then she clapped her hand to her mouth, stared at her husband and whispered, "Oh my God! The vicarage tea treat! I distinctly heard you mention bodies when you were talking to one of those Ackroyds . . . which means anyone else could have heard, too."

"Nigel Barclay?"

"And it serves you jolly well right. You're always teasing him."

George Dyson jerked his head towards the screwed up letter.

"Methinks I shall tease him some more. My honour is tarnished. The Dysons shall strike back!"

Various ideas were brought forward for discussion without anything being resolved then, after a lengthy silence, George asked what time they were due at St Cleer.

"The Mowbrays usually sit down to afternoon tea at four."

"Good. That gives us time to stop in Liskeard. I shall require you to slip down to that classy grocer's at the bottom of the hill and buy a couple of pounds of bacon bones. Ribs preferred. I shall pay Smiths a visit . . . there to purchase some obscure periodical such as Pigs and Poultry or Farmer's Weekly."

"Since you don't like pea soup, keep pigs, poultry or farm land, I feel left in the dark. Explain, darling."

"We shall break up the bones, char them in our sitting-room fireplace - carefully avoiding complete destruction - then I shall bury same in Nigel Barclay's garden. Hopefully, he will have a convenient rose bush . . . but almost anywhere will do at a pinch. This will be followed by a formal laying of information with the County Constabulary. We then sit back and contain ourselves with patience . . . until lots of Cornish country constables turn up with buckets and spades . . . "

" . . . to search for the remains of a dead body; concealment of which is a pretty serious offence? Ingenious . . . but suppose your handwriting is recognised?"

George explained this was the reason for his unusual choice in reading material. He would cut the necessary words from the magazine he bought in Smiths. Then: since it would appear to be a similar letter to the one which caused all that trouble with the chapel trustees, when poor Old Bill, the jobbing builder, was falsely accused of being a secret drinker, people would believe both letters had been sent by the same person.

"And we were out of the country when that first letter was dropped off at Snarling Aggie's cottage . . . "

" . . . so we shan't be suspected, will we?" George said happily.

"But Nasty Nigel will know it was you."

"Ah! But he won't be able to complain, will he? Because . . . if he does so, he knows full well that I shall make a counter complaint against him, concerning this letter he's just sent you."

"Which is just as much an offence. Clever old darling."

George Dyson smiled modestly, observing it was lucky for them that their vicar had a cousin in the village of St Cleer.

"Must give Tremain something for obliging with the lift."

"A pound of bacon bones?" Beatrice enquired with a laugh.

"No! And don't even mention bacon bones, whilst we're in the vicar's car. Just slip an ounce of pipe tobacco into his jacket pocket. That should keep him from asking what we bought in Liskeard," George ended, returning to his morning newspaper.

Everything went as planned, the Reverend James Tremain bringing the Dysons back to Polperro just after ten o'clock. George asked to be dropped outside the Crumplehorn Inn. Since it was such a mild night, they would walk home from there.

This was done by making a short detour round Nigel Barclay's garden wall, so that George Dyson could select a suitably placed flower bed . . . in which to inter his bacon bones at a later date.

Chapter Twenty-two

Timothy Hyde found Polperro harbour enveloped in a dense white sea mist when he awoke, on the following morning. He jumped out of bed and opened his window to get a better view, but saw it was hopeless to expect any foreign fishing crew to risk hazarding their boat in such adverse conditions, by attempting to draw near to Cornwall's rocky shoreline.

No brandy would have been landed at Lansallos Cove.

However, to make quite certain the whole coastline was covered by the same blanket, he pulled on trousers and roll neck pullover, then slipped quietly out of the cottage to walk up The Warren. Beyond the last cottage - set high above the footpath and almost hidden by several mature fir trees - the boy found gorse and blackthorn brushing his clothing as he hurried onwards. Dog roses and honeysuckle twined along the top of this undergrowth, with the yellow of a solitary broom occasionally to be seen as he approached a division in the path.

Disregarding the right hand fork, which he could see dropped down to the lighthouse - no more than a concrete cone, dated 1911, with a small lamp on top - Timothy continued upwards as far as Reuben's Walk. Then he branched right, walking out to the nearest cliff. He found the mist so dense that it gave him the unpleasant sensation of looking at a blank wall.

Shrugging his shoulders, the boy turned back towards the holiday cottage and reported his findings to the rest of the party.

All agreed it would be pointless returning to Lansallos Cove.

Debbie said she wasn't particularly sorry. Yesterday's long walk had left her with aching legs. She would be quite content to sit and read. Phipps murmured that she felt the same.

Bun told them she was quite happy to shop for food, in particular: a large boiling joint which would give them one hot dinner of ham, broad beans and new potatoes, with plenty of meat left on the bone for making picnic sandwiches afterwards.

Timothy expressed the thought that he would go up to Plymouth by train, if no one objected. "Might have a look at the place where Drake played bowls, or something."

"How absolutely thrilling!" Debbie exclaimed with a completely straight face.

Receiving no orders to negate his intentions, Timothy dashed upstairs to change immediately after finishing his breakfast, then hurried away to catch the bus for Looe.

Of course: there was still the outstanding job of sneaking into the grounds of Bay View House before the Ackroyd brothers returned from their yacht cruise . . . but that was night work.

Waiting at the bus stop, he wondered how they were getting on. Had they reached France, before this sea mist came down?

No. They had not.

Sixty miles due south of Plymouth Sound and the Eddystone Lighthouse, and about the same distance west of Guernsey, the Ackroyd yacht lurched fitfully on the swell . . . becalmed.

The vessel was shrouded in a dense sea fog and, from sounds all around, Richard concluded they had drifted near a busy shipping lane.

He could hear the thrashing of ships' propellers, indicating a steamer in ballast, together with the beat of heavy engines from diesel vessels, when one or the other was not drowning out all other sounds with the boom of its siren. Richard was extremely worried in case they were run down.

Ronnie said he could see them ending up as just another unsolved mystery of the deep. Richard told him to keep squeezing the rubber bulb of an old motor horn . . . their only means of indicating their own frail presence in the vicinity. Ronnie hoped the lookout on that nearest ship heard them in sufficient time for the officer of the watch to alter course.

"Just in case he doesn't, try repeating a few telling phrases from the thirty-first Psalm, by way of calming your fears."

"What's all that about?"

"Oh the usual exhortations: trust in The Lord; speedy deliverance; pull me out of the net . . . I only remember the last verse. 'Be of good courage, and He shall strengthen your heart', something, something, full stop. Seems to fit the present circumstances, wouldn't you say?"

Ronnie said he would rather have a louder fog horn.

Richard suggested food.

His brother said he wasn't very hungry.

"Well I'm starving. Just going to get a fried egg sandwich."

Halfway down the companion-ladder, on his way to their tiny galley, Richard paused and looked up at his brother.

"I wonder what sort of a night the Dysons had?"

"Oh yes. They'll have had most of yesterday afternoon and all evening to chew the fat. Well, as I see it: there were only two courses open . . . "

"Die laughing, or go to bed at daggers drawn?"

Ronnie said he was putting his money on the mother and father of matrimonial conflicts.

But this was far from being the case, back at Rowett's Cellars. George Dyson had enjoyed a night of dreamless slumber, followed by a substantial early breakfast, and was now about to begin his morning's work.

He brought wood, newspaper and bacon bones to the sitting-room, lit a fire in the grate and waited until he had a decent pile of hot red embers before adding the bacon bones, and stirring thoroughly.

Once nicely browned, they were retrieved and George admired the results. With odd slivers of flesh still adhering, he thought with a shudder, they appeared delightfully grisly.

At this stage, Beatrice came into the room, took one look at her husband's handiwork and asked if he was thinking of taking up a career in the cooked-meat trade.

"More like the rags, bottles and bones end of the game," George replied with wolfish smile.

"You don't think those scraps are too raw-looking?"

"No. They'll be all right once they've been buried for a few hours, and come up with earth stuck all over them. But I really do think some evidence of being in a fire adds authenticity. Nothing like attempted destruction, followed by concealment, to make our Cornish country constables believe they are digging up parts of a human rib-cage."

"You think of everything, darling . . . and I think you are quite wonderful," Beatrice replied, leaning down to pat her husband's head in passing, as a dog lover might signal approval to her pet.

George left the charred bones and went through to his study, where he seated himself at the desk, pulled a sheet of paper out and began scribbling.

'What happened to the previous housekeeper?

'Is she buried in the front garden?

'Barclay buried bones in his front garden but where's the rest of the body?

'Who did Barclay bury in the front garden?

"Ah! Now the last one's much the best, darling," Beatrice exclaimed, having come in to see how the clerical work was progressing. Pointing, she added, "This first line smacks of 'Murder in the Red Barn'."

"Forced melodrama, old thing?"

"Mmmm. Too Gothic. You'll make far more impression with something short and sweet."

George muttered words to the effect that he had never received any sort of formal training in the craft of anonymous letter-writing, as he bent to his task, now seeking suitable printed words from the Farmer and Stock-breeder, purchased at Smiths.

Horace Edgar Gundry, police constable, stationed at Pelynt, was also spending this part of the morning at his desk. On instructions from County Police Headquarters at Bodmin, he had interviewed Lilian Bunney on the previous evening.

The complainant had deposed that her brother - Alfred Jackett - had failed to visit her or in any way attempt to make contact for a period of almost twelve months.

She confirmed that she was the person who had telephoned Bodmin Headquarters on the previous morning. She now wanted her brother's absence to be treated as evidence that he was a missing person and called upon the police to find him.

Having taken due notice of Mrs Bunney's insalubrious appearance, Constable Gundry considered her brother was probably acting in his own best interests . . . by avoiding all further contact with his sister.

However, he reminded himself with a dismissive shrug of his burly shoulders, his was not to reason why. He continued with his report by admitting the matter did possess certain peculiarities.

Who was Miss Hyde?

Where had she come from . . . and why?

Could the complainant be believed when she said the Hyde woman spoke of a missing cousin, wartime marriage, and the possibility that the missing man had married above his station in life?

If this were found to be true: might it not explain the brother's non-appearance at his sister's home?

"Mrs Bunney is not a pretty sight," Gundry sighed. "But I can't put that in my report."

He completed his task, donned tunic and helmet, then proceeded in the direction of the village post office, with the intention of dispatching his findings to County Headquarters.

Chapter Twenty-three

The old Chief Constable had recently retired and a new man taken his place. Times were changing. Some of the County force were actually riding around on Sunbeam Lion motorcycles - six in 1931 with this number increasing each year - and now there were going to be a half a dozen two-seater motor cars available for some lucky people to use in the course of their duties.

More to the point - as far as Mrs Bunney and her missing brother were concerned - the Cornish force finally had their own Criminal Investigation Department!

According to old hands, The Standing Joint Committee had been considering the appointment of a detective inspector as far back as 1909 . . . but nothing had been done until the present year: 1935.

Cornwall County Constabulary now boasted one detective sergeant and two detective constables, seconded from the uniformed staff.

These were the men who would be cutting their teeth by conclusively establishing what had happened to Alfred Jackett, since he was last seen by his sorrowing sister on - or about - the seventeenth of August, 1934.

When Lily Bunney 'phoned to ask for police help, business was not very brisk in the new department at county headquarters.

Built on the outskirts of Bodmin in 1867, at a cost of £4,380, the Grand Jury had been so shocked that they had urged upon the Court of Quarter Sessions the necessity for observing a more rigid economy when public funds were being spent.

One critic had actually calculated the land alone had set the ratepayers back £1,162 per acre . . . at a time when agricultural wages were about ten shillings per man per week. Hardly money well spent if one considered that the County owned free building land down by the prison! No doubt this gentleman was now turning in his grave, at how costs had risen by 1935.

Activities in the CID room would undoubtedly have caused this critic's withered corpse to increase its revolutions.

Detective Constable Cedric Polkinghorne was making enquiries connected with a patient now being held in the County Asylum - at the other end of the town - concerning the death of a favourite son who had been struck down by blows from an axe. All rather pointless since the poor old man had confessed immediately after committing the act. Nutty as a fruitcake. No need for a trial. The prisoner would simply be detained during His Majesty's Pleasure. But procedural rules had to be followed, hence Polkinghorne's task on that particular day.

Detective Constable Edward Lipscombe was crouched over his desk, avidly reading Moriarty's Police Law, and dreaming of the day when he would be promoted to sergeant.

And the new department's present head - Detective Sergeant Thomas Bassett - was also dreaming of further promotion as he read Fighting the Underworld. This was a book of personal reminiscences by ex-Detective Inspector P. C. Norris, late of New Scotland Yard, which had been published a couple of years previously . . . and collected from the public library on the sergeant's way home from duty, the night before.

"Here! What d'you think of this?" Bassett said, pausing to look up from his book, "This 'ere bloke - Norris - first helped observe suspect premises when he was only ten years old!"

"That's starting young, Sarge," Lipscombe observed.

"'Course . . . wheels within wheels. His father was an inspector at Mile End Road, in the late 1890s."

"Ah! That's starting three rungs up the ladder by accident of birth," Polkinghorne grumbled.

"Even so: this Norris must have been a pretty smart chap. He was a detective inspector by the 1920s!"

"Not so much competition, in them days," Lipscombe pointed out with a shrug.

"And criminals weren't so clever, either," Polkinghorne said.

"Oh I don't know about that, Ceddie boy," Bassett replied. "It says, in my book, that Norris chased confidence tricksters. Caught 'em too. There was one called Hurricane Harry. He used to specialise in selling cargo ships to foreigners . . . immediately after they had been posted lost with all hands in Lloyd's shipping lists," Bassett told his assistants.

"Not much chance of finding a Hurricane Harry operating in Bude or Padstow," Polkinghorne mumbled as he returned to the recent exploits of that retired butcher's cutter from St Austell.

"More likely to catch one of the local shepherds doing something funny with one of his sheep," Lipscombe sniggered.

Then there was a knock at the door.

Books were slipped beneath blank files. Bassett pretended to be checking next month's duty roster, then shouted, "Come in."

A young constable entered, handed the sergeant some papers, saying this was from the morning's mail, and returned to the general office.

"New man?" Bassett enquired.

"Yes. Class 'B', poor devil," Lipscombe muttered.

This was no reflection upon the recruit's health or ability. It simply took into account the 1931 economy measures, when a lower scale of pay had been introduced for new entrants . . . who only received 55 shillings per week instead of the 70 shillings previously recommended by the Police Act of 1919.

Lipscombe closed his book and put it away in a drawer, expecting Bassett to pass across some work. This came in the shape of Constable Gundry's report. Having read it, Lipscombe glanced up in his sergeant's direction, saying this was a funny business, too.

"That woman enquiring about her long lost cousin?"

"Particularly when the complainant didn't know her brother was married, Sarge." He paused thoughtfully then added, "Come to think of it: I once came across a Sussex chap with that name."

Polkinghorne said he remembered an Archie Jackett playing in the Cornish rugby team.

Bassett observed neither comment helped clear up the present matter. "But Miss Hyde could be barking at the wrong door."

Lipscombe shrugged. "Either that . . . or the complainant isn't telling us the whole story."

"Yes! I agree. I'd have been prepared to accept this as just another time-wasting enquiry if the other woman hadn't turned up on Mrs Bunney's doorstep. But there has to be a reason why the Hyde woman went to Lanreath if, as you correctly tell me, there are Jacketts to be found elsewhere in the country. In any case, I should like to know how Miss Hyde found our Lanreath complainant . . ."

" . . . when her surname's Bunney . . . rather than Jackett?"

"Got it in one, Eddie. Get yourself on the 'phone. Ring up Looe and Liskeard stations. See if they've come into contact with any Jacketts, Bunneys or Hydes.

Lipscombe nodded. Bassett continued looking through their incoming mail, with one ear cocked as the constable telephoned.

"When was this?" Bassett heard his assistant ask. "And did you speak to the editor of the Cornish Times? I see . . . and she definitely asked about a man named Jackett on each occasion? Said they were on holiday in Polperro? Yes, got that."

Lipscombe covered the mouthpiece and said, "We're on to something fishy . . . but I don't know what. Yes!" The constable spoke into the 'phone again. "Ah! I see. But the owner's name is definitely Armstrong? No possible connection with Our Alfred?"

Bassett contained himself, while the usual pleasantries followed. As soon as his constable put the handset down, the sergeant stared at Lipscombe, raising his eyebrows expectantly.

"There's at least three of them, one not much more than a schoolgirl. Been making enquiries at the local newspaper office and our police station - in Liskeard - about an Alfred Jackett, on the pretext that his pension book had been stolen."

"And the real owner is a Mr Armstrong, I gather?"

"Yes. The editor of the Cornish Times suggested they went to Pelynt and they must have traced the Bunney woman from there. So it's not all darkness, Sarge."

"Agreed Eddie, but there's still a mystery to be explained. We'll have to have a word with these Hydes." Bassett got up to look at a wall map of the county, then turned round to give his subordinate a bland smile. "Polperro . . . not readily accessible by public transport from Bodmin. What a shame. We shall have to go down in one of the nice new cars."

Lipscombe asked if he should order one.

"Not just yet. This needs careful timing. Go too early and the Guv'nor will expect us back for lunch. Leave it too late and the miserable old sod will ask why didn't we eat before we went. I think you should call the garage just before eleven. We'll clear up any other odd jobs first . . . and have our tea and biscuits."

"I could ring up the War Office: get Jackett's army record. We've got the date of his enlistment in Gundry's report. That might give us a lead."

"And the alleged marriage to Miss Hyde's cousin?"

"I could try Somerset House. It must have taken place between 1915 and when Our Alfred was discharged with his disability pension. They won't have to cover a lot of ground."

Polkinghorne asked his sergeant what they would do, if there was no spare car available.

"Send Eddie by train, bus or his two flat feet."

"What about you, Sarge?" Lipscombe asked.

"I shall be unavoidably detained here, on office duties."

Chapter Twenty-four

Detective Constable Lipscombe found he had no difficulty in obtaining one of the police cars when he enquired, and put this down to old habits dying hard.

There were still men on the force who could recall the days when use of one's own bicycle, whilst on duty, required a red ink entry in the constable's journal . . . and even then, this was considered to be a special concession rather than a right.

Which meant few men had sufficient nerve to ask for such a luxury as a car. All knew the cars were available . . . but most thought them to be there for other people who were more important than themselves.

So Detective Sergeant Bassett was able to drive out of the yard promptly at eleven o'clock. He turned up the hill, towards Liskeard, saying they would run down by way of the Glynn Valley, then head out to the coast from Liskeard.

"I can justify the detour by stopping to have a quick word with the editor of their local newspaper . . . whilst you pick up a couple of hot pasties, for our lunch, from the nearest baker. Large size! We'll be twenty miles away from HQ by lunchtime, so we can claim it for meals taken in the course of duty."

Lipscombe smiled. This was the life! Being driven round the countryside, with free meals thrown in for good measure. He was going to like working in their new CID.

The pasties were placed on top of the engine to keep them warm, then Bassett drove down to Polperro by way of St Keyne, Duloe and Looe . . . where he parked at Hannafore Point, to enjoy the sea view whilst eating lunch.

The detectives reached Polperro by two o'clock, called on the resident constable to find out where the Hydes were staying, then strolled through the narrow streets to interview them.

A well-built woman opened their cottage door. She had a pleasant - though plain - face, with straight hair and no make-up.

Bassett noted the good quality skirt and blouse. The lady of the house. Not one of the Polperro temporary domestics. He introduced himself, saying he believed she had been making some enquiries concerning the whereabouts of Alfred Jackett.

Bun, admitting she was the Miss Hyde concerned, invited the men inside. Bassett asked if she was alone. He was told the lady's sister and niece had taken books up the path, intending to find a seat above the cliffs and read. Her nephew had gone for a walk in the opposite direction. Bassett assured her this didn't matter. She was the person he wished to interview.

Once seated, Bassett explained that the county police had now been asked to trace Alfred Jackett and he hoped she - Miss Hyde - would be able to help them . . . perhaps because she possessed information which was not yet available to the police.

"I'm sure I can't think what you mean."

"Cases involving a search for a missing person are often best approached from both ends . . . then, hopefully, we find the subject somewhere in the middle," Bassett explained. "I believe you have mentioned to a couple of people - Mrs Bunney and a newspaper editor - that you are related to a young woman who married Jackett. Can you give us her present address?"

"Imposssible. We've lost touch. Not seen each other for years."

"In that case: can we be told the lady's last known address?"

"Sorry. I never knew it. We never corresponded."

"Her parents' address?"

"Never met them."

"But she was your cousin, so you told these other people."

"We met, quite by chance, at the home of mutual friends."

Bassett knew that where families had moved around the country, it was often the case of one branch never having met those of another branch . . . but Miss Hyde was making him feel suspicious. "Could I have the address of the mutual friends?"

"Wouldn't help much. It was back in 1910 or '11. They've both passed on. They were quite elderly: my parents' generation."

Bassett contained his exasperation with difficulty, blandly saying, "But you have seen your cousin since then. I have Mrs Bunney's statement, in which you are said to have been in contact with the lady when she served as a VAD near Clacton."

Miss Hyde explained that she had spent the war years as a full-time assistant at a Brighton prep school, with VAD work in the evenings and at weekends. On one occasion she had acted as escort to some wounded men being sent to No: 8 Convalescence Depot, and met cousin Betty there quite by chance.

"I wonder you recognised her, if you'd only seen her once before that," Lipscombe suggested.

"Oh I didn't. She took me by surprise. Rushed up, just as I was making arrangements for an overnight billet in the nurses hostel. Betty told me she was living in furnished rooms, whisked me off there and gave me a bed for the night. We exchanged family gossip, parted next morning . . . and never met since."

Bassett decided to try mild sarcasm. Perhaps the wretched woman would be stung into making a damaging admission.

"Are you expecting me to believe you have gone to all this trouble, whilst on holiday, just to trace a person with whom you have such a slight acquaintanceship?"

"No trouble, officer. Nothing to do in Polperro, but sit and count seagulls. Thought it might be fun to look up Betty. Give her a shock . . . in exchange for the one she gave me at Clacton."

"Ah! Playing at detectives?"

"I regard my activities more in the nature of an intellectual exercise. Retired folk need an interest . . . and knitting does not exactly overstretch one's mental capacity, you know."

Lipscombe asked if Miss Hyde could describe the Clacton convalescence depot . . . or say where cousin Betty had lived?

"No. All the trains were running late. We were kept standing in small country stations for ages while troop trains ran past, going to the cross-Channel ferry ports. Dark by the time I reached Clacton. Didn't see much of anything."

By God! She's got an answer for everything, Bassett thought.

"Tell me: what sort of an impression did the husband make?"

"Never saw him. Away having his wooden leg fitted."

"What year would this have been?"

"Can't say for sure. '16 or '17 I suppose. Does it matter?"

"It could serve as corroboration of other evidence."

"Best not to rely on my memory. Nearly twenty years ago. Surely army records would be more helpful?"

Bassett was aware of that, but their telephone enquiries could not be answered at once, so the detectives were still waiting for official information. Whilst his sergeant was trying to think of what to do next, Eddie Lipscombe got one in below the belt, thereby earning Bassett's silent admiration.

"How do you manage to remember this surname: Jackett, when you are apparently unable to recall a single detail of the Clacton establishments?"

"We once had a parlourmaid of the same name. Not a great success. Mother used to call out 'Oh Jackett' in her sleep."

"And I shall call out 'Oh Jackett' in my sleep, after this," Bassett told his assistant, when they had left Miss Hyde and were walking slowly down The Warren.

"By the way, Eddie Boy: good work . . . for a brief moment I thought you'd got her on the run, in there."

"But it's all ended up a waste of time, hasn't it Sarge?"

"Not entirely. You know her trouble? Too many negatives! Miss Anthea Eulalia Hyde is covering up something . . . besides the fact that she is the embarrassed possessor of two incredibly unbelievable christian names."

Lipscombe observed that having Victorian parents appeared to be a bit of a handicap, for children who grew up to survive in the modern world.

"Yes . . . and that brings me to something else. If the Hydes were in the habit of using such antiquated names on their kids, why did Anthea Eulalia's aunt and uncle settle for something as working class as 'Betty' for their own daughter?"

"Meaning our Miss Hyde picked that name off the wall?"

"Damn' right. Ah! Here we are!" Bassett stopped outside the baker's shop window and pointed to a display of cream buns which were topped with a generous layer of plain chocolate.

"What about it? Shall I get us a couple? We can always charge in a few outside 'phone calls to defray the cost."

"Churlish to refuse," his constable replied with a quiet smile.

Bassett went into the bakery. When he rejoined Lipscombe, the pair walked on in silence, glad they were wearing plain clothes, because one couldn't eat cream buns when in uniform.

After Bassett had swallowed his final mouthful, and licked his fingers clean, he returned to the question of why Miss Hyde was stonewalling them.

"A perfect example of willing co-operation, Sarge." Lipscombe commented bitterly. "Every question answered without the slightest hesitation." He shook his head, adding, "What a pity she didn't actually tell us anything."

"That one ought to go in for politics!"

Lipscombe pointed out that evasion, in criminal investigations, usually indicated fear of being found out. But this begged the question of: what could such a respectable middle-aged lady have ever done . . . to make her so particularly apprehensive when policemen came to call?

"Dunno Eddie, dunno at all . . . but we'll find out!"

Chapter Twenty-five

Left to her own devices, Miss Anthea Eulalia Hyde made herself a small pot of tea, scattered a selection of sweet biscuits onto a plate, then went upstairs. Thoughtfully looking out upon the harbour scene, from a front bedroom window, she nodded to herself with a degree of satisfaction, at being able to recall such an apposite text from the Second Book of Timothy.

"'For God hath not given us the spirit of fear; but of power, and of love, and of sound mind'."

She certainly had no fear of the police . . . but saw nothing particularly lovable in her pair of bucolic detectives either. However, she recognised that she possessed a sound mind.

And power too . . . because, from their questions, it had quickly become apparent that she knew more than they did.

When confronted with news that Alfred Jackett's present whereabouts were now the subject of an official enquiry, Bun had briefly debated the course of her responses . . . and concluded it would save everyone a great deal of trouble if she avoided all mention of her family's investigations.

She had therefore answered all questions promptly, but in such a manner that no one would be able to check whether she had been telling the truth, or merely indulging her fertile imagination.

She had always accepted the fact that information would have to be passed on to the county police eventually, but did not want them getting too close to the heart of the mystery before she did so. The whole project was becoming quite fascinating and - as she told that sergeant with perfect candour - she did not find knitting taxed her brain nearly so much as the odd bit of criminal investigation.

She did not wish to be warned off at this stage in the game!

More evidence had come to light on the previous evening, when all four Hydes had gone out to Chapel Cliff, by way of Landaviddy Lane and the footpath through the woods.

Her nephew had forced the pace; pointing out that, although both Ackroyd brothers were known to be away from home, they could easily return to Bay View House at any moment. After all: it wouldn't have been much fun drifting about in fog for twenty-four hours . . . then finding themselves becalmed.

Timothy had first carried out a careful reconnaissance, mainly looking for lights which could indicate occupation. This had been done by strolling along the public footpath, in front of the premises. Then he had stationed his aunts and Debbie near the approaches.

It would be his sister's job to run and warn him, if the Ackroyds suddenly turned up, while his aunts engaged the young men in conversation, thus giving Timothy time to get clear.

Bun had felt most relieved when Timothy's prowl, around the coal sheds of Bay View House, was over without the need for her to make enthusiastic remarks about the Ackroyds' MG. She had heard men speak of such things as SU carburettors, soft brakes and crash gearboxes, but had no idea of the correct context in which to use such esoteric expressions.

Fetlocks and withers were more in her line.

When Timothy returned to his lookouts, he had been carrying an old, very well-worn, light fawn raincoat. Showing it to Bun, the boy had pointed proudly to three strips of coloured ribbon, two of which supported medals.

Timothy had already told the others of how he had discovered Plymouth City Library, on his day out, and gone into the reference room, where he had looked up details of the 1914-15 Star which Debbie found in Talland Hill.

Now he gestured at the piece of ribbon with its watered red, white and blue shading which, to Bun's mind, made it look as if all the colours had run together at the laundry.

"This is where Debs' medal came from and, what's more, these other two prove the point. The '14-'15 Star cannot be worn without the British War Medal - that's the silver one - and the Victory Medal . . . this bronze job."

Phipps had turned them over, shone her torch all round and confirmed Jackett's name was impressed on both. "So I suppose he was wearing this coat when he was hit by the car."

However, Bun had carried out a more general examination and had to admit it was surprising that she found no rents in the material . . . or even surface abrasions. To her way of thinking, this coat had been put out in one of those back sheds because it was no longer fit to wear: worn . . . but otherwise undamaged!

Phipps had made a few notes on an old shopping pad, then Bun had instructed Timothy to replace the coat and medals where he discovered them . . . or they might find themselves charged with concealing evidence of a crime.

Her nephew - keen to keep the medals as souvenirs - had expressed reluctance to comply with this order, but Bun had insisted.

Now . . . following the detectives' visit, she felt virtuously self-satisfied that she had put her foot down so firmly.

She reached out for a rich tea biscuit and began to crunch thoughtfully. Upon reflection, she felt fairly well-pleased with the way in which she had managed to find a ready answer for each question. But she was under no delusions. Those two policemen would check her replies against official records. That detective constable had been making a careful written note of everything.

However, she was not over-concerned about her imaginative account of taking wounded men to the Clacton convalescence depot. No doubt movements of that kind would have been recorded at the time, but she felt it unlikely such minutiae would have survived for so many years after The Armistice. Therefore: nobody could now prove she had not made the journey.

No. It was the man's personal records which bothered her. She had been unable to establish precisely why Alfred Jackett was drawing a disability pension. Even his sister had only used the word 'wounded'. It was Colonel Pickford's mention of lost arms and legs which had fitted their pre-conceived ideas, thus causing Phipps and herself to settle for a lost leg.

Pure guesswork!

Even the disability pension had entered the picture by coincidence. If they had not heard about Jack Penaluna's court case, would they have thought about that?

Yet there was no denying the evidence of Alfred Jackett's discharge paper and - as she'd said at the time - private soldiers only escaped being turned into cannon fodder if they could show they were unfit for further service in the field. It therefore followed this man certainly did have a disability pension.

Bun compressed her lips with irritation.

What about gas?

They had not considered that. Now, when did the first gas casualties begin coming back from France or Belgium? Some time during 1915 . . . following an offensive at Ypres. Which means: Private Jackett may have chest trouble and still possess all his arms and legs! And what about the colour of his hair?

Bun snatched up another biscuit and took a savage bite.

They - the Hydes - were looking for a ginger-haired man on the strength of finding leg muscle from such a person.

Now that was an incontestable fact!

But it did not necessarily mean Jackett had ginger hair. Yet, if only by coincidence, she now had equally incontestable proof that he was officially a missing person . . . because otherwise: why should those two detectives have come calling on her?

It might not have been the 'done thing' to make enquiries at that Liskeard newspaper office or the town police station, but it wasn't a criminal act either. Nor was her visit to Alfred's sister. So the police were not out and about, trying to trap her in any way with their questions.

Bun drained her cup and filled it up again.

Maybe the Hydes had jumped to conclusions without giving the meagre facts sufficient thought, but they must be on the right track. Why else should the police want to find Jackett?

Bun settled down to reviewing her answers to their questions. The cousin Betty story could never be exposed as a tissue of lies, so she was all right there.

And as for that imaginary wartime wedding . . . well everyone knew how moral standards had fallen in those four years. When the police checked with Somerset House and found no record of any marriage, then came back to tax her about this, she could always suggest her cousin had only told her of the event. She had not taken out her marriage certificate and waved it about as proof; so perhaps these two people had only been living in sin.

She shrugged, picked up her third biscuit and nibbled more thoughtfully. No. There probably wasn't much cause to worry. If the police managed to find that body, the clues would doubtlessly send them off in an entirely different direction. Trouble was: it would quite spoil her fun. What to do next? There was her idea of visiting Penaluna in prison . . . but that would serve no useful purpose because one could not discuss baiting crab pots with human flesh in front of the gaolers.

Well the Ackroyds couldn't have killed the man and left his coat in their shed . . . but Dyson may have put the coat there to throw suspicion away from himself. Which means Timothy must go back and make a closer search of Dyson's garage and car.

Further reverie had to be left for later because she heard her sister come into the cottage and went down to meet her.

Phipps said she had been chatting to an itinerant knife grinder.

"He was telling me he knew Alfred Jackett, dear."

Chapter Twenty-six

"'Behold, I will send a messenger . . . '" Bun intoned sonorously, raising both arms above her head.

"You sound like an Old Testament prophet, dear."

"Malachi, actually, old girl. Wouldn't put itinerant knife grinders in the same class as a general rule, but this one sounds as if he may well have come bearing messages. What did he have to say for himself, Phippsie?"

"That he lived in Torquay and toured Cornwall every summer, sharpening knives and scissors to pay his way. Since he pushed a two-wheeled workbench around the countryside, he naturally met tramps and other vagrants on his travels. Those who spent most of their time in the Westcountry got to know him and would stop for a chat over a mug of tea, brewed up at the roadside."

"And Alfred Jackett was one of them?"

"Yes. The knife grinder said he was easy to remember because of his wooden leg . . . and the fact that one had to shout to make him hear anything. Our poor old Alfred had apparently been blown up by a German shell, dear."

Bun roared with uncontrollable laughter.

Phipps asked what could she have said, that was so amusing.

Bun recounted the story of her interview with the detectives and the way in which she had been thinking about Private Jackett's supposed disability afterwards.

"We never really knew . . . somehow or other just took the loss of a leg for granted. And now you tell me he has a wooden leg!"

"Strange coincidence, dear."

Bun and Phipps made more tea and went into a long discussion about the police interest and what bearing it might have on their own future activities. Debbie, followed shortly after by her brother, turned up halfway through this. When her aunts stopped talking, the girl said she was most terribly sorry but she had done something which might cause further difficulties.

"You remember I wrote to my old biology teacher?"

"To have some hair samples examined under the microscope?" Phipps enquired.

"Yes. Well . . . when the reply was delivered I was on my own in the cottage. Miss Halford wrote that two hair samples came from human beings. So I thought . . . we can't do much more ourselves. This is now a police matter."

"Oh dear," Phipps wailed. "you haven't written an anonymous letter, have you?"

"Just a few words made up with cuttings from an old newspaper. Nothing which could be traced back. Simply: DYSON'S CAR. ASK COASTGUARD. I sent that old medal too, because it's got the man's name on it."

"Oh my God!" Timothy shouted. "You blithering idiot, Debs!"

Bun demanded to know why her nephew was carrying on in this seemingly ridiculous fashion. Timothy explained that he had purchased the three medals - together with the discharge certificate - at the corner junk shop. "On the first evening we arrived. You sent me out for food . . . "

" . . . and you met a Mr Chuggy Williams who told you all about the local smugglers and ghosts?" Bun prompted.

"That's right. Didn't say anything about the medals. Thought I'd sort of keep them in reserve. Then . . . when I thought we were a bit short on clues, I trotted them out to encourage everyone to greater efforts. Wasn't difficult to shove the 1914-15 Star into that roadside mud, for Debs to find, and I pinned the other two medals onto an old raincoat . . . which I found hanging on the back of a coal shed door, at the Ackroyd home."

"The police will trace this back to us, when they interview the junk shop proprietor," Phipps exclaimed breathlessly.

Bun disagreed, pointing out there was no reason for the police to go to the junk shop in the first place. They were looking for Jackett. Hopefully - upon receipt of Debbie's anonymous letter and enclosure - they could now be expected to transfer their attentions towards George Dyson and the Ackroyds.

Debbie reminded everyone that they were the only people who knew about those medals on the raincoat.

"That's right!" Timothy said. "But we can easily tip off the bobbies. Just send another anonymous note."

Bun suggested this might be going a shade too far. If the police received one note, they could be expected to take it seriously. But if they kept receiving similar notes, they would be more likely to regard the whole business as a hoax.

"Such as one might expect from those college boys," Phipps suggested. "I don't know if there's any truth in what I've overheard, when waiting to be served in the village shops, but there is talk of their having been sent down from Oxford."

"Oh yes. I've heard it too, Phippsie. One - or both - of them was involved in a midnight stroll through the grounds of a women's college . . . without the benefit of adequate clothing!"

"Starkers?" Timothy asked with a grin.

"Naked as the day they were born. Point is: if they would do that sort of thing . . . " Bun waved an open hand.

"There's no telling what they might get up to, when miles away from home and any form of adult supervision," Phipps concluded.

Debbie said she couldn't see how a midnight stroll, nude in the streets of Polperro, would help their own cause.

Her brother agreed . . . though suggested it might serve to start yet another smuggling legend, or something similar.

"Ah! Something similar!" Bun exclaimed in triumph.

"A wild rumour, dear?"

"What else, Phippsie? It is generally known the Ackroyd brothers keep their yacht just across the river from Devonport. We must speak of one of them having been seen in the middle of Plymouth - standing on the edge of a city pavement - wearing a light fawn raincoat . . . "

" . . . on which a row of war medals could be seen?" Timothy cut in, "And carrying one of those trays, favoured by beggars, displaying boxes of matches for sale."

"Masquerading as an ex-soldier?" Debbie laughed. "What fun."

"But it won't help to involve the police, because they won't know where to find the evidence," Timothy cautioned them.

Bun patiently explained that this would be amongst the facts to be incorporated into their rumour.

"We shall say that this story of the ex-soldier impersonation must be true because one of the women, who works at Bay View House, actually saw the coat . . . complete with medals. By the way Timmie: where will she have seen it?"

"Oh . . . yes. Of course. I hung it on a nail, at the back of the coal shed door."

"And both those medals have Private Jackett's name impressed on them," Debbie reminded everyone.

"So the Ackroyd brothers are going to have some explaining to do, when they return from their cruise, aren't they?" Timothy said with a laugh.

"But what about our imaginary cousin Betty?" Phipps asked.

Bun pointed out that the police were only interested in tracing cousin Betty because they wanted to find Alfred Jackett. Once his medals turned up, the detectives could be relied upon to forget Betty, as they concentrated their efforts in the general direction of Ackroyd and Ackroyd.

"To say nothing of Mr George Dyson," Debbie reminded them. His car has a dent. Everyone knows he's been involved in an accident and not used the vehicle since . . . "

"And thanks to your cryptic note . . . the bobbies will call on the coastguard, who will confirm that first medal was found in Talland Hill," Timothy added, "and they'll see the gashed hedge."

"All terribly complicated though," Phipps said with a shake of the head. "Perhaps it would be easier to admit we've been playing about. Throw ourselves on their mercy . . . before they charge us with wasting police time."

Bun scowled, replying that if they adopted this course they might all find themselves in the local lock-up. They couldn't let that happen or their eldest brother and his dear wife would never speak to them again. "Isn't one of your mother's relatives on The Bench?" she asked Debbie.

The girl replied yes, her uncle Gilbert Woods who was descended from a long line of brewers.

"Sort of chap who sells enough beer to make all the men drunk on Saturday night . . . then fines 'em five shillings on Monday morning, when they have to appear in court for disorderly conduct" Timothy explained. "A shining example of your typical English middle class, two-faced hypocrite!"

"Well there you are, Phippsie. Can't afford to take chances with the mercy - or otherwise - of the local magistrates. Best to send the bobbies off in the opposite direction."

"That's right," Debbie confirmed. "Nothing like throwing out a few good red herrings to confuse the issue."

"And those detectives are going to have quite a Chinese puzzle of clues by the time we've finished with 'em," Timothy exclaimed.

He rubbed his hands together. "Now then . . . what's for tea?"

Chapter Twenty-seven

As far as Constable Peter Trebilcock was concerned, it was not so much what there was for tea . . . as when he was going to find time to eat it. He was stationed in Polperro and had just received an urgent letter from his inspector at Looe.

Trebilcock read about the anonymous tip-off, featuring a recent burial of bones in Nigel Barclay's front garden, together with instructions to take a look 'in passing' . . . immediately.

If there were signs of digging, he was to call upon the householder and ask for an explanation. If the constable was dissatisfied with answers received, he was to request permission to examine the suspect site by digging . . . WITH GREAT CARE, underlined in red ink.

Hence the Polperro constable's thoughts about having a very late meal-break. Barclay was notoriously surly and known throughout the village for his irascibility. There would not be any co-operation forthcoming, that was a dead certainty.

Trebilcock heaved a sigh and went out to his garden shed. He selected a small trowel, returned to his office, where he wrapped the tool in brown paper, then stuffed it in a trouser pocket. Not very comfortable for walking, but one may as well go prepared for the worst, where the Nigel Barclays of this world were concerned.

When the constable reached Bella's House - now re-named The Anchorage - he found disturbed earth clearly visible and knocked at Barclay's door. The housekeeper answered, telling Trebilcock that the owner was not at home. Out fishing and not expected back until late.

The constable enquired who had been digging beside that rose bush, and was told he would have to ask old Jack Pooley, the jobbing gardener, who lived at the other end of the village.

"Sure you don't know, Miss Bascombe? Would save me a long walk," Trebilcock asked with what he hoped was a winning smile.

Miss Bascombe pointed out that her kitchen was at the back of the building, so she rarely knew what was going on, out front.

Fortunately for the village policeman, he found that Jack Pooley had finished his tea, so he was able to walk down to Barclay's garden and give an opinion.

Trebilcock was aware that old Jack was a notorious gossip, who would stop for nothing once he scented scandal, and regretted having to ask for his assistance. If there were any bones buried by the rose bush, everybody in the local pubs would know shape, size, number and sex by closing time. And old Jack would probably have to be taken home in a wheelbarrow, having been given too many pints by way of encouraging his imagination.

However, once inside the Barclay front garden, Jack denied all knowledge of the disturbed soil.

"All I does is a little light weedin', my son. Don't wanter dig no earth while the weather's so dry. Loses all yer moisture, boy!"

"In that case I'll have to dig up what's down there, Jacko."

"Well I don't want me lawn mucked up. You 'ang on 'til I gits a bit o' sackin' put down!"

Once this had been done, Trebilcock knelt on it to begin removing soil . . . slowly and carefully. To his amazement, he began to bring pieces of bone to the surface before the hole was six inches deep. Jack Pooley's voice piped in his ear.

"My Gor, boy! Them's ribs! There's bin murder done. You'll be turning up some poor beggar's 'ead in a minute! I'm off!"

Yes, I'll bet you are, Jacko . . . to the nearest public bar, the village constable thought to himself. I does all the work and the likes of him gets all the beer. Trebilcock looked up, then nodded. Last seen hurrying in the direction of Fore Street, your worships, where licensed premises known as the Ship Inn are situate.

It wouldn't be long now, before that handful of broken ribs acquired arm and leg bones . . . perhaps even a grinning skull, in old Jack Pooley's constant re-telling of the tale. Trebilcock got to his feet and hurried away to telephone his inspector.

A sergeant was sent over, by taxi, to collect the bones, saying that they would be dispatched on one of the northern night trains: first stop Bristol and the Regional Forensic Laboratory.

By then, Jack Pooley, having told all he knew in exchange for free beer at the Ship Inn, was on his way to spread the word at the Three Pilchards, down near the harbour.

And the landlord of the Ship had quietly slipped out of his bar to telephone the editor of the Western Morning News, who then ordered a district reporter to visit the scene of the crime.

Thus: Detective Sergeant Bassett read of this gruesome discovery in his morning newspaper before he even reached the office. Their Deputy Chief Constable had apparently done so too, for he summoned Bassett to report, upon arrival.

More annoyed at seeing the case reported so quickly, than concerned with forensic detail, Superintendent Davis had closely questioned his newly-appointed detective sergeant.

Bassett assured his superior that no newspaper reporter would ever benefit from items leaking out of their CID office, and was given leave to get on with his work.

By two thirty, that same afternoon, Bassett was blessing his good fortune that his name had not been linked with those Polperro rib bones, in the Western Morning News report.

He received a telephone call from an assistant at the Bristol Forensic Laboratory. The gentleman was more amused than irritated, saying the exhibit examined by him consisted entirely of fragments from a pig's carcase . . . and concluded by recommending Cornwall Constabulary keep their old bacon bones for making pea soup in future.

Bassett replaced the handset, spread out all the Polperro reports across his desk, and sat thinking things over.

Those chapel trustees had not complained to the police, when they received that letter which led to Old Bill's fall from grace, but Pete Trebilcock - they had both been stationed together in Callington when younger - had mentioned its receipt.

It appeared as if this second anonymous letter, relating to the bacon bones in Mr Barclay's front garden, had been put together in much the same fashion. Question was: did both originate from the same creative genius? Or was the second letter merely put together in the style of the first . . . but by a different person?

Bassett tapped his forefinger on the note about Dyson's car.

"And now we have a third," he murmured to himself. "Same style, but much shorter . . . and very much to the point. Is it the work of somebody who is improving his technique with frequent practice? Or do we have three entirely separate practical jokers resident in such a small village as Polperro?"

There was also now a question of what to do about this chap Dyson and his car? Best play safe. Do as the sender suggests and ask the coastguard first . . . on a strictly confidential basis, to save possible embarrassment if it turns out to be another prank.

Bassett smiled grimly. Providing all three letters originated from the same scource: this let those Hydes off the hook because they weren't present in Polperro for Old Bill's downfall.

"Which is a pity," he grumbled. "I rather liked the idea of blaming Anthea Eulalia Hyde. Would be poetic justice. I'm damn' sure she's been up to something she shouldn't be doing."

Bassett reached out and picked up Private Jackett's 1914-15 Star. The implication seems to be that a man named Dyson knocked down and killed an ex-soldier named Jackett, being observed by a coastguard. Curious nobody reported what happened . . . and where's Alfred Jackett's body? The detective sergeant shrugged. At least this was something he could settle by 'phone. He called Pete Trebilcock, outlined the facts - together with his own theories - told him to investigate and report back, then replaced the handset with a contented sigh.

Meanwhile, in Polperro, greater confusion was developing as Miss Philippa Hyde passed from one shop to another. She found everyone talking about the rib bones dug up in Nigel Barclay's garden, so it was a simple matter to suggest this had nothing to do with murder . . . but was merely yet another practical joke being perpetrated by the young Ackroyd brothers.

"I heard somebody from the village saw the eldest boy sitting on a low wall - out on Plymouth Hoe - dressed in an old fawn raincoat, displaying a row of war medals, and offering boxes of matches for sale from one of those small trays ex-servicemen use. I don't think he was displaying a card to say that he was an ex-soldier who was out of work . . . but the implication was plain enough," Phipps told people as soon as she had claimed their attention. "What's more . . . I heard one of the women who works for them - at Bay View House - saying she had actually seen the coat and medals hanging on a nail in the coal shed!"

Garbled versions of both stories - Ackroyd's begging and Barclay's bones - mingled together in the course of much repetition until they became one . . . the young Ackroyds had buried those bones in Mister Barclay's garden for a joke.

Nigel Barclay nodded wisely when his housekeeper told him.

"What one might expect from that pair. Got chucked out of Oxford! Running about, in the middle of the night, in their birthday suits. Not a pair of trousers between them! Well: if they can play the fool, I can act the goat! I'll fix those Ackroyds!" he snarled, picking up the 'phone to ask for Directory Enquiries.

Once he had obtained the number of a certain specialist retail establishment in Wimpole Street, London W1, Nigel Barclay called this firm and placed an order. Satisfied that the goods would be despatched in time for a next day delivery at Polperro, he gave a most uncharacteristic chuckle.

Chapter Twenty-eight

Timothy Hyde was awake before dawn's first light, next morning. This had been accomplished by borrowing an ancient alarm clock from the kitchen, after his aunts had gone to bed on the previous evening. He was certain they would have stopped him setting out alone for Lansallos Cove at such an early hour. A brief glance out of his window reassured him that it had been a clear night, for there was not a trace of mist to be seen.

The boy dressed hurriedly, crept down to the kitchen, stuffed bread, butter and cheese into a brown paper carrier bag, together with a generous hunk of rich fruit cake and the birdwatching binoculars, then let himself quietly out of the front door.

To his amazement, he found others were out and about, despite the early hour. Fishermen with canvas bags, presumably containing a day's food, were headed for their boats to take advantage of the clearer weather conditions.

Elderly gentlemen, easily identified by their townie clothing as being summer visitors, strode purposefully up The Warren carrying rods, doubtlessly bound for some rocky perch beyond the harbour entrance.

Timothy headed for Little Laney by way of Roman Bridge and Lansallos Street. He hurried up, past St John's Church, making his way out to cliffs just beyond Bay View House. Then he eased his pace for the long walk to Lansallos Cove.

In the sea, below and to his left, a local crabber chug-chugged close inshore, soon slowing as it drew abreast of a group of crab pot markers. About a mile further out, Timothy could see the sails of a large yacht heading up-Channel, indicating a stiff breeze was pushing in from the south-west. Nearer the distant horizon, the tiered lights of an ocean liner twinkled though, by then, it was almost full daylight.

In surrounding bushes, the boy could hear birds twittering; and shrews screaming with rage, as they met, whilst looking for food.

Glancing upwards, his ears alerted by a curious mewing call, he saw a pair of kestrels wheeling lazily in the sky above. As he progressed, he found the clean morning air scented with honeysuckle and told himself that a few hours later, when the sun had warmed surrounding gorse bushes, their muskiness would catch in walkers' throats as they brushed past.

By the time he reached the stream - falling to a tiny cove in East Coombe - at the beginning of Lansallos Cliff, Timothy wished he had stopped to make a flask of tea. As it was: he had to slake his thirst from the brook beneath his feet.

When he reached Lansallos Cove, the boy looked all round to make certain he had the place to himself. Then he took out his aunts' birdwatching binoculars, training them on that tiny white building almost hidden amongst the surrounding cliff top gorse and blackthorn bushes. Timothy smiled a satisfied smile.

The Riding Officer - who did it without a horse - was to be seen pottering about outside the Watch House . . . either cleaning the windows or urinating against the front wall, the boy concluded with sardonic amusement.

Dropping his carrier bag on the shingle, he hurried across to scrape away beneath the upturned boat. Upon removing the lid of that buried box - where the French money and shopping list had been found during his first visit - Timothy discovered a dozen bottles and some brown paper parcels.

"Just like in all the old books," he chortled. "Brandy for the parson, and baccy for his clerk."

Eagerly, he reached inside, and had his hand on the neck of the nearest bottle, just about to withdraw it, when he heard a rushing sound heading towards him.

Looking over his shoulder, the terrified would-be robber found Old Joe heading in his direction, tongue hanging halfway down his jaw and an expression of delight clearly discernible.

This could only mean one thing: Canon Prendergast, rector of Lansallos, was coming down to collect his spirits ration.

The boy grabbed his carrier bag, hastily thrust a handful of rich fruit cake into Joe's gaping mouth, then rushed away to throw himself behind rocks nearby.

As expected, Joe remained where he was to eat the cake.

Within half a minute, or less, Timothy heard the canon scrunch across the shingle. He paused to ask Old Joe whose cake he had found, then the 'clink' of bottles reached the boy's straining ears. He risked a quick peep.

Sure enough, Canon Prendergast was replacing the box top.

And standing on the shingle, near the canon's rump, were two green bottles. A brown paper parcel rested beside them . . . now being carefully assessed by Old Joe's questing nose.

Timothy withdrew his head while the clergyman was still busily rearranging the shingle around his cache. Wouldn't do to meet in the present circumstances. Could be embarrassing to all parties, the boy told himself.

Louder sounds of displaced stones - followed by a sigh and the sorrowful statement that one didn't get any younger with the passage of the years - indicated Canon Prendergast was standing up once again.

Sure enough, he was then heard calling, "Come on Joe. Time for breakfast!" And scrunching sounds, which became more distant with every step, proved man and dog were returning to Lansallos rectory.

Timothy Hyde stood up, stretched himself, looked around to make certain the coast was clear . . . and promptly dropped back into his hiding place.

A small boat was approaching from seaward.

The boy emptied his carrier bag then - holding it flat on top of his head - he peered over the top of his screening rock.

"That same chap who we saw, the other day," he murmured thoughtfully. "Now what did Aunt Anthea say he was called? Oh yes: Nigel Barclay."

Timothy shrank back into his hiding place to await events.

As expected, there was the sound of a boat's iron-banded keel scraping onto the beach, followed by the clump of feet as its owner stood up and stepped ashore.

More scrunching, dragging sounds - punctuated with the breathless gasps of a man totally unused to hard physical exertion - informed the boy that Mr Barclay had come to stay.

Feet scrunched up the beach stopping, as near as Timothy could judge, beside the upturned boat. Giving a final heaving gasp, Barclay could be heard sinking to his knees. Scrabbling sounds followed, then there was the dull scrape of wood against wood . . . and more 'clinking' of bottles being moved about.

Timothy risked a quick peep, heaved a disgruntled sigh, and sank down once again.

"Now Naughty Nigel's grabbed a couple of bottles," the boy whispered grudgingly to himself. "If things go on like this, there won't be anything left for me! And suppose the next person comes over this way? They would only have to stray a few feet sideways to be looking over the top of this rock and find me!"

Well there's only one thing to do, Timothy told himself while waiting for Nigel Barclay to clear off, I'll have to move up to a hiding place near the top of the cliff . . . where I can keep everything under observation without this constant fear of having the next member of the smuggling consortium trip over me.

The boy had only just got himself relocated between two gorse bushes - with a useful clump of grass to shield his face in case anyone chanced to look upwards from the cove - when he became aware of somebody tramping along the cliff path.

Cowering low, he asked himself if he could have been seen by the next person going towards that box in the cove, but it soon appeared this was unlikely because sounds from the path indicated the walker was passing on without as much as a pause.

Timothy waited until all was quiet, then raised his head.

"Good God!" he muttered. "Well that's torn it!"

Down below - and about to enter the cove - stood the horseless Riding Officer. The man looked all around . . . then marched straight across to the upturned boat, removed shingle, opened the smugglers' box and took out a single bottle.

This was slipped into a coat pocket, the cache re-covered, then the coastguard continued his foot patrol towards Polperro.

"They're all in it together!" Timothy exclaimed, feeling quite shocked at his discovery. He remained where he was, stuffing himself with food, while following the coastguard's progress. Once out of sight, the boy shrugged, muttering that this was where he let well alone, and returned to the holiday cottage.

Timothy told his sister and aunts all about it, when he was back in Polperro, "They probably have a gentlemen's agreement!"

"The proverbial 'blind eye' rewarded with a free bottle," Bun observed, adding that the local coastguard was taking a big risk.

Phipps thought not. If a senior officer saw anything, their man could always pretend he had only just discovered the cache.

Debbie agreed, pointing out that even if their coastguard was actually caught red-handed with the top off the box, he could still disclaim any previous knowledge. "No matter what happens, he's always going to come up smelling of violets."

Bun expressed her unequivocal approval of Timothy's immediate withdrawal. "If the coastguard had caught you with a bottle or two, I'm quite sure you would have been seized, along with the rest of the dutiable goods. But never mind, the Private Jackett mystery is becoming more interesting."

Timothy laughed. "Those Ackroyds will have a shock when they arrive home, to find the police waiting for explanations."

Chapter Twenty-nine

By the middle of that same afternoon, Detective Sergeant Bassett was beginning to wonder exactly who should be asked to explain precisely what. As he said to Lipscombe, every time they tried to separate real fact from the more dubious information reaching the office, they seemed to uncover yet more loose ends.

"This case is becoming more muddled than the old woman's knitting, after the cat's had a go at her ball of wool."

Shaking his head, Bassett thought he had good reason to feel frustrated. Details received by the morning's post, from Somerset House, stated there was no marriage registered between Alfred Jackett and any other person.

A search of the Births Register had revealed the subject of this enquiry was born on the sixth of July, 1897. There was no entry under Deaths, so it must be presumed Private Jackett was still alive, unless he had died overseas, or been killed - either by accident or design - and the body concealed.

A similar report from the War Office stated this man had been discharged with a disability pension . . . which appeared not to have been drawn for almost nine months. The subject was therefore still alive when he left the army, being no longer fit for service in the field.

The Brighton force had carried out enquiries in the vicinity of Brunswick Terrace. This established that two sisters: Anthea Eulalia and Philippa Hyde had lived in one property for many years, running their family home as a boarding house, following the death of both parents in the Spanish Flu epidemic of 1918-19. A young neighbour: Elizabeth May Derwent, had died at the same time. If she were still alive today, she would be forty-two years of age . . . which, Bassett reminded himself, was about the same age as those two Hyde sisters. Had Miss A E Hyde chosen the name 'Betty' for an imaginary cousin, because she had once known a Miss Elizabeth Derwent . . . as Betty?

Then there was the question of Number 8 Convalescence Depot . . . once situated at Clacton-on-Sea? No records existed, the wooden huts having long since been dismantled and sold off to retiring naval officers who were setting up chicken farms.

"Eddie!"

Lipscombe looked up expectantly.

"Can you tell me how the Hell our Miss Hyde could have known about this Con Depot at Clacton? The ruddy place is miles away from Brighton . . . where we know the Hydes were living, during the war years!"

"Heard talk at the one where she nursed in her spare time? You know: some bloke who had been wounded before and sent there. Or maybe our Anthea saw a list."

"Already thought of those ideas, Eddie Boy. They don't stand up to closer examination. It would mean the Hyde woman had remembered - accurately - part of a casual conversation heard something like twenty years ago. Or, in the case of a typewritten list, remembered one line from possibly dozens of similar items."

"Perhaps she really did go there, just as she told us, Sarge."

"Hmmm. Maybe. But I doubt it." Bassett grumbled, picking up Constable Trebilcock's report, and started to read once more.

Dyson's car had been inspected, damage being found to a front wing. The owner had declined to give an account of any accident, saying it was not a police matter.

Enquiries at a row of Coastguard Houses, near the top of Talland Hill, had produced a man who claimed to have been present in the road when a girl and boy - round about 16-17 years of age - found a war medal (ribbon missing). It had been buried in mud, near the bottom of a hedge. This had been gashed by an unknown vehicle within the past week or two.

Further enquiries in Polperro showed that the boy and girl were visitors. They had been interviewed by Constable Trebilcock in the presence of their aunts: Anthea Eulalia Hyde and Philippa Hyde. The girl deposed she had scraped the medal out of roadside mud. The boy - her brother - confirmed this.

Trebilcock ended with a brief summary of current rumours circulating in the village. These concerned buried bones, and a practical joker pretending to be an old soldier, on Plymouth Hoe.

Passing this report across to his assistant, Bassett made no comment, but sat waiting like a hungry cat - keeping vigil before an occupied mousehole - until Lipscombe finished reading. He looked up with an amazed expression on his face.

"These Hydes are a real mystery. Can't get away from them!"

"Keep cropping up, don't they?" Bassett replied grimly.

"And what about these bacon bones?"

"Unfortunately our forensic people couldn't tell me the name of the shop where they had been purchased . . . but you and I are going to Polperro tomorrow morning, to find out!"

"First stop the village grocer?" Lipscombe laughed. "I'll bet you a pint to a couple of cream buns them bones weren't bought in Polperro, Sarge. Even village folk aren't that dumb, whilst the incomers are too intelligent to be caught as easy as all that."

"Don't you believe it, Eddie. It's the little things that folk overlook, when they're planning to do wrong. Think they don't matter . . . but they do!"

Bassett glanced over the forensic report once more, before handing it to Lipscombe. "At least we've got something to help us: 'traces of brine and smoke curing' . . . the lab's even given the approximate age of the pig! If necessary, we should be able to find out who cures bacon sold in that part of Cornwall, thereby narrowing down the shop, if we can't get a straight answer when carrying out interviews. Tell me, Eddie: what d'you make of these rumour reports?"

"Which one? Undergraduate Ackroyd trying to pass himself off as a disabled ex-soldier . . . or the proposition that this same practical joker was responsible for burying bacon bones in Nigel Barclay's front garden?"

Bassett said he was not overwhelmingly interested in the content of the rumours, so much as in the reason why they had been started . . . and by whom.

"The way I see things: nobody knew Trebilcock dug up a bag of old soup bones except ourselves. Even Trebilcock thought he'd found fragments of human rib."

"But the bloke who put 'em there would know different."

"Exactly! Which means he's the one who started the rumour. Stands to reason whoever buried those bones wouldn't have been able to get hold of the real thing . . . from which it follows we're looking for a practical joker, but he isn't called Ackroyd."

"That's right! Our man in Polperro told you the Ackroyds were away in their yacht. And Mashfords confirmed they set sail for France. 'Course, they could have crept back ashore under cover of darkness, Sarge."

"Not a chance, flat calm, then dense sea fog. So the way I see it: somebody else is trying to make trouble for the Ackroyds, either because of personal dislike or . . . to put the blame on those two brothers, in order to shift enquiring eyes from himself."

"So what's the right direction?"

"Wish I knew. Haven't you got any ideas?"

Lipscombe shrugged, saying the only person who might have something to hide appeared to be Dyson unless - purely from reasons of malevolent spitefulness - Barclay had buried the bones in his own garden.

"Then sent us the anonymous note . . . informing on himself? Hoping we'd question Dyson? Hmm. Bit of a long shot, isn't it?"

The two men lapsed into a silence which was only disturbed by Detective Constable Polkinghorne's painfully slow tap-tapping on an ancient typewriter. He was struggling to complete a report on an unfortunate girl from Redruth, who had terminated her three-month pregnancy by throwing herself down an abandoned mine shaft, just outside St Day. Careful examination - of both body and location - gave no reason to suggest this fallen angel had been assisted by the expectant father's helping hand.

He looked up, thought for a moment, then pointed out that the tip-off about Dyson's car damage, and finding the medal in Talland Hill, could have been sent by the same creative genius who informed the police about Barclay's bacon bones. "You're misleading yourselves, accepting this rumour as a single information. Chuck out the bacon bones and what have you got?"

"Bloke in an old mac, selling matches on Plymouth Hoe," Bassett replied thoughtfully. He was about to tell Polkinghorne he'd be looking for another job if he didn't shut up, when the penny suddenly dropped. Snatching up Trebilcock's report, he read a paragraph, then threw the papers across to Lipscombe.

"The boy's right! That rumour isn't about bones at all. They are a known fact. It's what we have left . . . "

" . . . an old coat with medals. We've already got hold of one genuine Jackett war medal . . . and existing regulations state that it can't be worn without at least two companions: the British War Medal 1914-1920, and the Victory Medal 1914-1918."

"Well don't you see, Eddie? The person who started this rumour is trying to tell us where to look for the other two medals . . . and if young Polkinghorne goes on like this, I can see him ending up as a future Assistant Chief Constable."

Lipscombe reminded Bassett their rumour-monger suggested the Ackroyd house staff had seen a coat and medals hanging up in the coal shed. "Goin' to slip inside for a quick look round?"

"Without a search warrant? Bit risky, isn't it?"

"Tell the staff we saw a person behaving in a suspicious manner, out the back, as we were passing. Could be worthwhile."

Chapter Thirty

Nigel Barclay thought life very worthwhile, by the middle of the afternoon. His parcel had arrived, as promised by the specialist suppliers in Wimpole Street, and he had unwrapped it in the privacy of his study . . . away from his housekeeper's prying eyes. To his delight, he found the goods to be precisely what he wanted, and spent time fondling individual items while chuckling quietly to himself.

Late in the evening, when he judged it to be dark enough for dirty tricks and foul play, Nigel Barclay picked up the contents of his London parcel, finding he needed two brown paper carrier bags to transport them, on account of bulk rather than weight, and set out.

He made his way up Mill Hill, along Landaviddy Lane and Lansallos Street, then turned up Little Laney, negotiating this narrow footpath as far as the back gate to Bay View House, which he entered stealthily.

No lights! So those two college boys were still away on the yacht. Good. Barclay headed for the coal sheds, where he put down his carrier bags. Now then, where can one find a spade or shovel? Barclay went off for a prowl round the other outbuildings, finally discovering a wooden tool shed. He selected a small-bladed shovel and returned to the coal shed.

He dug out the centre of the coal heap, tipped the contents of both carriers into the hollow, shuffled them about to give a suitably haphazard appearance, then covered them over with the coal which had earlier been cast to one side . . . but not completely . . . because it was necessary to his plan that there should be a sufficient number of items, from the London parcel, clearly visible to anyone entering the premises.

Flashing his torch at the finished job, Nigel Barclay reached down a hand to make slight adjustments . . . a bit more exposure here . . . a bit less over there, then departed.

"That'll give those bounders something to think about," he muttered sardonically, as he made his way back towards the garden gate and home.

And - by then - 'the bounders' yacht was slowly creeping past Penlee Point, at the entrance to Plymouth Sound. Both Ackroyd brothers were dead tired . . . and extremely hungry, for they had run out of fresh food during the previous day.

They had abandoned their trip to France in mid-Channel, following delay by calms and fogs, so their principal interest now lay in making Cawsand Bay. Then they hoped to get ashore and persuade a friendly shopkeeper to sell them a loaf of bread, dozen eggs and quart of milk.

They intended spending the night anchored off the villages of Kingsand and Cawsand, working up past Drake's Island and Devil's Point to Cremyll on the morning tide. Then it would be back to Polperro, by car, for rest and recuperation.

Whilst engaged in this up-river sail, on the following morning, unexpected visitors were heading for Bay View House. Detective Constable Lipscombe was munching bacon sandwiches as his sergeant drove them both down the main road towards Looe.

They had only stopped once . . . when Detective Sergeant Bassett came across a motorcycle and sidecar combination parked beside an Autmobile Association telephone call box.

Bassett had asked the patrolman if he happened to be on first-name terms with any one-legged, ginger-haired tramps.

Once assured the two motorists were policemen . . . and not people with an unusual sense of humour, the man had replied that he did, in fact, know one.

"Result of The War. I got to know old Alf pretty well. Proper carrot top - ginger hair. Used to stop and have a cup of tea with him, if I saw him brewing up at the roadside. Got a sister down near Looe, Polperro or somewhere. Only trouble was: poor chap's deaf as a post. I had to shout. I didn't mind that . . . but he used to shout back! And I've got good hearing. Anyway: I can't help more than that." The patrolman thought for a moment then added, "Funny thing. I haven't seen Alfie for almost a year, now I comes to think on it. What's he done mate?"

"Got himself lost, according to his sister," Bassett replied.

"Same as you said . . . she hasn't seen hide nor hair of the man since sometime last year," Lipscombe added.

"Officially: he's now a missing person," Bassett explained.

The patrolman went into his call box, saying he would pass all this through to regional office. Maybe they could help.

Bassett thanked him, said any information would be gratefully received at Bodmin police headquarters, then continued towards Polperro, where they called on Constable Trebilcock. After complementing him on his helpful reports, and asking directions to the Ackroyds' summer home, the Bodmin detectives left their car outside the village police house. Bassett led the way down through the village, in order to approach by way of Little Laney.

This enabled them to check the back garden gate was unlocked . . . then they carried on as far as the public footpath, to call at the front door of Bay View house.

The woman who answered their knock was told of the imaginary intruder, who had run out just as the detectives reached her back gate. She directed the two detectives to a path which wound round to the back of the premises.

When he entered the coal shed, Bassett didn't even bother to glance at the floor, going straight behind the open door and reaching out for an old raincoat. Unable to read the impressed details on its two medals, he came back into the open. As expected, they had been awarded to A. Jackett.

To his surprise, low profanities curdled the air within the coal shed, then Lipscombe emerged. Bassett waved a hand at the medals. "Just as we thought, Eddie: Private Jackett's!"

Then he realised Lipscombe appeared somewhat shocked.

"What's wrong with you?"

"I think I've found his bones, Sarge."

"Not again, for God's sake! Well you know what to do: put 'em in a bag, take 'em home and make yourself a drop of pea soup remembering - as you do so - that this sort of joke can severely damage one's prospects of promotion."

Lipscombe returned inside the shed, could be heard shovelling coal, obviously found what he was looking for and rejoined his sergeant. "Ever seen a pig with a round head?" he asked grimly, holding out a human skull.

"You remind me of the graveyard scene in Hamlet," Bassett observed drily, to be told they hadn't studied Shakespeare in Port Isaac village school, when Lipscombe had been a pupil there.

Bassett struck a pose, one arm raised, declaiming, "'Alas, poor Yorick! I knew him well, Horatio: a fellow of infinite jest,' if you see what I mean, you ruddy Philistine! Yorick was the king's jester . . . and the gravedigger was holding up his skull."

"Meaning we shouldn't take this too seriously?"

"Use your brains! No one's going to hide a murder victim amongst the household coal. Can't have been there long, either."

Bassett reached out, took the skull and rubbed with his coat sleeve. "See what I mean? Spotlessly clean."

Lipscombe suggested he bring the maid out to the coal shed, on the pretext of questioning her about the raincoat and medals. Her reaction to the sight of this skeleton buried in the household coal, could indicate whether she had seen it before . . . or if it was a recent arrival.

Bassett agreed and sent Lipscombe to fetch her.

When the detective constable returned with the daily woman, he stood politely to one side, letting her enter the coal shed first. She glanced downwards to see where she was putting her feet, saw a human rib cage and skull, surrounded by coal and other smaller bones, let her breath out with a low moan . . . and promptly fainted. Lipscombe caught her falling body and pulled her outside to recover on the grass.

"A spectacular success?"

"Proves she hasn't seen them before," Bassett laughed

This was confirmed by the cook, when the younger woman had regained consciousness. What with the warmer weather, and the young gentlemen being away on the family yacht, there hadn't been any need to go out for coal.

"But I put that there ole yard brush inside the door, day afore yesterday," the younger woman stated, "An' there weren't no bones in there, then. I can tell 'ee for sure certain, 'cos I'd 'ave bin bound to see 'em. I mean ter say: they'm all white . . . show up something awful against that there coal," she ended with a shudder.

Bassett allowed both women to go back to their work, after he had asked where he could find the local doctor.

"Thought you said we shouldn't take this skeleton business too seriously, Sarge?"

"We're caught in the cleft stick, Eddie. We can't remove the medals without saying where we found them. And, if we do that, without reporting those ruddy bones, we'll find ourselves in the wrong, back at headquarters."

"So I've got to fetch a doctor, have I?"

"That's right. But you can take it from me: our skeleton's original owner won't turn out to be Alfred Jackett. It's too old and there's no bits of meat or gristle present."

The doctor's diagnosis, after a most cursory examination, confirmed this. He was brief and to the point.

"Some young medical student playing the fool."

"So we can leave it where it is?" Bassett asked.

"Unless you want to earn yourselves a fiver. I expect, if you sieved through all that coal, then laid those bones on the lawn, you'd find you had a complete skeleton. This is a perfectly normal anatomical specimen - non-articulated of course - and therefore the cheapest way of obtaining a complete set of human bones. Most of us shared a preference for the articulated version, in my days as a student, then we sold them on to the next lot of first year men when we'd passed our finals."

The doctor smiled at a recollection.

"I remember mine quite clearly - once an elderly female - she had nine notches carved into the back of her right tibia. My notch made ten. A few years ago, now. I wonder how many more budding doctors have learned their trade on her . . . and carved a notch to record the happy partnership?"

Bassett, puzzled by the term 'articulation' had to ask what it meant.

"All the bones wired together, making a full length specimen, which was usually supported by being hung in the upright position. Some men bought a special stand . . . but I hitched poor old Daisy to a gaslight bracket, on the wall beside my bed."

The doctor was just about to leave when Lipscombe enquired if one needed some sort of licence to buy such specimens.

"No! All the leading medical suppliers stock them. One just goes into the selected shop and asks for a skeleton . . . in much the same way as one might buy a few lamb chops at the butcher's. Probably set you back a fiver," he added, setting off down the garden path with a cheerful wave of his free hand.

"So it doesn't have to be the property of a medical student!"

"In which case, Eddie, you can find out who bought this specimen when we get back to the office. In the meantime: get out your official receipt book, enter the two medals, single ribbon (broken) and one shabby raincoat, then give it to one of those women with our compliments. You can say we're removing the items as possibly being connected with a crime . . . but don't say any more than that for the moment."

Bassett began to walk away, saying that he would have a nose around, though he didn't expect to find anything of interest. Then, as soon as Lipscombe was ready, they could go down into the village and begin questioning grocers about recent sales of bacon bones.

The two policemen met on Roman Bridge, just over an hour later. Each had visited several shops, few of which had been found to sell fresh bacon.

Sitting on smooth stones, forming the top of the parapet, lower legs dangling over the side, they watched a family of swans waddling awkwardly across the dried out harbour. They stopped beneath the balcony of a waterside cottage, where a woman was throwing out pieces of stale bread.

Bassett mentioned one shop, where the disgruntled proprietor accused many up-country new-comers of doing the greater part of their shopping in one of the nearby towns, such as Looe or Liskeard. "Pointed out there were those so-called 'high class grocers'. One could buy stuff not carried in a village store."

Lipscombe suggested making a few calls on their return journey to Bodmin but his sergeant doubted they would have time. "Too many people to be interviewed right here, in Polperro, and I'd like to stay as long as possible in hopes of catching those Ackroyd brothers . . . always assuming they come back today."

"Put the thumbscrews on them while they're tired and hungry, dying for a nice cup of tea and twelve hours sleep in a warm bed?" Lipscombe asked with a malicious grin.

"Sound police procedure, Eddie, but I know who I'd most like to put the pressure on . . . Miss Anthea Eulalia Hyde." Bassett went silent as a couple of visiting Americans paused on the bridge to say "Gee ain't this quaint?" and take several holiday snaps of the harbour views.

Once they had moved on in the direction of Fish Quay, Bassett heaved a sigh. "Between ourselves and in the strictest confidence . . . where Miss Hyde's concerned, I have to admit I'm more than a little prejudiced against the woman. I think - to be on the safe side - you'd better call on the Hydes."

"Put 'em through the wringer, Sarge?"

"No. Don't waste your time. She'll have an answer for everything. Just have a chat with the two kids about finding the first medal. You'll be looking for general impressions, more than specific answers."

"What about the Hydes' imaginary cousin?"

Bassett replied he would leave that to his constable's discretion, cautioning Lipscombe not to take all day because there were other fish to fry before the tide came in. "I'll slip back to Trebilcock's place and have an off-the-record chat about these anonymous letters. We've been put on the track of a possibly fatal car accident and Jackett's war medals. I wonder where the local Yorick is trying to lead us with that dud skeleton?"

"Probably up the garden path, Sarge."

Bassett stretched, then heaved himself off the bridge parapet, saying he didn't much care for being led by the nose.

"We're policemen, Eddie Boy . . . not farmyard bulls."

The detectives walked up to the corner, parting company beside The House on Props. Lipscombe turned right, walking up The Warren to call at the Hydes' holiday cottage. Bassett made his way through Talland Street, in the opposite direction.

The detective constable found Miss Anthea Eulalia Hyde all ready to receive him, when he knocked on her front door. She welcomed Lipscombe far too effusively as she invited him inside.

"Been expecting you to call again. Suppose you've dropped in to tell me that you've found my long-lost cousin Betty?"

"Er . . . no. She appears to be untraceable, unless you have remembered anything else which could help us in that matter?"

"No. Afraid not. All too long ago."

"Never mind. I'm calling about something else, this time."

"And would you have some tea, while you tell me all about it?"

This was a relief. Those bacon sandwiches had been rather salty and Bassett had been in too much haste to stop for elevenses. Lipscombe accepted with alacrity.

Miss Hyde went out to the kitchen and Lipscombe heard several voices conferring in low tones.

"All the family at home, today?" he enquired when Miss Hyde returned.

"Yes . . . banished to the nether regions."

Lipscombe told her it might be helpful to have everyone present, since he had really called to have a chat with the two children; reported as having found a medal in roadside mud, somewhere in Talland Hill, a few days ago.

"My nephew and niece. I'll call them. My younger sister will join us when she's made the tea."

Debbie and Timothy were brought into the room and introductions made.

Lipscombe at once checked that Debbie was the girl who had shown a muddy medal to one of the local coastguards.

"Yes. My brother and I had walked up the hill . . . "

"Any particular reason why?"

"No. Just wanted to see where it went. We met an old lady who said we'd come out onto the main road for West Looe, if we carried on. But we don't care for main roads . . . unless we're in a motor car, so we turned round and came back."

"And that's when you found the medal?"

"Yes. Then we brought it home, and scrubbed it clean."

At this point, the younger Miss Hyde - Philippa - brought in tea and biscuits.

While Lipscombe was drinking, the older Miss Hyde reminded him that this business of her niece finding a medal had been dealt with by the local village constable.

"Ah . . . but he failed to impound the object as evidence." Lipscombe slyly observed, hoping to trap the girl. Turning towards Debbie he said, "Perhaps you would let me have it? Can't keep it, you know. That could be 'stealing by finding'."

Debbie said she had not kept the medal.

"No. I told her it wasn't valuable," Timothy butted in, "so we gave it away to one of the village kids, next time we went out."

Lipscombe asked which one, to be told they all looked alike with their ragged short trousers, moth-eaten shrink-fit guernsey pullovers and oversize silly cloth caps. Oh well . . .

"Bought any bacon bones recently?" he enquired blandly.

"My dear young man," Anthea Eulalia exclaimed with a most superior expression on her well-rounded face, "if you are attempting to connect this family with what your village policeman dug out of Mr Barclay's front garden, I suggest you think again. Not guilty!"

"Didn't suggest you were, madam," Lipscombe replied blandly. Deciding on a change of subject, he turned towards the boy.

"Didn't find anything else in the hill, did you?"

"Nice little Riley Imp in an open garage, sir. Got a bent front wing. I just went in for a look . . . because I like sports cars." The boy reached into his trouser pocket and produced an old army jack-knife with the initials A.J. 1915 scratched on its handle. "I found this on the floor, sir," he added guiltily.

Lipscombe took possession of the knife, giving Timothy Hyde an evidence receipt in exchange. Nothing to be gained by asking further questions, he decided, so he thanked the family and left.

He found the Imp easily enough. Close examination revealed hairs caught beneath an RAC badge. There were more behind a length of metal trim strip, near a dented front wing.

The detective constable carefully removed samples, placing them in clean envelopes - just as he had been so recently taught to do at the up-country police college - then walked back into the village.

There was just sufficient time for him to eat a fresh cream bun, bought from the Talland Street baker's, before meeting his sergeant. "Must remember to charge in another couple of 'phone calls," he murmured, wiping his lips appreciatively.

Chapter Thirty-one

"Well that's sent the bobbies galloping away in the wrong direction," Timothy exclaimed with every satisfaction, once the detective constable had left Crago's Cubbyhole. He turned towards his younger aunt. "If your rumour-mongering hasn't got them to those medals in the Ackroyd coal shed . . . my hairs will most certainly have them baying at poor old George Dyson's heels before the week is out."

Debbie asked suspiciously what he meant by the phrase 'my hairs'. Her brother replied that he had cut off a few short ends from his own head and stuck them in appropriate places on Dyson's Imp.

"We already know they can be identified as human hair, thanks to that trial run when Debs sent some others up to her old biology teacher." Timothy smiled innocently. "Actually, I don't think there ever were any hairs stuck to that car . . . so I rectified the omission."

"Fabricating evidence in order to mislead the police?" Bun exclaimed. "I suppose you'll be telling us next that the jack-knife was another of your enterprising efforts, Master Timothy?"

Phipps grimaced wryly as she saw a modest smile spreading across her nephew's face. Then he admitted the knife had been purchased at the same time as he obtained Jackett's medals.

"It was a bit of a job lot: knife, medals, discharge certificate, a handful of French coins, small brass tobacco tin as sent out to all soldiers who were serving on the Western Front, and a couple of regimental cap badges. Ten bob, the lot! Not bad, eh?"

"Oh Timmie!" Phipps gently reproached her nephew, now realising why he had been giving Bun and herself all those pitying looks at odd times. Her sister remained ominously silent.

Debbie shouted "Pig!" and flounced out of the room.

After a few more moments of stunned silence, Bun asked how the discharge certificate had found its way into Penaluna's shed.

"It didn't . . . neither did I. Never went into the tarred shed. Just hung about in the shadows, above Willy Wilcock's Hole, 'til the rest of you had gone back to the cottage. Then I made my way home," Timothy explained with a dismissive shrug.

"And what about your chase: up the bed of our river?"

"Oh that was real enough. Not that it would have mattered if the village bobby had caught me . . . 'cos I hadn't been doing anything particularly wrong, if you see what I mean."

Phipps questioned her nephew about the filthy bundle of hessian which he alleged was taken from the boot of Dyson's car.

"Just what it appears to be. I wouldn't have bothered with it, but then I caught sight of the label and thought it might lend more colour to our mystery."

"Making things up as you went along?" Bun demanded with an expression which caused her sister to expect immediate reversion to a previous life, of prep school mistress. Would Bun lash out at Timothy with a request for a hundred lines before lights out?

Phipps went to his rescue, reminding Bun of her own recent activities, by saying, "Just the same as you did, dear . . . making up that story of 'Cousin Betty' and her wartime marriage, when making enquiries in Liskeard, Pelynt and Lanreath!"

"Hmmm. Chip off the old block stuff, is it, Phippsie?"

Debbie returned as Bun finished speaking. She said somebody ought to give her brother a good clout, or kick him in the shins, leading them all up the garden path, like that. She had just been searching his bedroom, in case there were any other items of so-called evidence lurking about . . . until such time as her silly brother could plant them in somebody else's woodshed.

"Didn't find anything, though? Did you, Debs?"

The girl agreed but said it wasn't for the want of looking. She had gone through his possessions with the proverbial fine toothed comb.

Phipps saw Timothy's face broaden into a wide smile.

Bun, also observing this change of expression, enquired if there were any more surprises in store for the rest of the party.

Timothy replied yes, he did have a few more tricks up his sleeve . . .

"Such as . . . ?" Debbie asked, advancing in a threatening manner.

Her brother replied that - at this stage - he must refrain from making boastful prophecies.

"Natural modesty prevents me from anticipating success."

Chapter Thirty-two

The two detectives from Bodmin police headquarters were brimming over with self-confidence, feeling certain they would be making an arrest by nightfall.

Lipscombe had found his sergeant with both feet firmly placed beneath Constable Trebilcock's kitchen table, when they met once again. Bassett was drinking tea, between taking hugely appreciative bites at a slice of Cornish 'heavy cake'. The detective constable had been invited to join them.

There were two notes - made up by pasting words cut from a newspaper or magazine onto sheets of plain paper - lying on the table.

One asked: 'Who did Barclay bury in the garden?'

The other advised readers: 'Old Bill drinks. Look in his car!'

"The chapel people didn't want to part with their anonymous note, but I guaranteed discretion," Bassett said. "There's a distinct similarity, isn't there, Eddie?"

Lipscombe scruntinised both notes for a while, observing that the base papers were of different quality and the printed words had even more obviously not been cut from the same periodical.

"Almost a year between one and t'other, Sarge. They could have been put together by two different people . . . but I go for the alternative."

"Same bloke each time! That's what we say, Eddie. Let's hope the forensic lab can confirm that."

"Analysis of the adhesive," Trebilcock suggested.

"There's the same pattern with that wording too," said Lipscombe.

"Main point is: those Hydes weren't down here when that note about the jobbing builder was received, and we all know the Barclay note turned up after those Ackroyds had put to sea . . . "

"So we're left with Dyson and Barclay?"

"Or some unknown person with an equally unknown motive."

Lipscombe suggested they should look on the bright side. With two sound suspects, why bother about the great unknown? "Either: one of them made up both those notes; or they each sent one. If we could establish a motive, we've got our man. And I think I've gone a long way towards implicating Dyson."

Lipscombe went on to tell his sergeant what had been discovered sticking to the Riley Imp.

"That makes it sound as if one of the Hydes sent the other note, together with the medal? Makes a mess of your theory, Eddie."

Lipscombe refused to accept this, pointing out the youngsters had said they gave the medal to a village child.

"Who threw it away, thereby enabling Barclay to come along and pick it up . . . which means both men sent notes," Bassett growled. After a pause he added, "I wouldn't believe those Hydes too eagerly. Suppose they kept the medal, then sent the note? Damn' sight more likely, considering that boy admitted entering Dyson's garage. He would have seen those hairs you found."

Trebilcock broke into the discussion at this point, to say that he had heard Old Bill carried out some building work for the Dysons, about a year ago.

"According to the parish pump gossips: Dyson alleged the job hadn't been done right and refused to pay for several months, though I think the dispute was settled eventually."

"So you think Dyson could have sent that note about Old Bill out of spite and sour grapes?" Basset asked.

"It's an idea, Sergeant."

"OK . . . but then we're back to the Hydes, as senders of the third note, because it stands to reason Dyson isn't going to do anything to encourage police interest in his car. If he's been involved in a traffic accident - which had fatal results for some poor old tramp - friend Dyson's going to keep his head down!"

"Which is just what he has been doing," Trebilcock chipped in. "It's common talk in Polperro that his car hasn't been seen, out on the road, since his front wing got dented."

Bassett swallowed the remainder of his tea, wiped his lips, burped and stood up, saying there wasn't much point in talking for ever. The time had come for some sort of action. They would call on Dyson. Giving Trebilcock a slap on the shoulder he added, "That little snack of yours has made a new man of me. I'm in the mood to roast somebody's chestnuts!"

However, when the Bodmin detectives arrived at Rowett's Cellars, they found both Dysons had gone to Truro.

"Vicar give 'um a lift in 'is car," the cleaning woman told Bassett. "'Ad to go see 'is bishop 'bout something or other."

"Who? Mr Dyson?" The sergeant asked in some amazement.

"No-o-o-o. Gisson with 'ee, yer great fool. Our vicar!"

Lipscombe, mentally adjusting to the fact that chestnut roasting would be delayed, asked the woman why Dyson did not use his own car.

"Lost 'is nerve, us reckons! Ain't never used 'un since 'is biff."

Bassett thanked the woman and led the way back towards the bottom of Talland Hill saying, "Behold: the Lord has provided."

"Perfect timing for a closer look at the Riley?"

"Yes. You go back to our car and collect something to take scrapings of paintwork, together with the necessary forms and envelopes. We can take further samples, then send everything off to Bristol forensic lab direct from Looe railway station. But don't bring the Black Bag. Better not to alert the entire village, if we make any significant discoveries."

When Bassett reached the garage where Dyson kept his car, he threw an old sack onto the floor. Laying down on his back, the sergeant looked underneath. He checked the track rods, together with linkages, suspension and front brakes, finding everything undamaged. No reason, so far, why the car shouldn't be used, he thought as he scrambled to his feet.

Bassett went round to the boot and opened it.

Bloodstains! Now we're getting somewhere, he thought.

The sergeant checked the gear lever was in neutral, let off the handbrake and pushed the vehicle out onto a small forecourt, where he had the benefit of full daylight. No doubt about it: spitter-spatter of dried blood spots . . . and what was this crumpled paper? Ah-hah! Once opened flat it was found to be Private Alfred Jackett's army release certificate.

This was shown to Lipscombe, then the two men began collecting samples. The detective constable also found a hammer, tucked away down beside the back seat, and this appeared to have dried blood on its striking surface. The hammer was carefully wrapped and slipped into a large manilla envelope.

While counting blood spots, and making a written note, Bassett was surprised to see stray hairs stuck to some. He told Lipscombe to slip these into separate envelopes. With any luck, the forensic people would get a match with those on the outside of the car, proving the dead man had been carried in the boot.

"Only one thing bothering me: if young Hyde was in here, why didn't he see these bloodstains and tell you about them?"

Lipscombe shrugged, replying that he had gained the impression the lad was decently brought up, and therefore would draw the line at interfering with anyone's private property.

"I think he just came in to admire the car, then went on his way. Couldn't avoid seeing that dent in the front wing, but wouldn't have looked in the boot, Sarge. And remember: he said he found that army jack-knife on the floor."

Bassett accepted this and encouraged his assistant to hurry up with collecting those samples before one of the locals came by, then rushed down to tell all his mates what was taking place.

"The last thing we want now: is anything getting back to alert Dyson when he comes home . . . and as to that point, I suggest you slip up to the vicarage while I'm driving into Looe with our samples. Ask what time the vicar's expected."

"But someone could put two and two together . . . and telephone Truro, Sarge."

"Then you'll have to adopt a convincing disguise, won't you Eddie? No one at the vicarage will know you're a policeman. Chuck your jacket and tie in our car, roll up your shirt sleeves to make yourself look more like a holidaymaker . . . then buy one of those silly straw hats for sixpence. You can charge it to expenses."

"But I'm wearing braces!"

"Good. Leave them in the car . . . and use your tie in place of a belt. The more informal, the better. And while you're at it: select a hat with Kiss Me Quick on the band, then you'll pass nicely!"

Lipscombe asked what he should say, to explain his presence at the vicarage, and was told to mutter something about wanting to get married, whilst down in the area on a camping holiday.

"And what about lunch? It's getting near time for afternoon tea!" Lipscombe complained.

"Have it . . . but mind you don't spend more than ninepence! Or the difference will have to come out of your own pocket," Bassett instructed. "Personally, I shall have six penn'orth of fish and chips, which leaves me twopence for five Will's Star fags, and a penny clear profit. That's the way to become a capitalist!"

Asked when he could be expected back in Polperro, Bassett replied some time after four o'clock. Eddie could have a couple of hours sunbathing or looking at the girls.

"Tell you what: I'll meet you out on the point . . . near that old fishermen's shelter, at the end of Bay View's gardens."

Chapter Thirty-three

When the detectives met again, Bassett was all a-bustle, giving Lipscombe the immediate impression that he had solved the case single-handed.

Whilst in Looe, the detective sergeant had made several telephone calls from the local police station. All were enquiries to trade premises situated in the Greater London area.

This had established that Messrs Warburton, Rennie and Childe of Wimpole Street, W1 - suppliers of high class medical equipment to physicians, surgeons and medical schools - had received a telephone order for a complete skeleton (boxed, not articulated) from a Mr N. Barclay of The Anchorage, Polperro, earlier in the week and despatched the goods on the same day.

"So that removes the skeleton in the coal shed from our enquiries?" Lipscombe suggested. "But what about the bacon bones?"

"Dyson!" Bassett replied. "I asked around the uniformed men at Looe police station. Wanted to know of any grocer who could be considered as purveying to the 'carriage trade'. One man mentioned a place in Liskeard. I gave 'em a ring . . . and yes! They remembered 'their Mrs Dyson' coming in for some bacon bones this week. It appears she particularly asked for pieces of rib . . . the only parts of a pig to resemble anything making up the human skeleton."

Bassett paused to receive words of praise from his subordinate then enquired, "What news from the vicarage?"

"I saw a maid servant . . . and got the impression I could have had a date with her. Said she liked tall men."

"Never mind your love-life. When's the vicar expected home?"

"A bit before six at the latest. He's got evensong, at the church." Lipscombe rubbed his hands together. "I can't wait to see the expression on Dyson's face when we turn up!"

"Complete with District Police Surgeon, of course!"

Lipscombe asked why they needed a doctor.

"For obtaining a blood sample . . . which we send to Bristol for comparison purposes. All our efforts on Dyson's car would be useless if he'd simply hit his own thumb with that bloodstained hammer. I hope to prove our samples are blood from a stranger. No sign of the Ackroyds, I suppose?" Receiving a negative answer, Bassett said it was time for tea and led the way down into the village.

Later, fortified by a Cornish cream tea of splits, strawberry jam and thick clotted cream . . . reimbursement to be achieved by skilful manipulation of his out of pocket expense claims, Bassett said it was time they got back to work. Since Dyson wouldn't be home . . . they would have a chat with Barclay.

The detectives found their man ready to co-operate, despite the fact that he had a reputation for being disagreeably cantankerous with strangers.

He offered no obstruction, once the policemen had stated the purpose of their visit, becoming almost friendly as he spoke of his belief in the Ackroyds' guilt, regarding those bones which had been discovered, buried in his front garden.

"I recalled passing that medical suppliers when I went for my annual check-up . . . responsible job in the City . . . had to keep an eye on the old heart . . . so when I realised those young fools at Bay View House had been playing silly practical jokes, I thought I'd give the bounders a taste of their own medicine."

"And promptly ordered a boxed set of human bones?"

"Yes. Expected to see the place over-run with police. Hasn't worked out that way, has it?" Barclay gritted his teeth. "Never mind. Word gets around in a small place like Polperro. People will look askance when the Ackroyds pass by. At least I've shown they can't play the fool with me!"

Bassett thanked the man for his frankness and left.

As they walked down through Fore Street, Bassett admitted to his companion that he would have been quite happy to charge Barclay with an offence . . . but none had been committed. The man had obviously not been responsible for sending any anonymous notes through the post - thereby causing a waste of police time - and it was not a criminal act to leave rubbish in another person's garden shed. Trespass to land and property came under Common Law . . . dealt with in the civil courts.

"I notice you didn't let on the Ackroyds were innocent."

"Common sense, Eddie Boy," his sergeant replied, tapping one finger on the side of his nose.

"Meaning: we're here to help keep the peace . . . rather than cause unnecessary trouble between fellow residents?"

Basset said he was thinking more along personal lines. They had enough problems to sort out, what with three anonymous notes, a suspected fatal motor accident, their missing ex-soldier, and his medals turning up all over Polperro.

"The last thing we want now: is Barclay trotting round to Dyson's place, intent upon causing a spot of criminal damage, by way of getting his own back for that bacon bone joke."

Lipscombe nodded agreement, observing that the local constable had already warned them Dyson could be a difficult customer, one way and another.

This was immediately apparent when they reached Rowett's Cellars, accompanied by the police doctor whom they had met at the junction with Roman Bridge.

A suggestion that this visit was only being made in order to eliminate Mr Dyson from their enquiries - concerning a matter of a possibly serious nature - was met with a shark-like grin, which bore no trace of friendliness, and the American ejaculation of, "Oh yeah?"

Bassett decided to use a more severe approach.

"Acting upon information received . . . "

" . . . from some filthy little snot-nosed sneak."

"I visited a certain garage, situated in Talland Hill, accompanied by Detective Constable Lipscombe. We examined a motor vehicle - registration number ARL 264 - and removed certain samples which are now on their way to the nearest forensic laboratory . . . at Bristol."

Dyson's face suffused purple-red in obvious temper.

"Get all you wanted?" he snarled.

"Yes, thank you, sir."

"Then what the Hell are you doing, calling here?"

"We need a little blood . . . "

"To drink?"

"No sir. For purposes of comparison.

Bassett smiled inwardly as Dyson glanced at the doctor and asked if he was about to be bitten in the neck.

The doctor replied that he preferred using a hypodermic syringe. "I found personal contact too messy. Always arrived home with blood on my shirt collars. The wife complained."

Dyson's face momentarily relaxed into a slight smile. "At least somebody's got a sense of humour . . . which is more than can be said for you other couple of po-faced objects."

"Then . . . may we come inside?" the doctor asked. "Don't much care for doorstep operations."

"Quite right," Dyson answered, gesturing for them to enter. "Too many germs flying about . . . some of them on two legs," he concluded, with a disparaging glance at the Bodmin detectives.

They were shown into a spacious living-room, with large windows overlooking the harbour, and introduced to Mrs Dyson.

Waving the three callers towards chairs, Dyson demanded to know their reasons for being interested in a few bloodstains.

"After all: it doesn't take much to start the old claret flowing; slip of one's penknife when sharpening a pencil; scratch from a blackthorn bush - they're real swines - or even barking the old knuckles, when a spanner slips, whilst tightening a nut."

Bassett replied blandly that was precisely why they needed a sample from the car owner. "Those bloodstains probably came from somebody else, sir."

"In which case, dear old peeler, may one ask how they found their way into my motor?"

Bassett said he was not able to say, at this juncture, but had every intention of finding out in the very near future.

"By the application of your county constabulary thumbscrews?"

Bassett assured Dyson there were other procedures . . . which often proved to be more effective than traditional methods for obtaining confessions.

By then, the doctor was ready to take his sample. Dyson removed his jacket, rolled up his sleeve and told the man to help himself.

He did so, packed his bag and departed with a curt nod.

The detectives made no move to follow suit.

Mrs Dyson asked her husband if they were staying to dinner.

He replied he doubted it, once they found there was only dry bread and water on offer.

Bassett explained there were several matters which he wished to discuss . . . starting with the discovery of a quantity of bacon bones in somebody else's garden. As to be expected, the Dysons denied all knowledge of the subject.

"We considered this possibility, sir, and I therefore took the precaution of making enquiries at certain grocery shops. We have been reliably informed that a person - known to assistants of a high class Liskeard store as 'their Mrs Dyson' - made such a purchase earlier in the week."

"Bunch of tell-tale-tits! Ought to be sent to Coventry!"

"Mrs Dyson . . . ?" Bassett said, looking enquiringly at the lady.

"I used them to make pea soup. Is that a crime?"

Bassett knew very well he couldn't prove the lady wasn't being entirely honest and changed the subject without comment.

"What can you tell me about Alfred Jackett?"

The Dysons' obvious bewilderment convinced Bassett that they didn't know what he was talking about. While he was silently thinking of his next move, Lipscombe got in a quick one, by asking if the Dysons knew any one-legged tramps.

"Is he called Hoppity?" Mrs Dyson enquired sweetly.

Bassett changed direction once again, asking if he might examine the Dyson waste paper basket. This was permitted with a shrug of the shoulders. To his disappointment, the detective sergeant failed to find any evidence - of words for anonymous notes - having been cut from a newspaper or magazine.

Lipscombe, suddenly inspired, asked if either person had received any anonymous letters within the past few days. The ghost of a cautionary glance passing between husband and wife convinced him his wild guess had paid off. He pointed out that contents of such notes frequently contained more suggestive innuendo than plain truth.

Husband and wife exchanged a second glance.

"Darling: under the circumstances . . . ?"

"The same bounder who tipped off these fellows?"

"Well George . . . bloodstains do imply bodies."

Dyson admitted they had received a note and brought it out from a nearby drawer, in a small occasional table, handing it to Bassett. Lipscombe leaned over his shoulder to read the final sentence of: "'So why not ask him where he's hidden this body'."

Bassett wondered if the Hydes possessed a typewriter and sent Lipscombe hurrying up The Warren to find out.

When the constable returned, to display a printed 'NO' on one page of his pocketbook, Bassett asked the Dysons if they owned a machine . . . because he would need a specimen for comparison or elimination. Mrs Dyson pointed out personal letters, which were typewritten, always seemed to lack the personal quality so: no, they did not own or use a typewriter.

Bassett changed course again, asking why Dyson did not use his car, to be told he had not needed to drive anywhere.

"But you've been to Liskeard and Truro . . . ?"

"Our vicar has a 'pash' on me," Mrs Dyson explained. "He likes offering us lifts so that he can be near me."

Dyson told his wife to stop playing the fool. "Plain facts are: we're infernally hard up. I can't afford the tax and insurance."

"Strictly entre nous," Mrs Dyson beseeched them, "or we won't be able to get credit with the shops . . . then we'll both starve!"

"May one ask how you intend to pay your bills?" Bassett asked.

"End of the month . . . when our rich relatives send an allowance. If we hadn't bought Rowett's Cellars before the Wall Street Crash, you'd be conducting this interview in the nearest Poor Law institution."

"So there's no truth in any current suggestions, concerning your apparent reluctance to use your car, sir?" Bassett pressed.

"Well: obviously we don't know what you've been told by those who would seek to do us harm . . . for reasons best known to themselves, but I'm telling you the truth when I say we haven't even salvaged enough to live on. All our shares are worthless! You can ask my bank manager, for all I care," Dyson replied.

Bassett decided he was speaking the truth and got up to leave.

Once out in The Warren, and walking back towards the village, Lipscombe suggested the blood samples would probably turn out to be a dead loss . . . in the same way as the Dyson interview had ended.

Bassett shrugged. "They may be skint now, but it's a recent affliction. The Riley Imp was only introduced last year. I had a chat with a garage bloke. He told me that model was still being developed in 1933 . . . long after the famous Wall Street Crash! It's based on a shortened chassis of the company's standard 'Nine'. Can be fitted with a Wilson pre-selector gearbox as an optional extra, but that's being discontinued.

"What d'you make of the Dyson note being typewritten?"

"Another ruddy Yorick playing the fool," Bassett grumbled.

They crossed Roman Bridge and Fish Quay, to climb the steps for Chapel Point footpath, calling at the Ackroyd home to hear the two brothers would not be back that evening. They had sent a message to say their yacht was aground in Barn Pool, below Mount Edgcumbe, so they wouldn't reach their mooring 'til after midnight.

Bassett and Lipscombe returned to Bodmin . . . leaving behind them a village seething with wonder and unrest.

Word had quickly passed from one cottage to another that plain clothes policemen were going round, questioning they-there up-country gentry. And a doctor had been called to Bay View House, when Jessie Peters found a human skeleton in the coal shed. " Whatever's goin' t' 'appen next?" Villagers asked each other. And Barclay abandoned all thoughts of repossessing his skeleton . . . hoping it would give the Ackroyds a fright anyway.

Chapter Thirty-four

Following Detective Constable Lipscombe's visit to Crago's Cubbyhole - making enquiries about a typewriter - Bun and Phipps, aided and abetted by their niece, were relentlessly cross-examining Timothy . . . who quite truthfully assured them he neither possessed one, nor would he know how to use it.

"Well . . . have you been sending out any anonymous letters?"

"I rather thought that was Debbie's current speciality."

"I only sent one!" his sister snapped.

"Which is one more than I've ever sent."

"Well I watched from the bedroom window, when that detective left here . . . and he walked straight down to Rowett's Cellars . . . " Debbie exclaimed.

"Which means they are now interviewing the Dysons, dear," Phipps pointed out.

"So what have you got to say about that?" Debbie demanded.

Phipps tightened her lips as she perceived Master Timothy intended reserving his defence and exercising his right to remain silent. Naturally enough, this attitude was taken as a firm indication of guilt by Bun and Debbie, who continued their cross-examination with renewed vigour.

Eventually, this combined assault wore away her nephew's will to resist and, to Phipps' consternation, he admitted having rigged some pretty damning evidence against Mr George Dyson.

"Whatever have you been up to now?" she asked.

"Laying false trails. The idea came to me as a result of your going round the village shops, spreading little white lies about the Ackroyd brothers impersonating an ex-soldier match-seller."

"Oh my gosh! Now what has he done?" Debbie asked the room at large.

"Taken that false clue of the hair samples a stage further."

"Go on . . . " Bun encouraged, with tone of voice and blackness of look suggesting she dreaded to hear more.

"I borrowed a needle from Debbie's sewing box, collected a few odd bits of hair, then nipped up to Dyson's garage just before going to bed."

"Why the needle, dear?" Phipps asked with some concern. Had the silly young devil punctured the poor man's tyres? She bit her bottom lip apprehensively.

"To prick a thumb, Auntie Phil. Needed a few drops of blood!"

"Whatever for?" Bun asked, head on one side and eyebrows raised.

"To make it look as if a dead body had been carried in the boot of his car. I squeezed out the blood, scattering it onto the metal sides, then carefully stuck pieces of hair across some spots." Timothy completed this description of his nocturnal adventures by explaining that he had caught the remainder of his human hairs beneath the car badge, and a bit of trimming metal near the car's damaged front wing. Best of all . . . he had discovered an engineer's hammer and smeared blood over the metal striking head.

"That must have taken more than a few drops of blood, squeezed from a thumb," Bun observed.

"Oh it did. I had to stick the bally needle into nearly every finger, before I was finished . . . but I think it was worth the effort. Anyway: one simply has to make sacrifices when faced with a sufficiently worthy cause," the boy concluded, with what Phipps thought a particularly noble smile.

Bun was more practical, asking where Timothy obtained his hair.

"Auntie Phil's dressing table. Picked them off her brush and comb."

Whereupon Phipps let out a sudden whimper of shock and dismay.

Her sister ordered her to be quiet. "Serves you right! I told you that hair-brush needed a good clean, days ago!"

Phipps retaliated spiritedly by telling Bun not to speak to her in the way Nanny Hudson used to do, when they were girls back in their late father's Sussex vicarage, then lapsed into silence.

After giving this latest development some thought, Bun expressed the opinion that Timothy had probably done them a good turn. From statements made by Debbie and her brother, those detectives knew he had been the only member of their party to actually enter Dyson's garage. But this was not in the least indicative of any intention to do wrong. All young lads would wish to pause and admire such an attractive sports car.

And the planted hair samples, if subjected to comparison tests, would not resemble his own hair. Turning towards her sister, Bun pointed out there was no cause for Phipps to show concern, because nobody would suspect her of being in the garage in any case. As for the bloodstains . . . no one could ever say for sure that they originated from Timothy.

"Just what I thought," her nephew interrupted, "because I read in Picture Post that blood is only divided into a few groups."

"Precisely . . . which means - at worst - if a sample of your own blood was taken for comparison testing . . . "

" . . . it would only show that myself - and about a third of the population - could be responsible," Timothy ended with a smirk.

"But the hair and blood spots will keep our Bodmin detectives running round in circles . . . always getting further away from us," Phipps said after giving the matter careful thought. "Anything else which you feel you should confess, young man?"

Timothy screwed up his face in a somewhat undecided manner, as if wondering whether or not to say more. Then he shrugged self-consciously. Well yes, there was one small thing.

"Out with it Tims!" his sister instructed.

"That discharge certificate . . . "

"Private Jackett's release from active service?" Phipps enquired curiously.

"Yes . . . I hope nobody wanted it for any reason?" Timothy asked, looking anxiously around the other three.

"Your property - so you've told us," Bun observed mildly, "so you were free to please yourself."

"But what have you done?" Phipps asked.

"Screwed it up in a ball - to make it look as if it's something of no importance whatsoever - then left it in the boot of Mr Dyson's car," the boy answered with a smile.

"A masterstroke!" Bun exclaimed.

Debbie burst out giggling. "No wonder the detectives are down at Rowett's Cellars . . . but that still doesn't explain their enquiry about typewriters, does it?"

Bun said she had reason to believe somebody in Polperro was writing the odd poison pen letter . . . seemingly for amusement purposes. One could only assume the Dysons had been in receipt of one.

"And the bobbies - already wondering what we are up to, because of our interest in locating Alfred Jackett - thought we might be responsible?" Debbie suggested.

"Give a dog a bad name . . . " Bun suggested with a wry smile.

When the congratulations had subsided, Timothy asked what they should do next.

Phipps, recalling the words of Josiah from the Second Book of Kings intoned, "'Let him alone; let no man moves his bones.'"

"That doesn't pose much of a problem, Aunt Phil," her nephew replied, "'cos we haven't found his bones, have we?"

Bun said she felt this was the moment to follow an old dictum of Nanny Hudson's and let sleeping dogs lie . . . at least for the next few days.

"Martin's coaches are advertising a charabanc day trip to Boscastle and Tintagel on the north coast; starting from Looe tomorrow morning . . . and picking up in Polperro, outside Central Garage. I suggest we pack sandwiches this evening and get right away for the day."

"Mmmm. Yes. Let everything simmer down," Phipps agreed, "without any more helpful interference from us."

Debbie was all for this because she thought it would be romantic to walk in the footsteps of King Arthur and his Knights of The Round Table.

Her brother agreed with his aunt's suggestion too, saying he had always wanted to take a look at Tintagel Castle - regardless of whether King Arthur lived there or not - because he'd seen pictures of the place. "Perched right on the edge of very high cliffs and crumbling into the sea. Most impressive!"

Consensus had also been achieved between the Dysons, once George had convinced Beatrice he really knew nothing whatever about any body being carried in the boot of their Imp.

"A pity you were sozzled when you ran into that hedge though, George. I'm surprised you didn't come up with some story about swerving to avoid a stray cow."

"My imagination shrivelled with shock. Not used to being questioned by the bobbies, leave alone donate blood for purposes of comparison and elimination."

And, in Plymouth Sound, a passing motor tug offered the Ackroyds a tow up-river, to their mooring. This enabled them to arrive back in Polperro just after dark.

They discovered an official evidence receipt - signed by 'Det Cons Squiggle-Squiggle for and on behalf of the Cornwall County Constabulary' - together with a brief note, in the middle of the scrubbed deal kitchen table. This stated the police had called twice, hoping to have a chat with the two brothers.

Ronald Ackroyd read the final sentence aloud.

"And please remove that skeleton from your coal shed."

Chapter Thirty-five

Richard Ackroyd stared enquiringly at his brother.

Ronald met his gaze with wide open eyes.

"More of your handiwork, Ronnie?"

"How can it be? I've been at sea for the past four days!"

Richard glanced more closely at the note in his hand. "Looks like Jessie Peters' handwriting - very school-girlish - but it's clear enough. The operative word is definitely 'skeleton'!"

"Doesn't exactly say which species though," Ronald pointed out.

"Meaning it could be a dead cat or dog, Ronnie? Hardly likely. Somebody would have smelt a decaying body, whilst flesh and fur were still intact."

"Should we take a look?"

"In the coal shed, Ronnie?"

"That's where the writer seems to want us to direct our footsteps. You don't suppose it's some sort of a trap?"

"Bucket of water on top of the door . . .?"

"First one inside receives a po-full of you-know-what down the back of the neck?"

"Or some sort of primitive booby-trap which goes off 'Bang'?"

"Tricky, what?"

"Perhaps you ought to slip out the back, Ronnie, while I put the kettle on for a nice cup of tea?"

"And put a large bath towel to warm over the stove? No thanks, brother mine. If we're going to go . . . we'll go together."

Richard drily observed that Ronnie could have hit the nail on the head.

"Hole in one, sort of thing?"

"Scored a bull's-eye . . . complete with crossed Ts and well-dotted Is. I mean to say, Ronnie old lad, how do we know there isn't a loaded shotgun pointing at the door?"

"Funny sort of a joke, Richard old bean."

"Might not be meant as a joke!"

"Shades of the jolly old shotgun wedding?"

"Well . . . you haven't been sneaking about in the middle of the night, have you Ronnie?"

"Assignations with a fisherman's daughter? Of course not!"

His elder brother looked thoughtfully round the room, then said he supposed they could walk down to the village and collect the resident policeman.

"On the grounds that all coppers are expendable?" Ronald shook his head. "I shouldn't like to hurt Trebilcock. We'd best manage by ourselves . . . crawl in on hands and knees . . . "

" . . . carrying umbrellas?"

Ronald asked their purpose. Richard replied they would give some measure of protection from over-full chamber pots, as they crept about below the level of any gunshot pellets.

Ronald started towards the back door. Richard offered him a handlamp. Ronald refused, saying he would open the coal shed door . . . while Richard shone the light about.

The brothers went out to the coal shed, where they dropped to the ground. Ronald tripped the door latch with a broom handle. There was no report of a gun being fired, nor did a deluge of unpleasant liquid spill downwards.

Richard stood up. "Obviously a false alarm."

He shone the beam of his lamp from side to side . . . and let out a strangled gasp.

"There . . . amongst the Derby 'Brights'!"

Ronald followed his brother's pointing hand.

"Well I'm damned! Anyone you know, Richard?"

The elder brother peered closer.

"Don't think so. No recognisable birthmarks, Ronnie, old lad." He picked up the skull, carefully scrutinised the lower jawbone, then added, "Obviously a stranger. All my friends still have a full set of their own teeth."

"What now, Horatio?"

"Best get rid of it, I suppose." Richard thoughtfully hefted the skull in his hand. "You're too good to waste, aren't you?"

"Down in the village?" Ronald suggested with a malicious grin.

"Special delivery! There's a potato sack just about empty, in the pantry. Shove off and tip the spuds out, then bring the bag round here. I'll just run a spade through the Derby 'Brights' and collect the bones together, in readiness."

"Can't go mooching round the village as early as this," Ronald cautioned. "The pubs haven't chucked out yet."

Richard assured his brother they would not be moving off 'til later, but they ought to have everything ready for when the clock struck half past ten.

"I thought we might rustle up some food."

"Fried egg sandwiches . . . or shall we consult Mrs Beeton and attempt a more ambitious repast?"

"Such as coq à la Riene?"

Ronald admitted he had been thinking more along the lines of an omelette au fines herbes.

But - as usual - they settled for fried egg sandwiches because this meal needed less effort spent on the preparation work.

Stretched out on settees in the lounge - the term 'sitting-room' being reserved for use by the 'old fogies' of the family - the brothers discussed possible reasons why the police should have called twice . . . and an evidence receipt concerning medals and a raincoat. Since they knew nothing of Phipps' rumour concerning begging on Plymouth Hoe, they reached no sensible conclusion and soon turned their thoughts back towards that certain-something-nasty-in-the-coal-shed.

"Tell you one thing Ronnie . . . about that raincoat. I don't recall seeing it before. I wonder if a tramp spent the night in one of our sheds and forgot his coat in the morning?"

"Could be . . . but a tramp wouldn't be hawking a skeleton around the countryside, would he? More likely Beatrice Dyson realised her typewritten note originated from Bay View House and set out to get even with us." Ronnie paused thoughtfully, "As for that raincoat: I say it's the gardener's."

Richard accepted these suggestions. Very possibly the beautiful Beatrice had realised they were responsible for the anonymous letter. But he rejected the idea that she had put the skeleton in their coal shed. "Dash it all: how many people do you know, who actually have real skeletons in their closets?"

Ronald agreed skeletons were pretty thin on the ground.

Then Richard, having considered any Dyson involvement more carefully, changed his mind completely. Neither the Dysons - nor anyone else living in Polperro - could have known anything about their recent purchase of that old typewriter.

"So nobody could have sneaked to the bobbies," Ronnie said.

"Which brings us back to those police visits. Could it be trouble in the family? Somebody ill . . . or falling off the perch?"

"The Old Man would have sent a telegram. Wouldn't have brought the police into things. At worst: he would have 'phoned the landlord of the Three Pilchards and asked him to find us."

"But then there would be other written notes lying around."

"Quite right, Richard . . . and there aren't any. Fair gives one the jim-jams . . . that's the worst of having a mildly guilty conscience. I've even considered the possibility of those chapel trustees having found out I sent them the note concerning Old Bill's secret drinking habits."

"Impossible! No, I reckon Jessie Peters went into the coal shed, discovered the skeleton, panicked and telephoned the local equivalent of Whitehall one-two one-two. We've got nothing to worry about. Some unknown person - with a curious sense of humour - making a nuisance of himself in our absence."

Ronald asked if his brother knew any medical students, up at Oxford, to be told the butchery section was avoided by all young gentlemen of good taste. "They emit a curious odour!"

"Ah yes: formaldehyde."

"Hands always covered in corpse pickle. Mind you: there's that chap Bunny Danvers . . . technical chemistry and allied sciences. Often speaks of changing to forensic medicine. Might well be seeking revenge for one of your more spectacular pranks."

"Y-e-e-s. Those fancy buns covered with laxative chocolate!"

"The poor chap failed to reach the bogs by less than four yards!" Richard reminded his brother.

"Embarrassing, I grant you . . . but he couldn't know we've come down to Cornwall. On the other hand . . . those bones are all as clean as a whistle!"

"I know. Not a morsel of flesh anywhere.

"They probably belonged to a medical student at some time."

"Yes, well . . . question for us to consider is: who shall become the new owners?"

After further discussion, the brothers concluded it might give the best return on effort, if they were to dump their bag of bones on the front doorstep of Crago's Cubbyhole.

"Of course, the trouble with this idea is that we'll never know just how much alarm and despondency we manage to create," Ronald pointed out.

Richard disagreed, reminding his brother of their favourite childhood game, for winter evenings, when they used to knock on people's doors and run away. However, in this case, they could hide round the nearest corner, where they should be able to hear all screams without even needing to strain their ears.

But when the young Ackroyds carried out their plan, they were very much taken aback by an all too obvious lack of predicted reaction, on the part of the people staying in the holiday cottage.

They watched as the boy came out - easily identified by the cut of his striped pyjamas - looked into the potato sack, glanced hastily to either side of the deserted thoroughfare, then pulled their special delivery inside and shut the door.

"What now, Oh Brother, dear Brother?"

"Curb your impatience, Ronnie. Wait and see."

To their delight, they heard the sound of a bolt being stealthily withdrawn about five minutes later. Then light spilled across that part of The Warren, from a slowly opening front door. Then a shadowy figure slipped out and hurried off in the direction of the village.

The Ackroyds followed at a safe distance.

They saw the person carrying their bag of bones stop outside a nearby cottage on the seaward side, drop the sack, knock at a door, then turn and run back the way he had come.

The Ackroyds silently faded into the darkness of a convenient alleyway, which served as access to the back yards of neighbouring cottages.

To their immediate consternation, the person who had just delivered the sack turned into the same cover. The brothers retreated to a back yard, hoping no dogs would start barking and blessed the fact that this was a fishing village . . . where cats were the favoured pet.

It was obvious this third person was following the same plan as themselves . . . now keeping watch on that door where the bones had been delivered.

A tricky business, because the brothers were well aware that the recipients were George Dyson and the beautiful Beatrice.

Time seemed to drag interminably. Neither brother was wearing a watch, and Richard realised it would have made no difference, in practical terms, if he had known the time. But a watch could have served to reassure him the endless minutes had not become hours.

Then, at last, there was a scuffling motion from the third person, who appeared to be easing forward, as if about to leave.

This happened as swiftly as one might blink an eye. One second the figure was still there and the next . . . it had vanished.

The brothers ran down their alley on tiptoes, then stopped to peer out into the relatively lighter darkness of The Warren. They saw a dark, crouching figure moving swiftly from doorway to doorway.

"He's tracking somebody else!" Ronald exclaimed in a whisper.

"George Dyson, carrying a bag of bones!" his brother replied.

The person in front turned left, just before The House On Props, crossed Roman Bridge, paused at the junction with Lansallos Street, then turned right. The Ackroyds continued to follow at a reasonably safe distance, first through Lansallos Street, then Landaviddy Lane. They came to a halt when the moving shadows up front faded away, going down into Mill Hill.

The person from Crago's Cubbyhole appeared to stop behind a low wall. Shortly after, a gentle knocking echoed upwards from somewhere beyond a bend, out of the Ackroyds' line of sight. This was followed by the sound of a door opening . . . then a sudden curse disturbed the peace of the night.

Finally: there was a distant crash . . . as if the householder had slammed his door shut in violent temper!

Another period of silent waiting was only broken when the person within sight began moving forward once again, dodging from side to side. The young Ackroyds moved out in pursuit.

They were led through to The Coombes, then back along Fore Street, in the direction of the harbour.

At this stage, though the brothers were unaware of it, Nigel Barclay was carrying the bones, with the firm intention of depositing them in the boot of George Dyson's car. Full of wrathful indignation, he turned left to go up Talland Hill.

Constable Trebilcock, who had been enjoying a quiet smoke just inside the garden gate of an empty property at the foot of this incline, silently ground his cigarette end underfoot and stepped out to follow an obviously suspicious person.

George Dyson, turning the corner from Fore Street, caught sight of the unmistakable outline of a policeman's helmet and promptly retreated to a nearby yard entrance.

Timothy Hyde hurrying past, stopped with an audible gasp of astonishment, turned on his heels and rushed back down the hill as fast as his legs would carry him. The boy dashed round the corner, into Talland Street, and made off towards The Warren.

Dyson followed silently, a few yards behind, with equal speed.

Thus, when the Ackroyds turned up Talland Hill, they saw nobody dodging about the shadows immediately before them and hurried upwards, fearful that they would miss the next act in this exciting midnight drama.

They reached Dyson's garage just as Trebilcock approached Nigel Barclay to ask him what he was doing, carrying a sack, and on premises clearly not his own, during the hours of darkness.

The Ackroyds stopped . . . stared . . . then turned tail, melting swiftly into the surrounding shadows of the night.

Chapter Thirty-six

Detective Sergeant Bassett heard Constable Trebilcock's version of the night's happenings, as soon as he arrived in the office, on the following morning.

Having listened patiently to the saga of the bones, Bassett made the observation that up-country folk living in Polperro appeared to be a silly bunch of Yoricks . . . apparently competing against each other for the title of King's Jester of 1935.

Trebilcock asked, "What's a Yorick?"

"Never mind. Office joke. So the Ackroyds have come home?"

Trebilcock replied he thought so. Lights had been observed in certain upstairs windows of Bay View House during the hours of darkness and, since the skeleton was last seen in their coal shed, it could be presumed the brothers had returned during the night, found the bones and promptly carried them round to Barclay's place . . . their reasoning for this not being readily apparent.

Bassett accepted the fact that no laws had been broken, so the rest of the practical jokers could be left to their own devices, but he told the Polperro constable that he - and Lipscombe - would be down in the village, as soon as they could get away from the office, to interview the Ackroyds.

"While you're waiting for us to arrive, nip round to where those two brothers park their car, and give it the once-over. Make a note of any outside dents on the bodywork . . . and take possession of any suspicious objects you might just happen to see inside the vehicle."

The detective sergeant spent less than a half an hour on reading reports and other paperwork, then went out to see if a car was available. It was, so he returned and nodded to Lipscombe saying, "Come on Eddie: time for round three in Polperro."

This time, they took the shortest route through Sweetshouse, Lostwithiel, Middle Taphouse and Pelynt.

When they had exhausted their feelings of dissatisfaction over the state of British cricket, Lipscombe brought up an item first seen in the previous day's Western Evening Herald.

"Terrible business: those two children finding that legless corpse, on the beach yesterday, wasn't it?"

"Haven't had time to look at my paper yet. What happened?"

"Down below Wembury parish church, it was: Devonshire side of the approach to Plymouth Sound. A couple of young kids, out after firewood, went down to look along the shoreline. Saw what they took to be a bundle of old clothes, washed up by the tide, and went across to see if there was anything worth having, like brass buttons, I suppose. They probably thought it was part of a uniform, chucked overboard from a naval craft."

"And discovered they'd found a body instead, eh? What was it? Ex-soldier who'd committed suicide?"

"No. The legs hadn't been amputated. The Evening Herald reporter said the body had been sliced in half, just below the waist, by a ship's propeller."

Bassett gave a shudder, saying it was a good job that body hadn't been washed up on the Rame side - in Cornwall - or they would have had the bother of it.

Lipscombe replied that it now appeared to be a fairly simple matter. He had bought a Western Morning News, on his way to the office, and they reported the body had been provisionally identified as that of a male passenger, lost over the side of a cross-Channel steamer, the week before last.

"A suicide?"

"Looks very much like it, Sarge. The boat was one of them on the Weymouth to Channel Islands run. According to the Western Morning News, several passengers remembered a ginger-haired man passing them on deck . . . then he passed no more."

"Hmmm. Open and shut case, as you say, Eddie. I wonder what happened to the nether half?"

"The what . . . ?"

"The bit below the waist . . . lower part of the body. Shakespeare used the term in his plays," Bassett replied, then swerved towards the hedge as one of Martin's charabancs came round the next bend, positioned squarely in the centre of the road.

"Ruddy coach drivers!" Bassett grumbled after the other vehicle had passed without slackening its speed.

"Got a long way to go, I suppose, Sarge"

"Won't get there if he doesn't drive better than that!"

But the charabanc did reach its destination - Tintagel - without any mishap . . . and Timothy Hyde couldn't wait to tell the other members of his party how he had finally solved the mystery of that human flesh, found in the Polperro crab pot.

"Pound to a penny it was cut off one of these missing legs," he told his sister and aunts, when they had all settled down in a convenient picnic spot on the cliffs, overlooking the ruins of King Arthur's Castle.

No one else had seen the Western Morning News, but the boy had been shown this story by his seating companion . . . who had turned out to be a pathologist from one of the London teaching hospitals, taking an early holiday in Looe.

"Decent sort of a chap. Not a bit of 'side', yet he actually teaches other doctors!"

Debbie told her brother to skip the hero worship and get to the point. Timothy did so; describing how the two Wembury children had found a half a body, when out beachcombing.

"The newspaper says it is thought to be the remains of a middle-aged, ginger-haired passenger on one of the Weymouth cross-Channel ferries. Lost without trace more than a fortnight ago. My friend - the pathologist - told me he expected the man had been sucked into the propellers, which chopped him in half."

"How terrible!" Phipps exclaimed, wondering if she really did want to eat this cheese sandwich with all its tomato sauce relish.

"Apparently they get quite a few cases like this, up in London," her nephew carried on regardless of other folks' finer feelings. "Sometimes it's a suicide which has been struck by one of the river tugs - very powerful engines, stop at nothing - and other times it's a docker or seaman who'd had too much to drink."

Debbie became impatient, demanding to know how this could have any bearing on something washed up on a Devon or Cornish beach.

"The tides! It's all to do with the tides!"

Phipps saw this at once, pointing out that when they lived in Brighton, the tide used to come right up the beach twice a day, and all that water had to come from somewhere else, didn't it?

"Up or down the coastline," Timothy agreed.

"Carrying all before it?" Debbie suggested.

"Absolutely. So there you are: this chap got himself chopped in half between Weymouth and the Channel Islands. The bits and pieces eventually became separated and Talland got a leg . . . "

"While Devonshire got the body. Clever old Tims," his sister complemented him with a proprietorial smile.

"Still doesn't explain the crab pot business," Bun commented.

"I think it does, dear," her sister said. "Jack Penaluna - or whoever owned those particular crab pots which Timmie saw outside the tarred shed - above Willy Wilcock's Hole, obviously found a leg washed up by the tide . . . and put the mortal remains to a practical use."

"And, since my clever brother has already confessed to spreading false clues about, concerning a certain Private Alfred Jackett, there's nothing more to bother us in that direction either," Debbie reminded her aunts.

"Oh well . . . " Phipps said wryly, "at least it gave us all an interest, for our first week's stay, in Polperro. I wonder what we'll find next week?"

However, back in that village, Detective Sergeant Bassett still wanted to finish sorting out the current week's many problems. He, and Lipscombe, were sitting outside the Three Pilchards, drowning their sorrows in a couple of pints of beer.

It was a day which had started full of promise. When they arrived in the village, Trebilcock had proudly produced a wooden peg-leg which he had found earlier, hidden beneath a seat in the Ackroyds' sports car. Added to that old raincoat, and Alfred Jackett's medals, Bassett had felt himself to be on very firm ground when he called at Bay View House.

But the two brothers had denied all knowledge of Alfred Jackett . . . his raincoat . . . or his medals. As for the peg-leg: they had given somebody a lift. "A one-legged ex-soldier who had been carrying it about to use as a spare." Richard explained.

"Oh really sir? Afraid of catching woodworm, was he?"

"Never thought to ask but you know . . . it's not an indictable offence to offer a chap a lift," The older brother replied blandly.

"And you can always check up on the veracity of Richard's statement - concerning this unusual gift of a wooden leg - by contacting the one previous careful owner," Ronald added.

"Now sir: about this accusation that you were seen begging on Plymouth Hoe?" Bassett said by way of changing the subject.

"I deny everything. I make it a practice to manage on my father's fairly generous allowance. And if I don't succeed, I generally manage to manage on that of a more affluent friend, if I can find one, which I usually do." Richard Ackroyd retorted.

"So the coat and medals are not your property?"

"Indeed not . . . and while we're on the subject of our coal shed, I should like to register an official complaint."

"What particular point do you wish to raise, sir?"

"Well I think it rather takes the biscuit, don't y'know, when one arrives home to find one's private property full of somebody else's old rubbish and cast off clothing. And it's not just your tatty old raincoat . . . we've had complaints from the maid that the Derby 'Brights' are full of human bones."

"Ah yes . . . those bones. Very mobile, aren't they sir?"

"Don't quite follow . . . ?" Richard Ackroyd replied cautiously.

"Well sir, my constable and I both saw the bones in situ yesterday and I think - if you care to look - you will now find that they are no longer in your coal shed."

"We've been robbed!"

"Shall I call the police, Richard?" his younger brother asked.

Bassett ignored this witticism, asking if either of the Ackroyds had visited their coal shed on the previous evening.

Ronald replied that it wasn't the sort of place one visited.

Richard added there was no comfort. Not even a deck-chair.

Detective Sergeant Bassett, fearing he might lose his temper, had then signalled to Lipscombe . . . and both men had withdrawn to the Three Pilchards.

After a long silence, Bassett had voiced his thoughts that if they disregarded the skeleton, and its nocturnal perambulations, as being a harmless schoolboy joke, they appeared to be left with a few bloodstains and stray hairs on Dyson's sports car . . . which brought them back to Timothy Hyde.

"We know the nephew and niece were involved in finding one medal, Sarge. Perhaps they found all three and separated them?"

"Exactly. This whole case started with those Hydes. If they hadn't begun asking questions about Jackett's whereabouts, his ruddy sister wouldn't have initiated these enquiries."

"Then we'd have never known about those bacon bones, medals, anonymous letters, bloodstained car boots or family skeletons . . . leave alone a wooden leg being carried round the countryside, in the same way as a motorist carries a spare wheel!"

Bassett set his lips in a thin, firm line.

"We're going to have it out with those Hydes! Come on!"

But this involved another period of waiting, for the detectives found Crago's Cubbyhole deserted when they called. So they spent the remainder of their afternoon sitting on a seat, at the end of Old Quay, from where they could keep 'the premises' under constant observation.

As soon as Bassett saw the two older Hyde women reach their front door he ground his teeth, shook Lipscombe, and they both set off to walk round the harbour at a brisk, business-like pace.

Anthea Eulalia answered their knock. Bassett said he hoped they were not calling at an inconvenient moment. Miss Hyde replied any time suited her . . . providing she could make a pot of tea before sitting down to yet another round of questions.

"I suppose you do drink tea - while on duty?"

Bassett replied it was specifically recommended when conducting interviews. "Helps to keep the mind alert!"

Once all were seated and tea poured, but no biscuits offered because Phipps said that would only encourage the policemen to stay longer, Bun asked them how she could assist their enquiries.

Bassett decided to raise the matter of the peripatetic skeleton as a starting point. He was no longer really interested in this subject, but felt a soft approach would disarm everyone. He explained they were investigating a series of disturbances, which had occurred during the middle of the previous night, and asked if the Hydes had heard any unusual noises . . . such as running footsteps, people knocking on doors or calling out?

Phipps glanced quizzically towards her older sister.

Bun frowned at Timothy . . . who raised an eyebrow, when giving his young sister a crooked smile.

Debbie giggled helplessly into her teacup.

Bassett looked from one to another.

"Have I just said something funny . . . or missed the point?"

Timothy shrugged. "Those naughty Tooth Fairies left a bag of bones on our doorstep," he explained. "I nipped over the road and passed the problem on to Mr Dyson."

"What made you leave them there?" Lipscombe asked curiously.

Timothy shrugged again. "Well . . . he was the nearest person who we knew."

"Do I take it you had been formally introduced on some previous occasion?" Bassett enquired, very tongue-in-cheek.

"Not me. The Aunts," Timothy gestured towards Bun and Phipps. "Terribly bad form to leave anything like that on a stranger's threshold. I mean to say . . . "

"He could be a vegetarian," Debbie added by way of further explanation.

The detectives exchanged meaningful glances, then Bassett changed tack, asking the older Miss Hyde if she had done anything further in her search for cousin Betty.

Bun shrugged this subject to one side in a nonchalant manner, saying no, she had quite given up. Obviously been on the wrong track right from the start without realising it.

"But no harm done, was there?" A positive statement rather than a polite enquiry.

Bassett replied that, to the contrary, she had caused a great deal of trouble . . . particularly to Cornwall County Constabulary.

Bun said she couldn't think how.

Basset explained: Jackett's sister had not seen her brother for almost a year, neither had other reliable witnesses such as AA road patrols. However, Mrs Bunney had not thought of asking the police to investigate . . . until a certain lady, giving the name of Miss Hyde, called and began asking questions.

"You started a panic! Now we've got to sort out the mess. It appears to us that Mr Alfred Jackett may no longer be alive. At worst: this could mean murder. Very serious. Do you follow me?"

Debbie looked covertly from one aunt to the other.

Timothy shuffled on his chair.

Phipps suggested they tell the sergeant about the crab pot bait.

Lipscombe pulled a face, as much as to say 'here we go again'!

Bassett responded with a darkening glower.

Timothy recounted how they had found this bit of human leg muscle, in a stranded crab pot, at Talland.

"My sister and I thought it could be interesting to search for the body," Phipps hastened to explain.

"Just like playing hunt the thimble?" Bassett asked.

Timothy said yes . . . but it had not turned out as easy as they expected. "However, I've finally solved the mystery, and it's got nothing at all to do with this chap called Jackett."

He rummaged in a nearby picnic basket, eventually bringing out a copy of the Western Morning News, which he had bought in Tintagel. Opening this newspaper at the relevant paragraphs, Timothy handed it to Bassett and told the sergeant of his conversation with a fellow passenger, during the charabanc trip.

"Bit of luck really," the boy explained. "We didn't book until the last minute. All the window seats were taken, so we had to push into whatever was left . . . which meant we couldn't sit together. That's how I came to be sharing with this doctor chap."

"And he told you a ship's propeller could cut a body in half?"

Timothy shrugged. "Said it happens all the time, on the Thames. Drunken sailors, mostly . . . but I gathered the odd suicide's body could end up like that if it got run over by a tug."

Lipscombe agreed with the doctor's theories, saying they had a similar case at Perranporth whilst he was stationed there. A Channel Islander had gone fishing, in a rowing boat which was later found smashed to pieces on the rocks.

"No body was recovered until weeks afterwards . . . when part of it turned up on our sands. The local doctor told the Coroner injuries were consistent with the body having been struck by a steamer's propeller at some time or other."

Bassett asked if the Hydes had found any bone, from which the flesh might have been cut, to be told everyone had searched the low tide rocks for some time without finding anything else.

"So we presumed this unknown chap with the crab pot had cut off the meaty bits, then thrown the rest back in the sea," Timothy explained, "to get washed up by the next onshore gale."

At this point, there was a heavy knock on the front door. Bun got up to see who was calling. She returned with Constable Trebilcock, who apologised for disturbing everyone, but said he was required to deliver an urgent police message to Detective Sergeant Bassett.

"Received at Bodmin earlier this afternoon, then telephoned through to me when I returned from foot patrol."

Phipps watched Bassett unfold the piece of paper.

His bottom jaw lowered slowly . . . as his dark eyebrows arched and drew closer together.

Here was a man experiencing genuine anguish, she told herself. Whatever could it be . . . in that message, to cause this dramatic reaction?

Bassett finished reading, let out his breath with a loud gasp and looked up at the cottage ceiling . . . muttering silently.

Phipps, who had never learned lip-reading, thought he might have been mouthing 'God give me strength'.

Trebilcock asked if there was any answer.

Bassett replied he could think of one . . . but present company prevented utterance. "Just say: message received, then remain silent . . . for the remainder of your time in the police force!"

Everyone waited with bated breath until Bun returned from showing the constable out.

Somewhat grim-faced, and decidedly tight-lipped, Bassett passed the message across to Lipscombe without comment.

Lipscombe read it, looked up, made brief semaphore signals with his brows, then swivelled his eyes left and right.

Bassett shrugged his shoulders.

Lipscombe passed the note to Timothy, who was sitting nearest, gesturing for him to circulate it after reading the contents.

When Bun had seen what was written, she observed mildly that, between them, they appeared to have solved all problems.

Bassett disagreed, saying there had - in his opinion - been a lot of jiggery-pokery from start to finish . . . such as those bloodstains in Dyson's car boot, Private Jackett's medals turning up all over the place and that same soldier's discharge certificate, together with his old army jack-knife, being discovered in Dyson's sports car, or its garage.

Bun stared fixedly towards her nephew

"As the Walrus said . . . "

"The time has come . . . ?" Timothy enquired wryly.

"To speak of many things," Phipps prompted.

"But you can skip references to shoes, ships and sealing wax," Bassett instructed, mainly by way of indicating he - too - had read Lewis Carroll's book. "Concentrate on: 'Alf Jackett'!"

Timothy made a clean breast of his activities, even admitting he had purchased the ex-soldier's war souvenirs in a Polperro junk shop, then scattered them about to make the whole mystery more interesting for his young sister. "Which proves our Alfred was short of cash, last time he came through this village, to visit his sister, or he wouldn't have sold these bits and pieces."

"I've a good mind to charge you with wasting police time!"

"But you won't be doing that, will you, Sergeant?" Phipps heard her sister say very firmly. "Because, if Timothy is taken before the Bench, everything will be reported in your local newspapers. He is nearly eighteen. You can't hide behind the Juvenile Court rules of anonymity, you know."

Bassett, guaranteed inspector's rank at the end of his first year, if he made a success of the newly formed County CID, realised newspaper headlines such as YOUTH TRICKS DETECTIVES or even worse: CID FOOLED BY SCHOOLBOY might well ruin all chances of further promotion.

"Yes well . . . taking that course can't help matters now."

"My old Nanny Hudson used to say: 'Least said, soonest mended'," Bun observed pleasantly.

Bassett got up to leave. Staring grimly towards the woman known to him as Anthea Eulalia Hyde, he remarked that Henry Ford had more suitable advice. "'If it ain't broke don't fix it'! Please Miss Hyde: don't attempt to fix anything else in Polperro."

Walking along The Warren, Lipscombe turned to Bassett.

"Would you believe it, Sarge? That ruddy bloke: Jackett! Tucked up - all safe and sound - right in the middle of Dorchester . . . whilst we were out looking for him!"

Bassett silently ground Trebilcock's message - from the prison governor - into a ball, before hurling it at a passing cat.

Other Bun and Phipps stories.

Published in 1999

TROUBLE IN TOPSHAM

Wind, rain and hail lashed their cottage on the banks of the River Exe in Topsham. And Bun had just run out of knitting wool. Far too wet for walking up to the shops, so she decided to have a poke about at the drawing-room walls.

Surely there must be alcoves hidden to either side of that huge Dartmoor granite fireplace?

Digging revealed a woman's body.

Getting rid of it should have been easy, but a young makee-learn detective became suspicious. And a scoop-happy newspaper reporter horned in on the act.

Then Phippsie found herself having afternoon tea with their murder suspect in a Dawlish seaside cafe.

Bun said he should be Put Down before he killed anybody else . . . such as her younger sister. So the retired schoolmarm, and the one-time lady's companion, set about plotting a fatal accident. A very tricky business when both are singularly lacking in previous experience.

In course of editorial preparation

SHOOTING IN ST TUDY

Bun and Phipps are staying at the Rectory, looking after their curate cousin, following his wife's riding accident. One evening, they attend a dinner party. A fellow guest is found shot in the churchyard next morning.

Several other guests immediately ask the sisters to provide them with respectable alibis. Bun and Phipps, ever ready to oblige their new-found friends, fabricate a suitably involved story which is passed on to the investigating detectives.

Later, Bun and Phipps find the murder weapon and begin their own investigation. A suspect postal package is taken to Bodmin Hospital for X-ray. It is found to contain old rusty horseshoes instead of the expected hand gun. The detectives are attacked by a belligerent peacock, the reasons for those false alibis are revealed when several extra-marital liaisons come to light, and bottles of the Rectory cook's famous parsnip wine have everyone legless . . . when they aren't exploding like defective hand grenades.

News of publication dates can be obtained by writing to:

TREVIADES PRESS
Falmouth, Cornwall, TR11 5RG